"Not long now, Glacier Ice. You seem well."
"I am, Barren Rock. And you? Come in
Silence to go in Truth?"
"As they foretell, yes."

<u>A Wolf to Remember</u>
Kali Brazier-Tompkins

Come to Say Good-Bye

by

Yvonne Wilson

DREAMCATCHER PUBLISHING
Saint John • New Brunswick • Canada

First Printing - August 2002

Canadian Cataloguing in Publication Data

Yvonne Wilson - 1927

Come to Say Good-Bye

ISBN - 1-894372-20-4
I. Title.
PS8595.I5912C64 2002 C813'.54 C2002-902896-5
PR9199.3.W49885C64 2002

Editor: Theresia Quigley

Typesetter: Chas Goguen

Cover Painting: Alan Weatherley

Cover Design: Dawn Drew, INK Graphic Design Services Corp.

Printed and bound in Canada

DREAMCATCHER PUBLISHING INC.
1 Market Square
Suite 306 Dockside
Saint John, New Brunswick, Canada E2L 4Z6
www.dreamcatcher.nb.ca

Acknowledgements

For this story I owe the moon, for putting on the show I watched till my back ached from standing at the window on Boxing Day 2000.

I owe the jet stream for the Ground Hog Day Gale of thirty years ago, that blew half the roof off the West Side Baptist Church.

I owe the earth for the fogs of spring, the strawberries of July, the brilliance of autumn, the sparkle of blue mornings after nights of freezing rain.

I owe Elizabeth and Joan at DreamCatcher for believing in my work,
Theresia Quigley for finding the weaknesses in the manuscript,
Alan Weatherley for his painting of Frank's inukshuk,
Dawn Drew for designing Alan's painting into the cover,
and Kali Brazier-Tompkins for allowing me to quote from her novel A Wolf to Remember.

Thanks for all the help I have received along the way, and for this opportunity to say my piece.

Dedication

This book is for all the people I have known throughout my already long life whose love for this beautiful Earth has formed my mind and heart-

I think of Elwood, who always found the first trillium; my father, who found us the brightest maple leaves in autumn, and my mother, who heard spring in the first crow's call - usually about the middle of January! of Mrs. Robs, who showed me my first robins' eggs; of my brother, who made so much noise learning to swim that a bald eagle swooped down over the lake; and of my daughters, Kate and Lucy, who share my delight in thunder storms and surf...

We have shared wondrous times and things. It saddens me that we have to come to say good-bye to so much.

Other Works by Yvonne Wilson

Of novels for adult readers:

Red Dragon Square

Of novels for children:

Slipper Hbr.
A Light Above the Sun

Among other writers' novels edited to publication:

Overtime by Brad Janes
The Making of Harry Cossaboom
by Jerrod Edson
Dancing With the Dead
by Vernon Oickle
To Hell or Melbourne and
Until We Meet Again
by Flora Kidd
The World That Is
by Alan Weatherley
Strange Lights at Midnight
by Allison Mitcham
A Wolf to Remember
by Kali Brazier-Tompkins

Chapter One:

The key slipped into the lock and turned, and I pushed open the door. A slight surprise registered in my mind - new lock, new key should have meant slight resistance; but there was none. I expected a good deal of resistance in this place, even, apparently, extending to the lock in my door. That I found none left me a little uneasy.

Inside I expected a cold, somewhat bare space, furnished with an assortment of reject tables, chairs, and a bed - and the latest in large TV sets. The suite would be bleak and empty. That resistance I expected and braced myself to meet: bleak and empty. I pushed open the door, stepped into a small foyer, dropped my bags on a carpeted floor, and straightened to come face to face with an astonished middle-aged female in a black dress, black shoes and stockings, and a frilly white apron.

"Good Lord!" I said. *I* said it, not she. She said, "m-m-Madam?" in a half gasp, half whisper.

Obviously she was not speaking to me. And just as surely the agency had not provided me with a housemaid. I might be beginning the assignment of my life. I *was* beginning the assignment of my life. But I had no illusions about my personal importance in the universal scheme. I was only one tentacle of

NEPP, a tentacle, moreover, with only a modicum of authority and less actual power. No housemaids.

This maid began to recover. She blinked. Her lips trembled. And again she squawked - perhaps croaked would be kinder and more accurate - "m-m-Madam..?"

At that I recovered enough to do what becomes automatic with accountants of my years and experience: I inserted two fingers into my waistcoat pocket, extracted my business card, and presented it to her. She took it with her right hand, passed it to her left, returned it right and so on, rather as one might toss an egg that came straight from boiling water.

I could think of nothing more to do or say. The door had closed behind me; I could not retreat. The way forward was blocked by the black-clad maid. I therefore watched and waited. And as I watched and waited I began to feel that my control of the situation was slipping away. I entertained the suspicion, which I instantly tried to quash, that I was sinking into something viscous.

It would not do for me to lose control in the matter of arriving at my own private rooms. No doubt existed in my mind that these were my own private rooms. House numbers, addresses, street names, floor numbers all bent to my will. I was an accountant - a good one - and if I couldn't find my way home, even to a home I had not yet seen...

The maid stirred. That is, the trembling or shimmer that I had observed about her lips and chin began to spread to her shoulders, then to her hands and knees. Her breathing deepened. Her lips steadied. She turned, moved toward an arch in the left-hand wall, and announced in a passably normal voice, "Madam, a gentleman..."

I followed her the few steps to the arch, which opened into a large room with a window wall that faced south. Pinkish-coloured drapes had been drawn back to their fullest extent. From where I stood, however, nothing was visible through the windows but a dark, storm-filled sky. The rattle of freezing rain was loud against the glass.

A slim straight figure in gray, gray hair pulled back into a loose bun, stood before the windows looking out. In a soft gown that fell from her shoulders to the floor, she all but vanished into the storm.

She did not turn but remained as she was, looking out of the windows.

"Madam," the maid repeated, "a gentleman."

"I am not at home, Jenny," Madam said. "Tell him I am not at home."

"But I am already here, Madam," I said.

I said "Madam," a word I had never used before, to my recollection, in my fifty-two years. "Madame," of course. "Madam," never.

Madam remained with her back to the room. "Then I suppose you are here for a reason," she said. "Come to the window." Her voice was vibrant; an impression of deep, flowing water touched my mind.

I shook off that impression - a metaphor of any kind would have been unwelcome; one of water doubly so. And still in my rain-spotted overcoat, my hat in my hand, my shoes no doubt leaving dark footprints on the carpet, I crossed the room.

The carpet was gray - a warm gray, if such a colour exists - and thick. Beyond the window the sky was thick and gray - cold gray. And the lady stood like sunshine. I thought so at the time. I, who had never understood music or poetry and was embarrassed, more often than not, by a fanciful idea; I, whose taste ran to a nice spread-sheet of nice gray numbers - I thought so at the time; not black, but gray numbers - I felt surrounded by sunshine.

Still in my outdoor clothes, I crossed the room and stood beside this lady.

Even then she didn't turn but reached out and took hold of my sleeve. "Look!" she commanded.

I saw a small, thin hand, the nails perfectly manicured and coloured a deep rosy pink, the hand of a woman who has come to the age when nail colouring looks best. I guessed that she must be about my own age, perhaps somewhat older than I.

"Look!" she commanded again.

"I..," I began to say, but I stopped, because I didn't know what to say next. What would she have me see?

As if she sensed my question, she tightened her grip on my arm. "Look out of the window," she said.

I looked down, and shuddered.

"No, no. Look! Look!"

I began to be annoyed. "What am I to look at?" I argued. "Surely on a day like this..."

I saw a wet parking lot. On a rainy day-after-Christmas... Especially on a rainy day-after-Christmas, even from the tenth floor, a wet parking lot offers little of aesthetic value. This one was almost empty. A few bits of paper - an old newspaper, some Christmas wrappings, a bag that someone might have carried gifts in... Across a narrow street a few old houses of wooden construction, one with a large green dragon sprawled across the facade above the ground-floor windows. All wet, all dark, the people no doubt gone away for the holidays, or closed in against the dreary afternoon recovering from the Christmas feast...

"What is it you want me to see, Madam?" I asked, in as reasonable a tone as I could manage. "I see nothing but rain and emptiness. There are no cars in the parking lot. There are no people on the street. Even the Chinese restaurant has turned off its dragon and closed for the holiday. If you can find anything out there of interest or importance, I'm afraid you'll have to point it out to me."

"You are not a singer," she said.

"I am an accountant, Madam," I announced. I felt rather insulted. Singer? What did she suppose...

"A singer," she said, ignoring my profession, "would first stand straight, then fill the lungs, and finally look out, out, out... to the back of the church, to the end of the hall, to the extent of the theatre.

"When I approached retirement," she went on more quietly, after a pause, "I feared that I would become inward-looking and tiresome, no longer looking out to the extent of my audience but inward to the little extent of me. But I found, on coming here, that I could look much farther than ever I could in church or concert hall... Oh, much, much farther. On a clear day... to the end of the universe.

"Not today, of course. Today the view is closed to the extent of the storm, to the density of the squalls that sweep in across the bay..."

I was appalled. I was to fill my lungs and look out? Out into that wind? That rain? Those squalls that beat against the windows?

I recalled a bird I had noticed briefly as I got out of the

taxi down below. "I feel like a bird that knows it can't fly in this weather," I objected. "There was one near the front door. A herring gull, huddled by the wall."

"Poor thing," Madam said. "Jenny, call the SPCA. They'll have someone on duty. At least it can die out of the storm... And take our visitor's coat and hat. What are we thinking of!"

"How do you know it was dying?" I demanded, as I was divested of my coat. "It may have been simply sheltering from the wind."

"If it had been able, it would have gone inland with its flock," she said. "They know when weather is coming."

This strange, slim creature, whose face I still had not seen, was beginning to frighten me. I confess it now. Though at the time I was not willing to acknowledge the feeling, she was beginning to frighten me.

I tried to move away, but she clutched my hand very tight. "Look," she whispered. "L-l-ook. Oh-h. Oh, Oh, Oh! Oh, look! Ah-h-h..."

This last, this "Ah-h" with a rising inflection, came on an in-drawn breath as if a great joy...

Appalled. Afraid. And now... baffled.

She had been rigid as she spoke; and her grasp of my hand, very tight, had been painful to me. But now she relaxed and clasped her hands together before her face as if in childlike delight. "Baffled" was hardly strong enough to describe my state of mind.

At last she turned toward me. I saw her face and forgot to breathe. She was beautiful, her eyes alight with a joy that must have been deep to the bottom of her soul. But at the same time, sad.

I acknowledged her emotions, and another gathering in me. At first I couldn't identify it. But when Madam smiled, I knew it for envy. I was envious of this woman. I admitted it for an instant - for an instant only - before I denied and rejected it because I was terrified. I suspected... No, I knew, that I was not capable of experiencing her total absorption into the moment; and my terror arose from a fear that she might make me try - or that I might want to try.

I blurted out the very words best calculated to betray me: "Madam, what is it? What is it you are seeing?"

She looked deep into my eyes, and I was again surprised, surprised that the power I sensed in her was centred in such a fragile appearance. She was lovely and limitless, I seemed to know, in the qualities I was glimpsing in her, as if seeing her through the sheets of rain that beat against the windows.

"And so you shall," she said softly. "So you shall."

As if I were a small boy, she took my hand and made me move closer to the window, for I had retreated a few steps the moment she released me.

"Slightly to the right," she said. "Look out and slightly to your right and you will see an island. A lighthouse stands near the summit of that island. Do you see it? Are we together?

"Yes," I managed to say, though my mouth had gone dry and my stomach felt as it might have felt had we passed through the glass hand in hand and sailed against the wind toward that lighthouse.

"To the right of the island," she went on, "you can follow a line of surf extending to a point of land farther to the right and a little closer to the city.

"Yes, I see."

I shuddered again, and Madam reached out with her free hand and patted mine, the one she already held.

That ended my self-control. "It's terrible," I cried. "Terrible. Terrible. The water pounds the island and boils over the reef. Why hasn't somebody done something?"

"Done something?" she repeated with a trill of delight. "My dear, they have long since done what's possible. That 'reef' you describe is man-made - a breakwater - put there to protect the harbour."

"Well, it's not working," I almost shouted. "The waves are coming over it and breaking *in* the harbour. If there are any boats..."

"There are no boats," she said. "Boatmen are like the gulls. They know when rough weather is coming and run for safety before the storm. We are free to enjoy the show."

There were no boats on the water as there were no birds in the sky.

"There is an oil-tanker behind that far point, away over to the left," Madam said. "Sometimes one can see her riding light when the rain lifts for a moment. She's been moored there for a day or two; discharging cargo, I suppose. But she's enormous and double-hulled. There's nothing to fear."

I began to think that Madam was probably right, that there *was* nothing to fear. And I began to breathe more freely and to study the animation to be seen through the windows.

To the left the sea swept into a shallow cove. The water there was brown from disturbed sediments. I tried to count the long, white-topped rollers that followed each other in, one after the other.

"You're looking at the white horses," Madam said. "The Celts believed that the sea god and his cohorts came no closer than nine waves from the shore. But I suspect that on days like this he comes closer, to remind us he's still out there and has lost none of his power."

I shuddered again and she laughed, but kindly. "You are too used to hunching over columns of figures," she said, "too limited to monitors full of little symbols to be peered at... Oh, oh, oh! Did you see that?"

"No."

"Watch. Straight ahead. On the foreshore."

I looked where she seemed to be looking, straight out over the town. Blocks of red brick buildings rolled down as on a monitor screen, and she laughed again as if she knew I was extending her analogy.

"You'll like the South End," she said. "Parts of it are very interesting, even beautiful. It goes back to the rebuilding after the fire of 1877."

I thought she was probably right once more, that I might indeed enjoy that part of the town. But my eyes, just then, were rivetted to the end of the buildings, where land met sea. A rail-line ran along the foreshore, and several tank cars stood there, black in the rain and sea spray; and a line of poles - power poles? telephone? light standards? stood behind them.

"Oh!" Madam cried, and again released my hand that she might clasp hers together. "Oh! Did you see that one?"

I had. A wave had reared up, higher than the rail cars, higher even than the poles.

"How high is that rail embankment?" I gasped.

"Oh, I don't know," Madam replied. "I never could estimate such things. But those who built it knew what they were doing. It is certainly high enough to withstand normal storm surges. Not today though. It's overwhelmed today!"

She sounded delighted.

"Today," she continued, instructing me now, "today is special. Perhaps, where you have been, people have not much attended to the fact, but down here by the water we see the effects of such things in a practical way."

"You are speaking, I suppose," I said, "about the moon's being closer to the earth than usual."

"Yes," she agreed, with wonder in her voice. "For these few days the moon's proximity, combined with the facts that it is full and that we have just passed the winter solstice, has brought the tides in very strong and high. But the weather, until today, has been unusually calm. We are fortunate to see this. It is our only opportunity. In normal circumstances this show will not play again for another hundred years."

I stood looking out at the scene that I now better understood. At past four in the afternoon the light was almost gone, but I looked and imprinted on my memory the breakers that pounded the island, the breakwater, and the point of land where city lights were coming on. I looked again into the shallow cove where the Celtic gods continued their immortal games. I looked for the lights of the tanker beyond the point and found them, brighter as the winter night closed in. And I watched the foreshore till I could no longer see the geysers that reared up over the rail cars.

"A hundred years or so, Madam," I said to myself. "Under normal circumstances. I wonder, Madam..."

Then I turned my back on the storm and looked into the room.

Chapter Two:

Madam had seated herself on a wicker couch at one side of the room, an ivory-coloured affair with pink cushions. Such a couch, I thought at first, as we used to have at my childhood home. Ours stood on the verandah through long, hot summers, slowly fading away. For a moment I was there, using the back of the couch as a fort and the cushions as camouflage. I could hear my mother coming. But Madam looked so... other worldly... on those pinkish cushions, wrapped in the robe of a medieval monk, that I reserved judgment.

No doubt more definitive words for Madam's couch and that particular shade, or hue, of pink exist; unfortunately not in my vocabulary. And I was, in any case at that moment, intrigued by the overall effect: grayish pink, or pinkish gray. Flashes of a brighter pink appeared at Madam's throat and wrists as she moved, and a sort of more-faded pink shone in her hair. I had never felt so fumblingly male in a female presence. Possibly, I thought, I was looking at works of art. Certainly the watercolour seascape on the wall behind her head was noteworthy.

"Jean Thompson," she said.

"I beg your pardon?"

"Jean Thompson," she repeated. "The picture you are

studying so gravely. What do you think?"

"I think it's probably very good," I said. "Not that I am a judge. Is it?"

"I think so. But if it were not, it would please me. She gets things right. I have several of her pictures; you shall look at them later. Now it's time to sit. I'm tired after standing at the window all the afternoon. And you were with me for a long time; you must be tired too. Come and sit down. Jenny is making tea."

I hadn't noticed that I was tired, but I had already put in a long day when I arrived, and standing had stiffened my back. The chair Madam motioned me to felt wonderful. The moment I sank into it, however, I was confirmed in my conjecture that any connection between it and our old wicker verandah set was tenuous at best and probably too remote to trace.

I sank into that chair beside the couch and thanked providence for the promise of tea. I needed tea - or something - or I would fall asleep, and the time had come for Madam and me to talk business.

I drew a deep breath, but again the lady forestalled me.

A low wicker table with a glass top stood between us. The table was bare, ready for the tea tray, except for a pot of cream-coloured poinsettias at the far end and a lone business card - mine - at the near end.

Madam leaned forward and picked up the card. "Richard Waterman," she read, and looked at me and smiled. "Doctor Richard Waterman, MBA, CA, etcetera, etcetera... Yes-s... 'How are the mighty fallen."

"I beg your pardon, Madam?"

"No," she denied quickly, with a childlike smile. "No, please. I beg yours. It just seemed... You don't think..? Perhaps a little amusing..? A touch ironic?"

Ironic? My degrees in business administration and accounting, ironic? The National Energy Planning and Procedural Council of Canada for which I worked, amusing?

Madam's eyes brightened. I have said I am not fanciful, and I believe that I am not. But just then, when Madam looked at me, I thought that she could see right through my head to the back of my skull. I was convinced of it.

"Forgive me, Richard," she said. "Of course your credentials are most impressive. But you are a Waterman!"

"There have been Watermans in Winnipeg since 1904, Madam," I said, a bit sententiously I am ashamed to say. "My great-grandfather, the first Waterman..."

"No, no," she said. "Your great-grandfather was not the first Waterman. The first of that name had never heard of Winnipeg, for Winnipeg did not exist in his day. He no doubt lived in England and followed a life in boats, Richard. Boats! On some British river. Perhaps the Thames itself. And he knew the tides and currents, the flights of birds, the weather signs in the sky, and the comings and goings of the moon..."

As she spoke I seemed to be on the surface of a broad stream engulfed in mist and rimmed with reeds. A flight of large white birds rose with a wet slapping of wings. Swans. But I had never seen... Had I?

I returned to hear Madam asking, "Have you a son?"

"No," I replied, when it dawned on me that she was speaking to me and that I was expected to reply. "No, I am the last of my family."

"And have completed the circle," she murmured. "It is well."

The skin at the back of my neck stirred. Fortunately at that moment Jenny arrived with tea, and I had time, while she placed the tray on the table and moved across the room to close the drapes, to recover myself and regroup for another foray.

"Now, Madam," I said, when we had finished the business of preferences and I had received a cup of clear, unsweetened tea and a small turkey sandwich. "Now, Madam, we must settle the problem of my being here."

"Is it a problem?" she asked. "I am enjoying your visit."

"I suspect you enjoy everything..."

"No, no. Not everything."

"No. Well..." I refused to be drawn. "Madam, you have hit upon the very word to describe the problem," I said. "You are enjoying my 'visit,' but I am not making a visit. I am here to stay."

"You will be very welcome," she said.

"Thank you, but you must understand. The government agency I work for has bought this building, and frankly, Madam, this apartment is now my apartment. I am surprised to find you still here."

"Really?" she said. "I thought we had made our position clear to NEPP - I and the other owners."

I picked up the fact that she was acquainted with my employer, but I barged on. "There are no other owners, Madam," I insisted. "No owners at all except my agency. NEPP owns this building."

"Your lawyers were down just recently," she went on, as if I hadn't spoken. "And they went away confounded - if I read the situation correctly." She twinkled at me. "They hadn't a leg to stand on, you know, though of course they couldn't admit it."

I hardened my heart. "I can see that you have lavished a great deal of thought and money on your home here, Madam," I said, "and I am truly sorry. But you must understand that the new owner - my agency, of which I am the chief representative in this area - expects occupancy of the building - the whole building - forthwith. We must decide on a date for your removal."

"For many years," Madam explained, almost dreamily, "this building belonged to a philanthropic society - at least the first eight floors of it did."

"I have read the history."

"The society used part of the ground floor for its own purposes," she continued, ignoring me, "and rented out the rest."

"Yes, of course. And the agency, I understand, has been generous in its dealings with the tenants."

"Very generous," she agreed. "Those of us who are left have said good-bye to one after another of our former neighbours, and waved them off smiling."

"And there we come to the nub, Madam," I insisted. "You should be gone too."

"About five years ago," Madam continued, looking off into the distance... "About five years ago, the owners of this building, as it then was, wanted money - lots of money. And a plan was conceived to add two floors of pent-house apartments that should be spacious, well appointed, and very desirable. These - four to each floor - would be offered for sale."

"But I understand that they were not sold."

"And there, as you say, lies the nub. The real nub. Five of the suites were sold. The other three were fitted out by the society and rented, from time to time."

"You are telling me, Madam," I said, "that you believe you bought your apartment."

"I know I did."

"Can you prove it?"

"I can. And I employ a very expensive law firm to do it for me."

I groaned. I could see years of litigation stretching ahead. The agency had bought the whole building in good faith, no doubt. No doubt the previous owners had sold the building in good faith. But someone had messed up, and the mess had landed in my lap. I would have to sort it out. It would be up to me...

"The previous owners," I said, "as I understand it - I will have to look up the records... The previous owners stated that the monies paid by the tenants of the ninth and tenth floors were rent in perpetuity, and the agency..."

"Oh, yes," she agreed. "I received a cheque in compensation for four years' so-called rent. So did the others. We sent them back."

"I heard nothing of this."

"Oh, well, you know... bureaucracies. Especially over the holiday season..."

I shook my head.

But Madam smiled. "This is a wonderful opportunity!" she cried. "To practise good fellowship. Or brotherhood. Or something. Why can't we share the building? There are only five of us owners, after all. Your people can rattle around in the rest of it. You will have eight floors for your offices, or flats for your people to live in, or whatever it is you want to do with the place. We won't be in the way."

I turned over the possibilities of her suggestion in my mind. If the other owners were anything like Madam, I thought they wouldn't be security risks. Anyway, security would be tight. On the other hand, if they were in the building, sharing the elevators, getting to know some of the agency staff... Here was I, for example, top gun himself, already taking tea with Madam. The next thing I knew...

"Oh, Lord!" I moaned. "This is terrible."

"It's not all that bad," she soothed.

And I began to laugh. "It is, Madam," I assured her. "It is very bad indeed. And the least of it is the obvious tip of the iceberg: I have no place to stay. I was supposed to live here - here in this very suite. Now do you know what's going to happen? We'll be short of VIP accommodation, and every time we're full up, which will be every other day or two, I'll have to move to a hotel.... Or bunk in with the janitors!"

"You can come and stay here with Jenny and me," Madam said, and reached out to pat my hand. "We'll keep the guest room ready for you."

I gave up and laughed as I hadn't laughed in years.

"Have another cup of tea," she said, and poured me one. But it was cold before I had calmed down enough to drink it.

Madam allowed me to have my laugh out. Then she pounced. "Am I to understand," she demanded, "that you, Richard Waterman, are the senior officer of your agency in this city?"

I nodded. "City and area," I said.

"And what exactly is your area?"

I might have known she wouldn't miss that slip.

"Oh, the town and some kilometres round about," I told her.

"How many?"

"How many..?"

"Kilometres."

"Oh. I don't know. That is, it varies. Other jurisdictions encroach, so we can't simply take La Tour as centre and draw a nice neat circle out from it."

I couldn't tell her the average was two thousand kilometres - roughly twelve hundred miles, give or take a few hundred here and there, except southward where it stopped at the US border. My American counterpart, with whom I was to work closely, took over at the international line and worked south to the New York megalopolis, which the US authorities, after much agonizing, were going to have to abandon. Westward my territory extended to the eastern edge of the Great Lakes Basin, which meant most of the St. Lawrence River Valley, and took in Montreal, but not Ottawa, which, of course, was our Canadian headquarters and discrete. Northward, then, from the lakes, I followed the Canadian Shield, responsible for small settlements in continental wilderness, as far as that variable called "permanent ice." My authority ended to the west just short of Hudson

Bay, and eastward reached into the North Atlantic, taking in Newfoundland, St. Pierre and Miquelon, and the Sable Island gas fields. I, Richard Waterman, being by no means assuredly in his right mind, had solemnly sworn to undertake the biggest scam since the Napoleonic Wars and to do the best he could... My God.

I sighed, and relaxing for a moment in Madam's very comfortable chair noticed that the storm had abated with nightfall. The wind had dropped. The rain no longer beat upon the windows.

I think we were quiet for several minutes before Jenny returned to clear the table.

"The storm seems to be over," I said then.

"It's snowing," Jenny murmured.

"Snowing!" Madam exclaimed. "How lovely. In the morning everything will be clean and white."

"Clean and white," I thought, and a shudder passed through me.

Madam saw, and waited only until Jenny had left the room before demanding, "Why are you here, Richard Waterman?"

The woman was uncanny.

"I thought that was common knowledge," I hedged. "We are preparing to shut down the Lepreau nuclear plant - eventually. And searching out sites for alternate sources of energy."

"It makes a good story."

"You don't believe it?"

"Do you?"

I caught myself thinking, "Dick, for God's sake, couldn't you have found a nice, fuzzy-headed little lady to walk in on?"

Then I looked her straight in the eye and told her the first bare-faced lie. "I know it," I said.

"Do you indeed," she snapped back at me. But I got away with the story that time and passed the point of no return. I was committed. Forward ho! And if I could convince Madam, I could probably convince enough people to allow me to accomplish a good deal of valuable work before the leak in the dyke split wide open, if it was going to.

I glanced at my card, which still lay on the table. My string of degrees and affiliations was impressive, but those letters alone had not earned me this promotion. Two other qualifications had been needful: one, the ability so to believe in the project that lies became truth, and not even in one's dreams at night did one betray one's dedication. The other? No wife. No dependent children. No unreliable friends or lovers. No personal weaknesses. Utter dedication to the work - and a bare-faced liar.

I believed in the project. Change was coming, gradually if we were lucky; cataclysmically if we were not. And I thanked God that influential politicians in Ottawa and around the world were listening at last to their scientific advisers and allocating funds for research and long-term planning.

My agency: NEPP, the National Energy Planning and Procedural Agency of Canada, was to study Canada's most vulnerable areas and try to foresee events, and to set in place means of meeting problems that could be brought to bear quickly as soon as need was identified. We believed that, given even a little time, with just a little luck, we could probably prevent some of the chaos that would result when Canadians began to understand that climate change wouldn't mean the comfort of milder winters and earlier springs, but that, as year followed year, deserts would appear where we were used to growing our food, rising water in New York, London, Tokyo, not to think of the teeming cities on the coasts of China, India, Bangladesh...

This was Boxing Day. I banished the pictures of hell on earth that I was visualizing and caught Madam watching me with a light of speculation in her eyes. She'd be a worthy opponent. If I could fool her...

I pulled myself together and stood up. "Thank you, Madam," I said. "Perhaps now you can suggest a hotel where I might find a room till I sort out this problem of my accommodation. I think there are several good ones in or near the centre of town?"

"You're tired," she said.

"Yes, I am a little," I confessed.

I was. I had been up most of the night. I had been buffeted by strong winds while travelling in small planes. I had been bored by long delays in airports where most of the passengers were hung over or remedying the situation by topping up again. And these last few hours with Madam would have taxed my powers at the best of times.

"I *am* tired," I said. "And I must go."

I expected Madam to recommend the Hilton or the Delta, and then to say, "Of course you may use my phone. Call Diamond. Or Royal. They're near."

Instead she said, "My dear Richard, you must stay here. You expected to spend a lonely evening and to sleep the night in this apartment, did you not? Then you must do so - at least, the staying here part; I hope you won't be lonely. Come. I'll show you your room. Jenny has already put your luggage there."

For a moment I had visions of Jenny unpacking for me. What had I in those bags? Was there anything that..? Of course not. But my heart was thumping. I was going to have to learn to be very careful, so careful that I need never fear a sudden rush of adrenalin or the need for a convincing denial, a plausible lie.

Madam was watching me. Our eyes locked. Again I felt that she was seeing to the back of my head. But I was worn out. I couldn't deal with this enigma in female form till I had rested. I let her see into my soul till she was satisfied and herself turned away.

"You'll find everything you need here, Richard," she said, and I had the feeling that I could, if I were not so tired, read that statement on many levels.

"Jenny and I will rest now too," she went on. "We'll have a light dinner at eight. And then you and I shall visit my neighbour, Dr. Brownrigg."

I raised my eyebrows.

"G.P. That is, family physician," she supplied. "Retired. Widowed. With a yen for Honduras."

"Oh," I said. "You mean..?"

She took my arm and led me to my room. "I think he'll deal - if you can agree together," she whispered. "You'll like his place. Mine is best, of course, looking south. But Robert's looks west and is only slightly less desirable than mine. Second best, but only just. You'll see."

Chapter Three:

"Robert, I've brought you a visitor."

"Not another lawyer!"

"An accountant," she whispered behind her fingers.

The old man eyed me with suspicion. "Suppose you're from that damned NEPP mob that's making life a misery around here," he growled.

"Guilty," I agreed. "Sorry about the misery. Perhaps I can help."

"Not likely," he grunted, "but you'd better come in... You're looking well this evening, my dear."

This last he said with a sort of toothless leer, such as a decrepit cougar might practise upon a new-born foal. I warmed toward the old fellow.

Madam paid no attention but led the way into the living room, leaving the doctor to close the door and follow us - to follow me into my childhood.

A few steps, a nanosecond passed, and I was in old Tom Verachuk's waiting room. I smelt the Lysol and felt my mother's iron grip upon my wrist. For there on the floor was the same Persian rug rucked up under the same low, round table - except that this rug was not dusty, not very. Across a corner of the rug Tom's brown leather couch stood, one leg anchoring the fabric; but this couch, smooth and taut, rolled back to a time long before my visits to the Verachuk waiting room. Even Tom's round table, that stood on the Persian rug in front of the old brown couch, was there, but not there; Dr. Brownrigg's had never been a dining table.

In childhood I believed that Dr. Tom used the same saw to cut off the table's legs that he used on people. Pete Yakovitch said he did, and I never dared ask my mother if it was true. What if she said it was?

Even a pile of old magazines... I was speculating how far out of date they must be by this time, when a gray tomcat with white paws stalked into the room and I breathed easier - Dr. Verachuk never had a cat. Dr. Brownrigg's was a fine fellow, a little portly, a little stiff, a little grizzled among the whiskers, but very much *Monsieur de la Maison*.

"Good-evening," I said. "How-do-you-do? My name is Dick. And you are..?"

"He is Pericles Rex of Regina," Madam said, "a displaced person like all the rest of us."

Pericles looked me over, walked around me for the view from all angles, raised his tail straight up, and rubbed against my leg. I bent down and scratched him under the chin. He purred and buried his face in my hand.

We had reached this stage of intimacy when Dr. Brownrigg joined us. "Well, will you look at that!" he exclaimed. "Old Perry never makes friends. Not with anybody. Not since Sarah Jane... my wife, you know. He was her cat."

I suspected that Perry's interest in my hand might be traced to Madam's cold roast turkey. I had washed, but perhaps I had missed a spot, and sage and onion is not easily removed. I kept my suspicions to myself, however; I felt I needed every advantage.

Madam went straight to a corner of the couch and curled up there. She had changed before dinner into a brownish-pinkish silky outfit - trousers and some sort of short jacket, with a cream-coloured shirt showing at her neck and down the front. She sat on the couch and disappeared. Only the strip of shirt and her big gray eyes remained.

I could see that the doctor habitually sat in the other corner of the couch. It bore his imprint in the cushions, and the remains of his dinner littered the table opposite. A coffee cup and sherry glass both contained liquid; the sherry bottle, in fact, stood on the floor beside the couch.

I hesitated, waiting for the doctor, but Madam motioned me away from the door to the chair next to the old man's place. I wondered why, but I picked up the cat and crossed the room.

"Just finishin' my dinner," the doctor muttered, gathering up his plate and coffee cup. "Beg your pardon." And he shuffled off to some dark place - I supposed the kitchen - while Perry and I settled into the chair.

Rummaging sounds came from the other room. They indicated, I thought, that the old man might be a few minutes.

I looked at Madam.

She straightened her shoulders, filled her lungs, and gazed straight across the room.

She was sending me a message. I knew that. But to see what she was looking at, I would have to crane my neck through a very awkward angle. She wouldn't make me sit where I couldn't see whatever it was. Would she? I twisted as far as I could, but without result. Then light dawned. Up and out.

Up. Out. And on the wall opposite, a pair of western grebes stretched their beautiful white necks to see beyond the reeds that fringed their melt-water pool in a slough. They floated in the cold air of early prairie spring, their reflections rippling in the water. Around them new-growth reeds flushed green, and last summer's brown grasses sheltered horsetails and small native flowers.

I set the cat on the table and walked home.

A wind from the far-away north we never saw rustled the dry grasses, and stirred the universal, sour smell of spring. Red and yellow shoulder patches flashing, red-winged blackbirds rose in a whirr of wings from nests in the reeds. The high-pitched piping of frogs filled the air.

Soaked to the knees, my nose running, my feet on a pan of ice that had sunk beneath my weight to the bottom of the slough, I froze. The grebes knew I was there.

They knew I was there, and they knew I had found the nestlings they had hidden in a clump of cattail stalks.

Tiny pink and yellow flowers blossomed all around the nest. I would have seen only them had not the nestlings also stretched their necks, gray necks for safety, and opened their yellow beaks wide to be fed. I hadn't heard their demands over the shrilling of the frogs. Nor had I seen the parent birds at all till they turned, their necks like lighter stalks against the reeds.

One of the birds slid onto the nest and covered the little ones from view. The other... slowly... turned... toward me. And the ice under my feet split in two and I went down.

I heard a roar of many wings, then only the rubbing of my pants together as I fled toward home - not even the eternal sighing of the wind.

"Like that picture, do you?" the doctor demanded.

He was standing by the table with a sherry glass in each hand.

"It's perfect," I whispered. "It's the prairie, living and breathing."

"God's country," he agreed. "That's just north of Winnipeg."

"I know," I said. "I grew up there."

"Good God! And I was about to offer you sherry."

So it was that I spent the evening of the day-after-Christmas swapping prairie stories with an old doctor from Manitoba, and wallowing in nostalgia.

The old man had thirty years on me and remembered things that were gone before I was born. He told me about the Great Depression, when they couldn't give the wheat away and it was a long winter after the ducks and geese flew south in the fall, until, one day in spring, the V-shaped strings of them appeared again, dark against the softening sky, and you heard them calling.

He had known real cowboys: old men, even then, but still with the ring of spurs about them in their walk, in their way of slapping dust from their hats against their thighs, in the way their eyes gazed into distance when the wind blew the smell of horses and cattle into town.

I had never seen a cowboy, but I had seen that look in the eyes of old men of the Plains Nations. At the time, when I was a child, I understood only that those strange men wore their hair in pigtails, like girls did. But I remembered the look. Was it

horses on the wind with them? Or the eternal herds of buffalo they must have seen when they were children?

For a little while I blew across that land in the clouds of dust that destroy horses with heaves and mothers with the endless fight to keep things clean, till I dropped into a corral beside a railway station, where they were setting up for a rodeo.

"Not real cowboys!" Dr. Brownrigg was saying.

Madam laughed. "Don't tell me," she said. "Real cowboys couldn't have matched the fellows who go down the road these days."

"Nor these fellows stayed sane on the plains alone," the doctor barked. "Sleepin' with their heads on their saddles. Livin' on bacon and beans. No TV then, my lady. No radio. No Hockey Night in Canada. No... No Metz brothers. No Terry Sawchuck in the net, nor Foster Hewitt hollerin' the play-by-play."

"Who?"

"Foster Hewitt. You wouldn't remember him. You wouldn't go back past Danny Gallivan, if that."

"Danny Gallivan was a Maritimer," Madam murmured.

As if she had uttered blasphemy, we both turned to look at her.

"Well, he was."

"But Foster Hewitt trained him," the old man snapped. "And he sounded just the same. Not like this bunch they have nowadays."

Back and forth across the years and across the plains we went, till we reached Saskatoon on a day a girl called Sarah Jane stopped her bike by the little building that was the original university, to correct the balance of her load of books.

"That university was founded by a Maritimer," Madam murmured.

We didn't bother to challenge that remark, because on that day of Sarah Jane the sun shone brighter than on any other day in the history of the world. The air moved so gently that dry leaves crushed sweetly under her feet. And the harvest moon rose full and golden before the sun went down...

* * *

At last I stretched out in Madam's guest bed and groaned

from weariness. No sound from the world obtruded. No light annoyed. Only a slight oscillation behind my eyes marked present moments as they passed. But no sleep came. I had been sleepless too long. Too many time zones, too many frustrations, too many new faces, too much nostalgia - too much good whiskey probably. My body lay in the bed, grateful for the luxury, but my mind went back to Colorado.

Two days, was it? Maybe three... Last night in Toronto. That flight got in at... seven? I had thought it was about dinnertime, but Toronto was already well launched into Christmas Eve. No, that couldn't be right. Back to Colorado and try again.

I must have been drifting in and out of sleep, but I didn't think so at the time; and by and large there was a pretty lucid continuity to my thoughts, though they never slowed. And before my body had rested enough to fall truly asleep, I think I went through all the meetings I had endured over several days, and then reviewed the important details time and time again...

I met Jack Davidson at the Denver airport and had a beer with him.

"Dick?" he said. "I thought it was you."

He spoke from behind my shoulder at about the time the sun disappeared behind the mountains, and I knew his voice. By sight I wouldn't have known the man who stood beside me in jeans and a turtle neck, carrying a fleece-lined suede coat bunched up under one arm and a camera bag over the other shoulder. I had never seen him before out of the uniform of a brigadier of the US Marines.

"How about a beer?"

The sun would have gone. The sudden winter night would have taken over the west. We sat in a bar knowing that only the shape of mountains would be visible where we were going, had we been going then, and commiserated with each other for being away from home on Christmas Eve. I didn't tell him I had no home to go to but a furnished apartment I didn't know, in a small city I had never seen, down Canada's east coast that I didn't understand, by a sea that scared the hell out of me.

"Cold in Ottawa this time of year, I guess," he remarked.

"It can be very cold."

"A lot like Chicago."

"Something."

"I've heard ambassadors get bonuses for going to Ottawa. Don't guess there's much truth in it."

"Oh, I don't know," I said. "It's a story we like to believe. They say there's only one capital that's harder on the diplomatic corps, and that's Outer Mongolia's."

He laughed. "How come?" he asked. "I mean, it's not all that cold, is it? Lots of places are just as cold."

"Or worse," I agreed, remembering the wind howling down Portage la Prairie. "It's the expense."

"For God's sake! Those guys get everything provided - heat, light, rent... Florida vacations..."

"It's the furs," I explained. "Very expensive. And the women have to be well dressed. You can't be an ambassador's wife without a mink coat."

"Oh," he said, and grinned as if he understood.

I didn't ask. No attachments.

He checked his boarding pass. "Window seat," he said. "I like that. No matter how often I fly over this country, I never get tired of looking at it."

"You won't see much on this flight," I replied.

He looked surprised. "Don't think so? It's the emptiness I like," he said. "Just the odd sentinel light showing up now and then. The odd little town hunkered down. The occasional city off in the distance..."

He left me with a touch on the shoulder and a "See you around, Dick."

"Enjoy the holidays," I told him.

I didn't know if he observed Christmas or not, but I meant the wish. Marine general or no, I liked him - not like some of those bastards...

As I sat in that bar in Denver, I heard again the plummy voice of our British chairperson: "Dr. Waterman, we haven't heard from you for some time..."

I wondered how long it would be before a man could think of hitting a woman without the automatic taboos cutting in. At that moment I had almost wished the day had come. But I pulled myself together and presented the official Canadian point of view. What I wanted was to jump to my feet and let her have my personal point of view. Let them all have it. Even Jack Davidson, who thought of the Great Plains as two or three hours of emptiness unrolling under his wings. What did he know? What did any of them know?

What did they know about being down there on the ground in Christmas week? About hoping against hope the car would start without a new battery. About that pinch of the nostrils that meant it would be a night of deep cold. About roasting turkey, stuffed with sage and onion, filling an overheated little house. Or about bundling up till you could barely move and taking a snowmobile beyond the lights that men put up, to lie on your back on some frozen lake and send your soul into the night. Did they know the crunch of snow? The faint singing of the Aurora when it dips close to the ground? The almost imperceptible colours of those curtains of light that sweep with mathematical precision around the pole?

"You've been to Churchill?" Jack had asked me.

"Yes."

"They say lightning never strikes twice."

"But we know it does."

"Yes."

Chapter Four:

I saw Madam and Dr. Brownrigg often; in fact, I soon came to agreement with the doctor and moved into his spare bedroom pending his departure for Honduras.

My logs show that I also spent about ten days of January in Colorado again, and then went to Ottawa. So it was not until about a week after Robert left at the end of January that I saw Madam alone for more than a few minutes.

I was on my way home at noon, crossing the park in front of our building, when I heard, "Richard! Richard! Isn't this wonderful?"

She was dark green, head to toe - pants, parka, gloves and boots, even the fur on her hood. And her park bench was green. I had walked right past her.

"Madam! Is this a game you play?"

"What? Feeding the birds?"

"No. Disappearing at will."

"Do I?"

"You're at it again!"

She laughed as if delighted by the idea. "Do I really? Come and explain."

I was not dressed for park benches in February - not for

any length of time - but I settled on the edge of the one she had chosen and helped her scatter cracked corn and bread crumbs to the pigeons.

"It's illegal, you know," she said, as a fan of corn left her hand and fell among the birds.

"Sitting in the park?"

"Feeding the pigeons."

"Then why do you do it?"

"They're hungry."

"Fair enough."

After awhile she laughed, a bubbling sound much like the pigeons made. "They're hungry," she said. "That's the only reason now. But some of my friends who used to live in our building - your building - fussed about them. It was more fun then."

"Feeding the birds."

"Of course. Isn't it a beautiful sight?"

"The birds."

"No, no, Richard. Really, dear, I worry about you. The birds are always the same, except a little scruffier in winter. I mean the trees - everything - the whole town."

"Is it? I hadn't noticed."

"Exactly. You've been accounting again," she said with a sigh. "Now sit back on the bench. Lift your head. And look... Look at that elm tree."

It *was* wonderful. The tree sparkled, every twig and bud encased in ice. The sun shone from a clear sky, and the tree sparkled wherever the light touched. We gazed at it for quite a long time, while the pigeons moved closer and closer and finally pecked at our boots to remind us of the business at hand.

"How about lunch?" I said, rising from that freezing perch.

"A lovely idea," Madam exclaimed, and immediately emptied her sacks of corn and crumbs in two neat piles on the ground... "Do you see that bush?"

"What bush?"

"That one. I'm afraid it's going to..."

Before our eyes the bush disintegrated. One moment it was scintillating with the colours of the rainbow. The next - a pile of twigs in the snow, like the corn and bread crumbs.

"Ah, bravo!" Madam cried. "A disappearing act with a vengeance."

I stood mesmerized. “It’s gone!” I gasped. “Just like that, it’s gone! I’ve never seen anything like it.”

“It’s all right,” Madam murmured. “It will grow back next summer. That kind does.”

She took my arm - it was a good thing she did - and started me across the park.

“But I’ve never seen a bush disappear before,” I insisted, still looking back over my shoulder. “Not until just now. Does it happen all the time? Have I..?”

“No, no,” Madam soothed. “That was serendipitous, I’m sure.”

“But it...”

“But if it happened today, has it happened many times when you might have been looking but weren’t?”

“Yes. Perhaps I...”

“Perhaps you had your head in a cloud of numbers.”

“Yes.”

“Or perhaps,” she conceded with a chuckle, “perhaps such things are rarer in Manitoba - or Ottawa - than they are here on the coast, where we often hover between rain and snow, melting and freezing. Perhaps disappearing bushes are more common here than they are.. other... where...”

“Perhaps they are.”

“After all,” she said, “burning bushes appear only in desert country. At least, the only instance I know of did... That’s a Manitoba maple over there, a young one. Tomorrow it will stand straight again. Not like the old elms. They can’t bend and may break. But I think they can bear much more weight than this little ice event has piled upon them.”

She squeezed my arm and I wondered why. I never knew with Madam, but I always felt she understood more than I ever told her.

“I went to the theatre last night,” she said as we left the park. “The one just there on the square. Have you noticed, Richard, how dreary coming out of a theatre can be? The magic is gone, and one sees worried faces, unhappy faces, faces of people with nothing to do and nowhere to go...”

“Chewing gum stuck to the sidewalk,” I added, “and the wrappers collecting in corners.”

She glanced at me, her eyes sparkling, but she said nothing; and again I searched my mind for an explanation. None came.

"You were saying..?"

"I was saying," she replied. "I was getting around to saying that coming out of the theatre last night was better than being in it. Everything sparkled under the park lights. I didn't want to go home. And I couldn't wait for the sun to come up this morning... Where shall we lunch?"

"How about that little place in the corner of our building? We can get a good meal there and still see the park without freezing to death."

"It isn't really all that cold, you know," she said. "For someone brought up in Manitoba, this should be positively balmy."

"In Manitoba," I said, "I would have been wearing longjohns."

"There is this," she conceded as we crossed the road.

A grouping... No, that's an accountant's word; it was more a dancing or a babbling. Good Lord! That from Richard Waterman! Start again. A group of children overtook us and ran by - on their way home to lunch, I supposed.

"Hi, Madam," some of them shouted.

And one little girl with bright blue eyes and a strawberry-blonde ponytail turned and danced backwards for a few steps. "I saw Amos, Madam," she called. "He's all better. Maybe he went to see Dr. Robert."

"That's an idea," Madam answered with a wide smile.

"Who's Amos?" I asked.

"A pigeon."

"A pigeon!"

"That's right. A pigeon who spent his winter holiday in Honduras."

"And found time to visit Robert between flights."

We stood on the street shouting with laughter and went inside the restaurant with better appetites than even the silver morning had given us.

During lunch I warmed up considerably, and Madam, having undone a number of zippers and peeled back layer after layer of her green snow clothes, settled at last with her elbows on the table. She was down to a yellow T-shirt with a banana tree splashed all over the front.

"Robert brought it from Central America after one of his trips there," she told me with a fond smile, having noticed my raised eyebrows.

"You must miss him," I remarked.

She looked away, in peace and silence, for a minute or two. Then she studied my face, sighed as if she had made up her mind, and said, "No, Richard. No, I do not."

"Madam!" I cried. "You never cease to amaze me, but this is above and beyond. I thought you and Rob were great friends."

"We are!"

"But you don't miss him."

"How can I miss him? I know where he is."

"But you can't see him."

"I can, Richard. I know just where he is. I could describe it to you."

"Do it, then," I challenged.

"All right," she agreed, after another pause. "Yes, I will describe it, for you... If I can get it right, for you."

I waited.

She took a deep breath.

"Robert," she said, "sleeps in a small narrow bed in a small narrow room with a door and one window, both small and narrow. The window has shutters painted a deep, strong blue, but no glass and no curtains; and the door has a latch but no knob and no lock. It is painted the same strong blue. The walls are white. The ceiling is poles fitted close together. And the floor is rough, red tiles. He has a small table and a straight chair, both painted green - a deep green. On the table is a clay candlestick, and on the wall a picture of the Virgin..."

"Robert is not a religious man."

"Robert is a happy man."

"In this place you describe."

"He sleeps well. He works. He keeps fresh flowers for the Virgin on his table..."

"He isn't even Catholic."

"It isn't necessary."

"How old is Rob?"

"Robert is eighty-two."

"Then he should be..."

"He should be where he is. It is where he wants to be. He lives with Father Luis, and together they look after the village."

"But at eighty-two someone ought to be looking after him."

"And so they do. Father Luis and all the villagers. Old men and grandchildren, birds and lizards, flowers and vegetables. They love him, Richard. And he loves them."

"And it doesn't matter - to you - that you cannot see your friend."

"Try to understand, Richard," she said, "that I do see him. And so do you."

I ignored the last part of her statement. "But you can't talk to him," I argued.

"I talk to him all the time. I'm talking to him now."

"You are talking to me now."

"And you are..?"

I shook my head. "I am an accountant lunching with a woman who baffles him," I said.

"And I," she countered with a happy laugh, "am a woman full of a very good lunch. You will be late to work, accountant. Go back to your numbers and think of nothing else till the sun goes down."

* * *

I did that, not from choice but from necessity, but as I took the elevator home about eight I thought of Madam again and of some of the baffling things she had said to me.

I returned to Robert's suite, and it was exactly as he - and I - had left it. Our agreement was that I should use his furnishings in exchange for room, board, and veterinary care for Pericles - I threw in a lap to sit on, a hand to lick, and frequent displays of affection on my part. Although I drew the line at allowing him to sleep on my bed, I made no distinction among the chairs and tables, and on the whole I think Pericles was satisfied, as I was.

That evening I opened the door and, for the first time, noticed the floor in the foyer.

"I should get rid of that carpet," I thought.

Not till then did I see Perry waiting for me by the closet

door. Only the part of him that was not backed by the carpet was visible.

"Good Lord, don't tell me you do it too," I exclaimed, and he unfolded himself and strolled toward me, his white paws like small snowballs moving against the gray.

"We're going to have to do something about this," I told him.

I nearly turned around then and there to fetch Madam, but I picked up the cat and carried him into the kitchen instead. It was well past his dinnertime, and I forgot the hall carpet in the evening ritual as I served his dish and watched him settle down to eat.

I noticed then that the cushion flooring in the kitchen was a dingy, faded green with a complicated pattern of red arabesques. No wonder that room always struck me as dark and gloomy, even when the afternoon sun was pouring in.

I went into the living room and looked at the floor there, expecting better things but not finding them. The Persian rug was truly beautiful, but it covered only a small portion of the total area - less than it should have, being rucked up as usual. I had mentioned that problem to the cleaning staff.

"It's because it's laid on top of wall-to-wall," they told me. "They'll do that. Every time."

I looked and found the same no-colour wall-to-wall that I had examined in the hall.

Madam. This time I reached out my hand for the phone, but changed my mind again. It would do no good to demand of her who in the world had decorated this flat. Perhaps it had been old Rob himself. Perhaps his lost Sarah Jane, but I doubted that. Never Madam - though with her penchant for disappearing into the woodwork...

And there she was. The doorbell rang. Perry and I answered at a stately run. And Madam entered with coffee, sandwiches, a bowl of strawberries, and some chocolates, on a tray.

I took the tray from her and set it on the round table that I had never been able to accept for anything other than a cut-down dining table, and she went directly to her place at the end of the couch.

I had not adopted Robert's place - that was still his - but that evening, for convenience in dispensing and despatching supper, I made an exception. I was suddenly very hungry.

Madam made no excuses, nor advanced any reasons for her appearance bearing food. She merely sent me to the kitchen for plates and cups and a knife or two for the fruit.

"And bring a few napkins," she called after me. "I meant to include some but I forgot."

We polished off her roast beef and pickle sandwiches in short order. If I was hungry, so was she. We said nothing beyond "Uum-m," and "This is good," and "Would you like another?" till the sandwiches and berries were gone and I suggested I bring out Robert's bottle of Oloroso to go with the coffee. This proved a very sound idea, which encouraged us to eat the chocolates as well, without ever saying "I shouldn't," or "Here goes that New Year's resolution again."

"Madam," I began at last, relaxed and in expansive mood: "Madam, the cleaners tell me that I can't hope to keep Rob's Persian rug smooth while it is spread over what they call wall-to-wall."

"Bravo!" she cried. "You're moving in."

I let that pass. "Is it true?" I demanded.

"Yes indeed," she told me. "If it were not that one corner is anchored by the couch, and the table holds down the bulk, your rug would have worked its way out the window and down to the harbour long ago. Where did you think the idea of flying carpets came from?"

Naturally I had never thought of flying carpets at all.

"You mean it would lie straight if I took away the carpet underneath?"

She sighed; almost, I thought, with relief.

"Why did you sigh?"

"My confidence in you has been confirmed," she said.

I frowned, baffled again.

"Because, my dear," she explained, "you said 'If I took away the carpet underneath,' not 'If I threw the damned thing out!"

"Throw out old Rob's Persian rug?" I howled. "It's the best thing in the place - next to the painting of the grebes. I would rather throw out Perry."

"I was sure of it," she said with a wide smile. "But one does like confirmation. We must have our signs and wonders."

"What would be under the carpet," I mused, "if I were to take it up?"

"Oh, I can tell you that!" she cried. "It's only the coarsest of under-flooring. Isn't that wonderful? You won't have to decide whether or not to salvage anything. What do you think you'll choose?"

"Choose?"

"For your new floor."

"Oh. Well... What would you choose?"

"I? Parquet beyond a doubt," she said. "It's warm and inviting, and you could have it finished in the shade that would make the very best background for your Persian. If I had owned a rug like that, I wouldn't have put down wall-to-wall in my place."

I noticed that she referred to "my" rug, but I was concentrating on the subject of parquet at that time and went on with that enquiry. "You are talking about those little pieces," I began. "I mean, short lengths, or... whatever... which..."

She took pity on me. "Of course," she said. "Hardwood, naturally, but you can have it laid down in all sorts of patterns depending on what you want - depending on what the rug demands, that is. Of course you will have the real thing, not those prefabricated blocks that stick down like cushion tiles. I should think something fairly simple but not too plain. The rug needs to cuddle up to it but not to disappear into it..."

I studied her face and decided she hadn't meant anything beyond the obvious meaning of what she said.

"...or fight with it for attention," she finished.

"It sounds expensive," I hedged.

"Oh, of course," she broke in. "Is that a problem? For if it is..."

"No, no," I assured her. I had the money from the sale of my mother's house. Accountant-like, I had invested it at a good rate of return, but, in the last little while..."

"No," I said. "Why not? I expect to be here till I retire, which, in the normal course of events..."

My voice trailed off as I assessed how likely it was that the normal course of events would last another ten or twelve years, and Madam caught me out. I was beginning to see why the powers that be in Ottawa, and elsewhere, were so adamant about no personal attachments. But one could hardly avoid... Perhaps I was not the man for the job after all... If I had to choose between Madam and Perry and old Robert and...

Madam said nothing, but she read my face like a book.

"You keep referring to the rug as mine, Madam," I said, to change the train of thought. "I'm afraid I will always think of it as Rob's. You see, it's twice his..."

And I began the story of old Tom Verachuk and the German measles inoculation, the time I dove under the table and wrapped myself around a leg, screaming as loud as I could, "No, Momma. He hates kids. He uses horse needles on them."

"Don't be ridiculous, Richard," my mother scolded. "Come out of there."

"No, Momma. He does. Everybody says so."

"You're making a spectacle of yourself, Richard. Would I take you to a horse doctor?"

"You don't know, Momma."

"I certainly know more than you do, Richard Waterman," she announced in a loud voice. "Come out of there this instant."

"No-o-o-o-o-o!!!"

Dr. Verachuk poked his head out of his consulting room and glared. "What's going on out there?" he shouted. "Can't you keep that boy quiet, Elsie? What's the matter with him?"

"Don't you yell at my mother," I yelled at him. "Horse doctor! Horse doctor! Horse doctor!"

He still scowled, but he came out and his shoulders hunched up in a funny way. "You ever seen horses in my waiting room, boy?" he demanded.

"No-o."

"Nor horse manure on my Persian rug? Eh, boy?"

"No, but you're a horse doctor all the same. Pete Yakovitch told me. He said he seen you..."

"Saw," my mother corrected.

"...saw you at his grandfather's barn with a needle as long as your arm. And he said you stuck it in a horse's rump as far as it could go and that horse bucking and kicking..."

"Elsie, you're coddling that boy," old Tom said, turning on my mother. "How is he going to learn the difference between truth and what the Yakovitches of this world tell him if you never let him see for himself?"

My mother drew herself up. “Are you suggesting,” she demanded, “that I should leave the education of my son to Pete Yakovitch and that disreputable old grandfather of his? For if you are, Tom Verachuk, though you brought him into the world, and me before him, and no doubt my mother and father before that...”

The old man chuckled. “No, no, Elsie,” he said. “The boy, yes. You, too. But I’d have had to qualify at the age of ten for the founder of your clan. Don’t get on your high horse. You know perfectly well... Now, now. Bringing up a boy without a father... Can’t be easy for you... Nor for him either...”

Tears had started up in my mother’s eyes and were running down her cheeks. “I do the v-very b-best I can,” she said, and reached for a bunch of tissues out of a box on the table, which she yanked out and punched at her eyes to stop the crying.

“Now, now, Elsie,” the old man said again, and came out and put an arm around her shoulders. “Come into the office and calm yourself, girl. We’ll have a cup of tea and talk things over. Nobody thinks you’re not doing a good job with the boy. But he’s a smart little fellow and bound to grow up...”

He began to chuckle, and I heard him say as they disappeared into the consulting room, “...and believing that young hoodlum Pete Yakovitch, Elsie. Now I ask you. You know yourself no Yakovitch this side of St. Boniface ever said good-morning without exaggerating... Know the old man, do you?”

My mother murmured something that I didn’t catch.

“Yes, dishonest old rogue,” the doctor said - he seemed to be agreeing. “Untruthful, we all know that... But maybe he has reasons...”

I still couldn’t hear my mother’s words, though they had left the door open, but she sounded indignant.

The doctor began then to tell her about Pete Yakovitch’s grandfather and I stopped listening. His voice reached me, but I heard only snatches of what he said: “Straight out of the Ukraine, you know, Elsie... Life wasn’t easy... No. No. No excuse for lieing and cheating. You’re right. And you’re right to...”

I stayed under the table, but their voices receded to a murmur in my ears because I wasn’t interested any more. I had discovered the carpet. I felt it with my hands. I smelt the dust in it. I scraped a patch of it with my fingernails and watched a deep red colour appear. A little more, and I found a brilliant blue. Another patch, yellow as sunshine...

"Well now, Elsie," the doctor said at last, "if you've recovered, we'd better retrieve that boy from under the table..."

I crawled out and left, shutting the door softly but firmly behind me...

"And?" Madam prompted.

"And, would you believe it? The first person I ran into on the street was Pete Yakovitch. But I knew him now. He was two years older than me, but that didn't matter any more. I didn't have to believe him. We spent the afternoon jumping in the hay loft of his grandfather's barn, that had been a livery stable long ago and still said 'Livery Stable' over the door."

"And did she?"

"My mother?"

"Did she get over her fear of Pete Yakovitch and his grandfather and let you grow up on your own?"

"She came to terms with her problem," I said with a smile... "We went to the old man's funeral. In the Catholic church. I wondered even then how an old reprobate like him could deserve such a pretty funeral... Have another sherry."

"Thanks," she said, "and finish your story."

"I thought I had finished."

"I doubt it," she said. "Your mother would have remembered the injection you hadn't had."

"Naturally," I chuckled. "My mother never forgot an injection. We went back in the evening."

"And you behaved like a lamb."

"Yes, I didn't even yell, though I can remember the sting to this day."

Madam smiled. "While your floor is laid," she said, "you can send your rug out to be cleaned and repaired. You'll find the most brilliant colours will show up this time too."

She looked around the room with a speculative eye, and I felt a sinking sensation in my stomach.

Chapter Five:

Soon after that day - I realized afterward that it was the day on which I first lifted my head and looked out of my own volition... Soon after that I received notice of a planning session for the North Atlantic basin to be held in London the weekend of February fourteenth, in ten days' time. I was to represent the Canadian east coast: bays, islands, inlets, and estuaries, from the international border to permanent ice. It meant a great deal of preparation.

The decorators were coming, too, to lay the new floor, and to paint, paper, and polish - all the things that had to be done if walls and ceilings were to be fit to associate with the Persian and the parquet. I supposed, however, that since the workers would go home at night, I would sleep in my own bed, shave in my own bathroom... in short, that my personal life would not be disturbed at this time when I had so much to do.

"Oh, no, no!" Madam assured me. "You'll never stand the confusion. Or the smell. Think of it - glue, paint, cleaning compounds. Dreadful."

She had come over to see how my plans were progressing.

"And what about Perry?" she went on.

"Yes. Perry."

Now Perry and Madam treated each other with dignity and respect. Perry greeted her politely whenever she visited us, but he never suggested that he might sit on her lap or that she might scratch behind his ears. And Madam talked to him as she might have talked to an elderly gentleman caller, one who would never presume to rearrange her pink cushions or to sit on her glass-topped coffee table.

Jenny, though, treated Perry like some oriental potentate with the intelligence of an infant chimpanzee. She called him her "lovey-dovey little man" and her "dear sweetums handsome Pericles." And he lapped it up. He slept on her bed, shared her meals, sharpened his claws on her grandmother's handmade, antique rag rug - did whatever he liked. And she loved it.

"Of course Perry can't stay alone while you're in the UK," Madam said. "And you'll need to keep him out of the way of the decorators. You'd better bring him over to Jenny."

"He won't be a bother?"

"Not at all. She adores him. Bring your own things at the same time. When did you say you were going to London?"

"Friday next week."

"Lovely. People always say, what a pity you're going in winter: wet, damp, and draughty. But I would go to London any season of the year. If it weren't for the fund-raising drive for the symphony, I'd be tempted to come with you."

The thought struck me - with some surprise - that I would enjoy having Madam come with me; with so much surprise, in fact, that I almost missed her next remark.

"I'm having a party on the Wednesday."

I supposed there was a connection. "I'll make myself scarce," I said.

"No, no. Of course you won't," Madam scolded. "I intended to ask you anyway, and naturally you'll come. It's just that staying in the house there'll be no escape."

"I'll make myself useful, then," I said.

"I don't think you like parties."

"I don't, much. But I can pass drinks and canapés with the best of them. I'm assuming it's that kind of party?"

"Yes," she agreed, but absently, as if her mind was not on my question but possibly on the list of things she had to see to before next Wednesday.

Then she looked at me and saw me again, but with a puzzle in her eyes. "Where was I?" she asked.

"I was saying I could help serve your guests," I repeated.

"Oh. Yes. It's a pre-concert party. Six to eight. Nobody will come before seven, of course, and they'll all have to be out by a quarter to eight, even if the concert *is* just along the street. Only there's always someone who won't budge."

"Have no fear," I promised. "They'll all be out by ten to. You won't have to miss a note. What's on the program?"

"The string quartet... And guests."

Again her mind went absent. I waited.

"I have a seat for you," she said presently, with a return of vigour. "I don't think you're musical, but you need to be educated."

"Well..," I started.

"It's necessary, Richard," she told me. "A man in your position."

"In my position," I said, "I am not required to appreciate Bach and Beethoven."

"You wish!" she exclaimed, and laughed. "There won't be any B and B at this concert. We're having Virginia McKellar and Jeremy Squill."

"Never heard of them, I'm afraid," I said. "They sound like a comedy team."

Madam only laughed again. "You'll see," she said, and my blood chilled. I was growing used to her cryptic pronouncements, and that one always filled me with dread.

"Highbrow?" I croaked.

"Very."

"But, Madam, I know nothing, nothing..."

"Sergeant Schultz won't help you either," she said. "Present yourself in my living room on the dot of six - in formal clothes."

"I don't own formal clothes."

"Look in Robert's wardrobe. He had a very good tuxedo. Real old wool, the kind that's cool and slightly damp to the touch, not one of the new ones with synthetic fibres to keep a crease. And no made-up ties."

"I can't wear Rob's clothes!"

"Why not?"

"You wouldn't want me wearing yours."

She cocked her head on one side, her eyes sparkling. "No," she said at last. "No, I think not. But you may wear Robert's with his - and my - blessing."

"He left me his furniture," I argued, "but I don't think... Anyway, he's taller than I am."

"There's a good tailor on Charlotte Street. Drop in tomorrow and he'll alter things for you."

"Madam," I howled, "you're incorrigible. You're talking about a man's dress suit. I can't go having the coat taken in here and there, the trousers shortened, to say nothing of..."

"Robert doesn't want it," she said.

"He will when he comes back. I don't know what he'll say about the redecorating, but I do know what he'd say if he found his formal coat wouldn't meet around the middle any more and his formal trousers couldn't quite cover his ankles."

"No, Richard," Madam said. "Robert will not leave his village again. Whatever he left *with* you, he left *for* you. Now whether you know it or not, you're somebody in this town. People want to meet you, and you'll have to look your part."

All this time I had been standing in the kitchen doorway, having just given Perry his supper. Madam was just inside the living room in front of one of the windows, standing with the light of the setting sun making a halo around her head. She looked very young, and I wondered how old she was.

I walked into the room and led her to a chair where the light still shone through the window. The chair was already covered with a drip-sheet, but I shoved that aside and settled her there. I leaned against a semi-circular drum table from which I had removed Robert's bric-a-brac. The table too was covered with a drip-sheet, but the painters had not yet started their work so it was safe to sit there.

"Madam," I started in when I had her seated so that I could tower over her. "Madam, I don't know how to say this. I don't want you to think me ungrateful... or anti-social... or... or... But you really mustn't... I really think I... I mean.... You know, if I were to... But I..."

"You're like your native prairies, Richard," she said, and laughed at me. "You begin, but you never end."

"Yes, well... The thing is, Madam..."

"The thing is, Richard," she said, "that you must. It's expected."

"Anybody who knows me," I argued, "knows that I... well..."

"Knows you are never happier than when you have your nose in a column of figures," she said.

"No, no. I wouldn't go that far. But..."

"But there's truth in it, isn't there," she said. "You're a darling, Richard..."

"Me!"

"Yes, you. But you need to be brought out. Your career demands it, dear."

"No, not that," I said with conviction.

"Not your job career, your life career. Lots of nice people in this town would make you very welcome if you'd let them. But you have to come out and be seen. I'm giving you an opportunity to do that, and I expect you to take it."

"I don't think it's an opportunity," I said, "because it doesn't include an escape clause."

"Exactly. So have Robert's suit altered, and stand up to be presented."

She stood up to go, but she beamed at me. "You may quite possibly like it," she said.

No, I wouldn't like it. I would do it. For Madam. But I couldn't see that any good would come of my being known around the town. Eventually I would be that fellow who knew all along that the salt water was rising, the fresh water table dropping; that we were not going to have warmer summers, but more fog; that milder winters were going to bring ice storms to the east coast, not the delights of Florida and Cuba. How many of them would want to know me then?

My thoughts were sombre as I followed Madam to the door and opened it for her. But Perry and I moved over to "10 South," and I had Robert's tux altered. I never felt right about that, but there was no way I could have a suit made before Wednesday week, and Madam seemed to think I really should dress for the occasion.

When she had gone, I wandered back to the window, where the setting sun had disappeared behind the buildings that slid steeply down to the inner harbour and that part of the city known locally as the foot of King. I stood there for some time, thinking, musing, till my eyes began to blink and I realized I was standing straight and looking out into the winter night without having been ordered to it. My breathing seemed deeper than usual too. I shook my head and laughed, and turned on the news channel.

* * *

I had rarely worn formal clothes, though I knew how it should be done from watching TV, and therefore, on the Wednesday I walked into Madam's living room only half an hour late, looking, if I say so myself, quite distinguished.

Madam looked me over and approved.

She wore some shade or other - possibly shades - of the pink she seemed to prefer. I have no words to describe her dress except to say that it swirled around her knees and made her look happy and playful. She made me smile just looking at her, which pleased her. Her hair shone, her nails shone, but not even the diamonds in her ears and around her neck shone like her eyes.

There was something different about her though. It took me a moment, but I realized in time! She'd had her hair cut. Cut very well, I decided. It swung just below her ears and looked... well... pinker. And younger. I now knew her age - she was fifty-eight - but nobody would ever have guessed on concert night.

My tongue stumbled, but she seemed to know what I meant. No doubt my face said it all.

"Thank you, Richard," she murmured. "It's fun to dress up now and then, isn't it."

"Uh-h."

"Don't you agree? Aren't you really rather pleased with yourself tonight? You look very well."

"I feel like the head waiter at the Green Dragon across the street," I said.

"Nobody would ever take you for a waiter," she told me. "Don't worry. You'll knock 'em dead."

I laughed. "If I can forget I'm wearing a pirated suit," I said.

"You will. You'll see."

And I was wondering how much I had left "to see" when the bell rang and Jenny admitted the first guests.

"We're on," Madam whispered, and I suspected that she was as keyed up as I was.

She was duck to water; though, come to think of it, more a Pacific dolphin than any duck I ever saw - every movement graceful, every word gracious, her voice pitched to be heard but not to dominate the room. I, on the other hand, seemed to have ten or twelve feet, each going in its own direction, and I usually had to repeat what I said - when I could think of anything to say in the first place.

"You were right, Elsie," I thought. "I should have stayed home when you had the ladies in, but it was much more fun to run with Pete Yakovitch and the other kids instead. Too bad I couldn't have done both."

I soon got the hang of party behaviour, however, if not the rhythm, and bowed and smiled, and shook hands as if I had listened to my mother back there on the prairie. I never caught anybody's name, of course; they all came at once, all shouting at the top of their voices. When we talked them over later, I had to refer to "the old fellow with the paunch... the slinky blonde... the one with the fake German accent."

They all came. They came in good time. And we had them out by ten to eight. But it was a long night even so. Madam had taken a box at the Imperial, and I sat through two hours of the most excruciating, modern, so-called music that a man ever had to endure - in full view of the house too.

And then there were the intermissions.

"Isn't it wonderful, Dr. Waterman!"

"Very interesting. Very talented young composers."

"We are so lucky to have them come home and play for us."

"Here's Dr. Polowitz, Dr. Waterman. Dr. Polowitz taught Virginia when she was only six and went to school here - just around the corner, actually."

"Don't you agree, Dr. Waterman, that Virginia's etude is exquisitely tuneful for such a serious work?"

I hadn't been able to find two tuneful notes in the whole piece, but I smiled at the lady who had, and put my special talent to work. "I must meet the young lady and congratulate her," I said.

I said it without the flicker of an eyelash, and had to eat my words later, at the reception for the musicians.

Miss McKellar was a plain, angular young woman, who wore thick glasses that magnified her weak eyes, and did nothing with her hair but let it grow long and thin. Only talk of her music brought any animation to her face or figure.

Someone introduced me, and I heard suitable - even appropriate - words pour from my lips. I wondered at the time at my fluency, appalled but at the same time rather pleased. The truth is that I performed almost as well as Virginia had, smoothly applauding her performance. She glowed. Drank it all in. And I didn't feel guilty in the least. Thinking about it afterward, I wasn't sure how to feel about that.

At the time, however, I dealt with Virginia perfectly. But I paid for it when a deep, syrupy voice oozed from just behind my shoulder, "Dr. Waterman's opinion is very worth having, Virginia. He has a vast experience of music."

A boa constrictor had snuggled up to me. "Oh, no, no," I murmured. But my reputation as a connoisseur of modern atonality was made. What can a man do, sandwiched between a girl who desperately wants her work to be understood and appreciated, and a lady of fifty-something who desperately wants to be understood and appreciated for herself? I am old enough to know that there is precious little any man can do.

At the end of the evening I reached Madam's door wanting only to free myself of Robert's clothes and stretch out in bed, but Madam needed to talk.

"Sit down for a minute, Richard," she said. "I need to unwind before I can sleep. Tell me what you thought."

I sank into a chair - my chair at the end of the coffee table - and kneaded my forehead with my fingers.

"Well," I said, "I thought, 'How in God's name could a scared little wisp of a girl like Virginia McKellar create such an instrument of torture."

Madam shrieked with laughter. "You didn't like it!" she cried.

"And you knew I wouldn't!"

"And you're honest enough to admit it."

"And I'll bet you, so are ninety percent of the people who were there, now that they're back in the privacy of the master bedroom suites of this town."

"Oh, no," she said, and didn't smile at all. "I would put the figure at much higher than ninety percent."

We sat and howled together. Madam kicked off her shoes and curled up on the couch. I undid my tie and removed the first stud from my shirt front.

"Now tell me who they were," I demanded, as soon as we could both talk. "You made me meet all those people. Who were they? Start with the paunch. I thought doctors these days had everyone on diets by the age of fifty-five or sixty. The paunch must be well over seventy and still first to the food and drink."

Madam laughed. "Hostesses count him as two," she said. "That's Dr. Farrinburg."

"Doctor!"

"Professor. English literature. Shakespeare a specialty."

"Oh. Still teaching?"

"A little. They don't come like old John Farrinburg any more. Did you meet his wife? Edna? Mousy. Mustard coloured."

"Oh, the one you told me to dig out of the corner whenever she tried to fade behind the radish roses?"

"That's the one. She's as smart as he is, but you'd never know it... Did you meet Harv Portman?"

"The architect? Yes. Nice fellow, seemingly."

"Harv built these suites. I think you'd like him and Annette."

"Girl with light hair, nice smile?"

"Yes. And I saw you talking with Alexa Carmody at the reception afterward. That was good."

"I'd met her before. On business. Was that Maggie Murchison with her?"

"In person!"

"And what about the one with the voice like an all-day sucker?"

Madam laughed so hard Perry ambled in to see what was going on. "The one in that awful bright blue velvet?" she asked. "I don't know."

"What?"

"They were saying she dresses out of Frenchie's," she

howled. “But Frenchie wouldn’t have that rag in stock. It looked like it came out of some little girl’s dress-up box. You’ll be hearing from her.”

“God help us!” I cried. “I hope not! She kept creeping up behind me. I wouldn’t know she was there; I would be opening my mouth because I had finally thought of something intelligent to say; and I’d hear, ‘Dr. Waterman is from Winnipeg, you know.’ She got that one off at least three times, maybe four.”

“She only wanted people to think she knew you better than they did.”

“But who is she? So I’ll know how to avoid her. She’s already made me out to be an authority on that noise that passed for music.”

“I told you. I don’t know.”

“But she came to your party!”

“The Farrinburgs brought her. I never saw her before in my life.”

“But... Do people do that?”

“They do if they’re shy like Edna, and fall into clutches.”

“Good Lord! Am I in danger of falling into clutches? I may stay in London and resign there. How would you feel about adopting Perry permanently?”

Madam cocked her head at Perry, who was taking part in the conversation from his favourite station under the coffee table. “Jenny would be delighted,” she said. “But you won’t.”

“I’m not so sure about that.”

“I’ll help you,” Madam promised. “When she rings, say you are having drinks, or lunch, or whatever, with me. I’ll back you up.”

“I could tell my secretary to deny me,” I said, “but I don’t know the woman’s name!”

“Oh, don’t worry about that,” Madam said. “I’ll find out. Edna is sweet, but she’s not stupid. Shelley must have caught her unawares.”

“Shelley. It would be. There’s something about women called Shelley. They seem to think I can’t tell a female strangler when I see one. And why must they all look as if they came from a fire sale?”

Madam’s eyes danced. “Richard, my love,” she said, “tell me. I must know. Have you never married?”

"Once," I said. "It didn't last. Maybe I didn't know enough about women's dresses. Maybe I didn't know enough about women. Maybe because her name was Shelley."

Madam couldn't contain her delight. "So that's it!" she cried. "Robert would be delighted his suit was having so much fun!"

* * *

After a night flight, a gruelling Saturday - ten hours of acrimonious meetings at which I had had to be unusually vigilant and more alert than ever - and I was standing at the window of my hotel room in London, looking out over the city and the river. I was very close to the glass so that I could see, through the streaks of partially oxidized hydrocarbons that had accumulated there, away off to the left, the Tower and the lights of Tower Bridge. A light rain was falling.

I had no recollection of how I had arrived at that window - perhaps transported from some earlier time when the river took its natural course and reeds grew and swans slatted away, flapping low over clean pools shrouded in mist. It took me a moment to reorient myself, but there I was when I was aroused by a siren below in the street and the simultaneous ringing of the phone beside my bed. I thought I must be more tired than I knew.

I realized, as I came to myself, that I had been thinking of home. Not the little town north of Winnipeg where I grew up, but my new home by the sea. I had expected to find the Persian rug and the polished parquet I was having installed in the living room, the afternoon sun pouring through the windows, the grebes in their slough. Perry. Madam. Robert...

I thought especially, I remember, of Rob and of how the other considerations affected him. I could see, in my mind's eye, his impression in the cushions of the brown couch, his sherry bottle standing on the floor. I almost heard him speak.

I must have been asleep on my feet. They say horses sleep on their feet, which, of course, led me back to old man Yakovitch's barn, to Tom Verachuk and his needles, and so to my mother and the wicker couch on the verandah. I shook myself, trying to free my mind of too little sleep, too much work, and too much caffeine over the past forty-eight hours, but as I picked up the phone, I felt almost that I was eight years old again, the disrespectful, cheeky kid I used to be, and my voice, when I spoke, surprised me with its depth.

"Dick," I heard. "Downstairs. Quarter of an hour. Beef Eaters Room."

"I'm bushed, Frank," I said. "Unless you..."

"Somebody I want you to meet," he said. "Quarter of an hour. Beef Eaters."

The coordinator of our agency was, in fact, not the retired MP who sat in the big office and drew the top salary; in reality, our organization was directed by Frank Quarters, ostensibly our senior security officer. Once a Mountie, then an official of CSIS - Canada's CIA; some say, KGB - and now seconded to NEPP, Frank Quarters was a top administrator - nobody could deny that - and dedicated to the project. But he was an odd, misanthropic, physically burly man who had never weaned himself from his first posting, above the tree line. Mentally he still lived among the scored rocks, the ice age ponds and streams, the permafrost, the ducks, and the bugs. He went armed against blackflies and mosquitos; never left home, they said - even to attend an opening of Parliament - without a bottle of insect repellant in his pocket and a wild light in his eyes that many found repulsive but I knew to be love - love of the free, harsh country west of Hudson Bay that he had patrolled as a young constable.

Of our government's servants who go down into the north, most shrivel in the long, dark winters, the fly-infested summers, and live only to be reassigned. Frank Quarters left reluctantly, when his orders came, and lived to return - again and again, farther and farther afield. The names of the north rolled off his tongue like endearments: Moosonee, York Factory, Rankin Inlet, Aklavik, Inuvik, Tuktuaktuk... Strong men who had worked in those places blanched and moved away when he spoke. "What kind of soul must a man have..?" their faces asked, and they left him alone with his memories.

But Frank had grown up in Brandon, and he and I had become friends. We trusted each other. We understood each other. Our roots were entangled. We shared that frame of mind that the rest of Canada recognizes as "the squashed-beetle mentality" - that lonely, sad acceptance of a foreordained, limitless universe that all plains dwellers know. We explain it as being able to stretch one's elbows. We talk of big country, big sky, big air. And we cope in our individual ways.

I, apparently, by losing myself in numbers, had denied the heritage and tried to block it out. Perhaps the Waterman genes had not had time to adapt. Fifty years? Nothing, on the prairie. Frank's mother had been part Cree. He carried the unmistakable mark of her genes in the bridge of his nose, and of her heart in his passion for the land. I sometimes envied him. But I was feeling the plains awareness more, now that I had become a coastal dweller, than I ever had felt it at home - or even in Ottawa. I was glad of my new awareness, long in coming but welcome, even at the eleventh hour. Ironic that I should begin to belong to the plains now that they lay vulnerable to whatever global forces should decree. Or perhaps not ironic; perhaps only perverse - human nature - since in all their history the plains had lain vulnerable to global forces. Whatever it was, I liked the sense of identity the plains' acceptance of me - or in me - brought, even though with shades of loss and pain.

My new neighbours didn't always know quite how to approach me. "You're from Manitoba," they often told me. It was their way of saying, "You're alien here, so we'll make allowances."

My reply was always to ask, "Been there?"

I could tell by their faces what they would say next, before they opened their mouths: "No," in a tone, and with a shake of the head that meant, "No, and I haven't any intention of going there."

A few: "Once. Didn't like it. Too flat."

Commonly: "Seen it from the air. Loneliest feeling I ever had in my life."

"You're right," I would say. "It's not for everyone. You have to be born there."

No offense, and none taken. They'd go to Manitoba to fight fires, to clean up after floods, to help their brothers face drought or plagues of insects in the fields, but they'd always be glad to be home again: "Too flat. Felt like a squashed beetle all the time I was there."

The truth is that the Great Plains breed humility, and no other part of the country does. Humility. That quality Rob

Brownrigg talked about the night of the day-after-Christmas. Humility in the broad, biblical sense: the plainsman endures.

On the coast, they fight back. For centuries they've been hanging onto the rocks with broken nails. They say with pride, "We have weather down here on the water. Other places only have climate; we have weather." Under the jet stream, that constantly drives storms over them, back and forth, back and forth, at sea they live and they fight - or drown; ashore they defy the wind, the ice, the snow, the rain, and the heat of summer, or perish. And they believe... No, they are convinced, that their bleak coast loves them and smiles upon them with a love that they return. The outsider - certainly myself, at first - sees more grimaces than smiles, and feels precious little love on a cold, raw day that rains one minute and snows the next. But the easterner's enthusiasm is insidious; I was beginning to feel it.

Down on the coast, I saw life to be good in many ways, but bounded by the length of one's anchor chain. On the plains, infinity: clear, geometrical, beautiful, and inexorable. The coastal people *apply* geometry - watch a tug boat in action. To my plains-imprinted mind, sheer arrogance; to the Maritimers, common sense. That's what one does. That's how things work. "Take you out someday. Catch a few fish. Cook up a chowder." And I was employed to understand and reconcile all this! I'd better be good.

I must have been sound asleep on my feet. But I appeared in the foyer of the Beef Eaters Room at the appointed time.

"Mr. Quarters' table."

"Dr. Waterman? Yes, sir. Mr. Quarters and his other guest are expecting you."

"Dick! Right on time! What are you drinking? This Scotch is pretty good."

I nodded to the waiter and looked at the other guest, a tall, lean, slightly stooped, sandy-haired man of about my age. I'd seen him somewhere. Since I had come under Madam's influence, I had been observing more than I had ever done before, but my brain was not yet processing all the data my eyes sent it. I felt I should know this man, but who was he? Well, presumably Frank would tell me.

"Dick, Jon Carmody," he said. "I thought you should know each other."

Instantaneous recognition. Once in Ottawa at some social function, no formal introduction but a brief few words about the weather, particularly foul at the time. And twice this morning in the corridors of the building where we had been working all day. Twice I had passed him and wondered where we'd met before; once he had looked as if he wondered whether he should speak. Moreover I had seen his photograph on an office desk soon after my arrival in La Tour. A family portrait: this man; the beautiful, red-haired woman I had gone to see; a school girl and a small boy, also with red hair.

I smiled. "I had a brief chat with your wife Wednesday night," I said. "I attended a reception for some musicians, at the Imperial Theatre. Mrs. Carmody had been at the concert with a guest, Lady Maggie Murchison."

I glanced at Frank, but his face held no clues. I would have to follow his lead. Jon Carmody was married. That broke the cardinal rule of NEPP recruitment: no personal attachments. I wondered, momentarily, if Frank knew that his guest was not only married, but married to a beautiful, brilliant, high-powered specialist in my own field of accountancy, Alexa Aldebaron. The question answered itself. Frank Quarters knew all about everybody he introduced to anybody these days. And if he didn't already, he would soon know all about Lady Maggie Murchison as well.

We had a good dinner - New Zealand venison, as I recall - and I had sense enough not to drink anything more than the one Scotch; after that, only bottled water. I even stayed alert enough to wonder how long it had been since the world became afraid of tap water. I didn't know, but I felt sure it was far too long.

The conversation lagged while we concentrated on our dinner plates, but Frank finished first and then, under the influence of a good Burgundy, the name Moosonee oozed between his lips.

"My father knew the old bishop," Jon murmured, and sat back with a slight smile softening his face. I remembered then: diplomat, former judge, now liaison for the La Tour Project - the reason I had gone to see his wife. Very well connected. Old money. Discretion stamped on every cell. And his father had known the old Bishop of Moosonee. Of course Frank had known all about Jon Carmody, and about his wife.

I went to bed at last clear headed enough to think of Madam: warm and pleasant, grateful thoughts. Companionable thoughts. I promised myself to remember to notice a few things I could tell her about when I got home. But a good dinner and no coffee? My thoughts soon passed into oblivion.

And it was Robert who had my attention when I awoke. Heavy rains in Honduras had brought down mud slides, and several hillside villages had been obliterated.

"Are you all right, my friend?" anxiety asked.

I checked the location. He was. But the tragedy was near. They would be needing doctors.

Chapter Six:

Home again I found Madam subdued. She was pleased to see me and came over the first evening I was back with one of her impromptu picnics. But something was wrong.

"I thought you'd be ready for a quiet, relaxed meal in your own home," she said as I took the tray from her and set it down on the table by the couch. "Travel is wonderful - all the new places, the new restaurants, new dishes..." She sighed. "But one finds," she went on, "when one comes home again, that one... is... rather weary."

She herself looked rather weary, and I suppose I must have looked concerned.

"Listing to port, am I?" she asked.

"Maybe a tad to starboard," I murmured. "But not so as anyone else would notice."

Her smile grew warmer. "You're learning the lingo," she said. "You're really very bright. I thought at first that you knew exactly what the ground looked like, but little else. I was wrong, wasn't I. You don't miss very much."

"I haven't missed the fact that you're tired," I said, and was moved to take her in my arms and hold her. "You've been doing too much, haven't you. What is it? The symphony in the red again?"

"Honduras," she said. "Conditions are very bad. They need everything, particularly medical supplies and personnel. I'm sure Robert is doing too much - far too much. He thinks he's a young man still, and they need him so desperately."

For a moment she laid her head on my shoulder, and I fought down the urge to whisper words I would regret. This woman was becoming important to me. I never should have touched her. I knew that. I also knew I wouldn't be the one to end the embrace.

For a few moments neither of us moved. Then Madam drew back. "Thank you, Richard," she said. "You are a wonderful friend. I thought, when I brought you and Robert together, that I was exchanging an amusing neighbour for one I would rarely see. Instead I have found in you... the kind of... new... friend... I never thought to find again, here, and now. I've told you before, you're a darling... Come and eat your supper."

I was not supposed to have friends - friends of any description. And a woman? An intelligent woman? No, no. Especially not an intelligent woman. I felt a strange mix of emotions, but Madam was pouring mushroom soup from a thermos and talking about crocuses.

Later, when she had gone, the obligation to analyze my feelings nudged my conscience, but my mind wandered and I heard my mother's voice: "Richard, you are being rebellious again! I've warned you against that failing. When you were a child, you insisted on playing with Pete Yakovitch. And when you were in high school and imagined yourself in love with Evelyn Hammond..."

Instantly I was standing outside Wong's Wok on the corner of Assinaboia and Crown. It was summer. The day was hot. And the smell of fried fish was strong in the air. I was waiting for Evelyn to come by. She would be barefoot and wearing her long, full skirt - I remember it as striped vertically in some sort of ribbony arrangement of red and yellow and black. She would be wearing, as well, a white blouse pulled off her shoulders, a small purple scarf over her long hair - blonde as wheat straw and just as dry - and hoops in her ears that she told everyone were pure gold but I knew even then were only copper washed with gilt. She would be carrying an armload of sweet peas in a basket, and she would thrust them, stem by stem, at everyone she met, whether they wanted them or not. Most people wouldn't accept flowers from her grubby, green-stained fingers, but I never refused.

Once I got up the courage to ask her into the Wok for a Coke, but she only patted my cheek. She was a violet, she said. She drank nothing but water and only sat in the sun. The smell of Wong's, she said, polluted her fragile being and caused her to wilt in her soul.

Nothing my mother could do or say moved me an inch. I hung around the corner and polluted *myself* with fried fish fumes till cold weather came again and Evelyn disappeared with half a dozen hippies from North Dakota who were headed south in a converted school bus painted all over with geraniums and palm trees. On the back a legend read "The Universe Loveth Cheerful Vegetarians." That, on the Great Plains!

I hadn't thought of Evelyn Hammond in years and went to bed chuckling. The reason my mind might have had, to remember her, then, didn't concern me. It never even struggled into consciousness.

* * *

Early on Easter Sunday a FAX came to my office. Robert had died in his village in Honduras. Pneumonia, brought on by overwork and exposure, and fatal because he would not use for himself any of their scarce supply of medicines that were needed for the children.

He wouldn't have minded; Sarah Jane was waiting. I would mind, though, and so, I thought, would Madam. I found her in her living room, sitting lotus fashion on the floor and gazing out of the window at a heavy, late-season snowstorm.

"Madam," I said, "I have sad news from Father Luis."

"I know," she murmured. "Robert passed away on Wednesday."

"You've had a message too?"

"Yes," she said, and turned her head to look at me. "Yes, but I have been waiting for signs and wonders, and now that they have come by your communication devices, we can talk about it."

"Madam..."

"Richard, we must go to church!"

Far from talking about anything, she reached out one hand for me to help her up. "Go and dress," she ordered, "or we'll be late."

"Madam, there's a blizzard out there!" I howled.

"But it's only across the street. We can get that far. Dress for it, dear. The Lord won't mind if you're informal."

"I'm not worried about what the Lord thinks of informality," I argued. "I'm thinking there won't be anybody there on a day like this. They'll have to cancel."

"Cancel Easter? Never! Go and dress, Richard. I'll be ready in five minutes."

So much for a quiet Sunday and a perfect excuse to stay home. Every one of Madam's points told. It *was* Easter; somebody was sure to be there. Door to door it was only obliquely across a narrow street. And Rob was dead; a message had come. He himself might laugh at us, but I was out of excuses.

Madam was waiting by the elevator ten minutes later. Her hood with the green fur was still thrown back and she carried her mittens in her hand, but in all other ways she was ready for the Arctic. So was I. And so we should have been. We stepped out of the side door into a maelstrom.

Snow was falling heavily, but it was the wind in the narrow street that was lethal. It seemed to blow from every direction at once, and it took our breath away.

Madam ducked back inside. Good. She had changed her mind. But before I could open the door to let myself in, she was back with a snow shovel from the vestibule in her hand.

"We'll need this," she shouted, close to my ear, and set to work to dig a path through a drift that had formed in front of the doors, blocking our way to the street.

I took the shovel from her - at least *I* could shovel faster than the wind could fill in the hole. Then, once we were out, crossing the street was not as difficult as it might have been. We had to cling to each other and bend double for stability, but the pavement was largely clear. Out there, snow was blowing away as fast as it came down.

The churchyard, however, was one of the places where it was accumulating. Deep footprints indicated that someone had been before us, but they were already indentations only, mere indications that someone had been there. And a large mound had built up that filled half the distance between the gate and the door. Madam could be stuck till spring. I set to work again with the shovel, following the contours of the drift, looking for the easiest way through.

The clock in the tower struck the quarter to the hour. At this rate we would be late, but it looked to me as if we would be the only congregation there, and I expected to be welcomed with open arms.

While the clock struck, we stood still, Madam listening to the sounds of the bell shredding on the wind, her eyes shining; I leaning on the shovel, hot and glad of the rest. But when the chimes had ceased and, to my ears at least, no sounds came but the wind whistling around the corner of the building... when I was hard at work again, with Madam, as I imagined, still behind me... after a shovelful or so, I heard a sharp little cry followed by laughter. Madam had tried to cross the snowbank where it was loosest, without waiting for a path, and she was stuck. One leg had sunk into the snow; the other extended straight in front of her.

My first reaction was, "Oh, my God! She's hurt herself!" But even as I thought that, I heard her laughter ringing against the stones of the church and bouncing back into the storm.

"Richard!" she shouted. "Richard, help! I can't move."

I was already plowing my way through the snowdrift.

I pulled her free and swung her behind me into the path I was digging, but she protested vigorously. "No, Richard. Over there. Where I was going. Help me over there. Something needs us. I don't know what it is, but I heard little cries for help."

"Over there, Madam?" I argued. "What would be there? If anyone wanted to escape the storm, there are lots of better places."

"Not any *one*, Richard," she said. "Something, though. Perhaps a cat. I don't know."

She slipped out of my grasp and tried again to wallow her way through. I shrugged. There being nothing for it but to abandon the path to the door and dig another in the direction she wanted to go, I again swung her to a position of safety behind me and doubled my efforts with the shovel. The snow flew.

About that time the church door opened, and an elderly man and a half-grown little girl with bright blue eyes, who looked vaguely familiar to me, stood in the opening, both bundled up against the storm. Each grasped a snow shovel in one hand. The little girl's eyes grew round when she saw us, but she smiled when she recognized Madam, and set to work to clear a narrow passage down the church steps. The old man came down and advanced as far as he could on their side of the drift. He looked puzzled, but he called out cheerfully, "Welcome to Trinity and a Happy Easter to you. Not a day for spring bonnets, is it!"

I waved a mitten at him and continued to dig.

As often happens, the drift that was keeping us out filled most of the yard but did not extend right up to the building, so that the old man and the child, who had followed him, reached the spot Madam was heading for with little trouble - at least a lot less than we were having. We soon met on either side of the barrier, and Madam directed that she be helped over the remaining mound, which she accomplished by holding my hand while she slid part of the way, then switching to the two from inside, who pulled her over the rest. She arrived white with snow, but there was no difficulty keeping her in view against the wall.

When I had broken through, I found Madam, the old man, and the child bending over something sheltering in a corner made by a buttress of the stone facade of the building. Whatever it was, it was out of the wind there and in a little nest made by the swirling snow, but I could not see for the three heads that were in the way and the bulk of the three bodies in their winter clothes. I didn't know what they had found till the little girl stood up with something cradled in her hands. A bird. A male robin, its eyes glazed and its head hanging on one side. I thought its beak opened slightly as if to gasp for air, perhaps from shock, but I wasn't sure.

"I'm afraid this one is dead," she said to me, "but there are two others."

With that she waded around the buttress and disappeared up the steps to the porch.

As I turned back, the old man was just straightening with a bird held between his mittens. This one was alive. Though it was not making much objection to being handled, the old man kept a good grip on it as he made his way cautiously, close to the wall, and disappeared as well.

Madam was struggling with the third bird. It seemed to be in better condition than the others and was objecting to being handled. I bent down, scooped it up, and held it tight against my parka as I too hurried to the porch, Madam right behind me carrying our shovel.

The little girl had found a small carton and some warm clothing - I'm told there are always sweaters, mittens, scarves forgotten in churches by parishioners who needed them when they came but not when they left. The child and Madam placed the box on an old-fashioned hot-water radiator in the foyer, with scarves and sweaters in the bottom and a place for the birds on top. The old man's bird still fluttered feebly; the child's lay on its side. I deposited mine with the others. It fluttered with a good deal of determination, but Madam reached in and smoothed its feathers and it settled down with a faint cheep.

The clock in the tower struck the hour of the service.

"It's time to begin," the little girl said to me, "but the rector isn't here. His name is Mr. Reeger. My name is Gerda MacKenzie, and that is my grandfather. He's the verger in church. What is your name?"

"I'm called Richard," I said. "Richard Waterman. This lady is always called Madam."

"Oh, I know who the lady is," Gerda said with a smile for Madam. "She feeds the pigeons, and so do I."

"Of course!" I exclaimed. "That's why I thought we had met before. Amos!"

"Do you know Amos?"

"No, but you spoke to Madam about him one day when we were crossing the park. You were running home for lunch - at least, I suppose you were running home for lunch. Were you?"

She looked at me as if trying hard to remember, for my sake, but not succeeding.

"You said maybe Amos had gone to Honduras to visit Dr. Robert," I prompted.

Her face lit up. "I remember now," she cried. "Was that you? I didn't know. Do you think he did?"

"He..?"

"Amos. Do you think he went to see Dr. Robert?"

"Perhaps..," but I shook my head. "Honduras is a long

way from here," I said, "and I believe that pigeons are not very good fliers."

"Yes," she agreed with a sigh. "They're too fat. I guess Amos just stayed home... to get over his cold or whatever."

"Probably ate something that didn't agree with him," I suggested.

She nodded. "Sometimes kids give them their school lunch," she told me, "if they don't like what their mothers pack. Darren MacMillan's mother makes green, yucky stuff. He throws it away all the time. Maybe Amos ate some of that. Darren said he would if he ate it. Be sick, I mean. When I feed the pigeons, I give them corn. But not in the park. I feed them when they come to our backyard, which is every day when I come home from school."

At that moment a group of "snow people," who looked to be a family of four, appeared in the porch. The verger hurried to greet them, and seizing a broom that stood with the shovels just inside the door, began to sweep them down. I gathered that the tall one must be the rector - his clerical collar became visible when he began to undo snaps and zippers, and to unwind a heavy, plaid scarf from around his neck. He bore down on us, still stamping his boots free of snow as he came.

"Good morning! Good morning!" he exclaimed. "Have you ever known an Easter like this? We've been on the road for an hour and a half with a plow blade on. Usually it takes us ten or fifteen minutes. Thank you for waiting."

He looked around. "Nobody else here? I was expecting a churchful! It's Easter!"

The young woman who had arrived with the rector appeared then with two small boys. Her eyes danced with fun. The children danced all over with excitement and the need to be quiet in church.

"What's in the box, Gerda?" one of the boys hissed to the verger's granddaughter. And the other wanted to know, "What are you looking at?"

"Birds," Gerda replied quietly. "Robins. We found them in the snow."

"Let me see," the little one demanded, and both boys had to be lifted up to see the visitors.

"That one's dead," the older boy said, pointing to the bird

Gerda had carried in.

"Maybe," she replied, "but I think it fluttered a bit when I picked it up. Maybe it's not dead."

"Maybe it will come alive again," the smaller boy said. "Jesus did."

"Maybe it will," Madam agreed, "if we don't frighten them all to death. They're cold now, but when they warm up they'll be hungry. I wonder what they'd like to eat."

"Worms," Gerda said, with a hopeless shrug of her shoulders.

"Of which we have none," Madam agreed. "What else do they like?"

"Better to ask, what else do we have?" the rector suggested. "Elizabeth always carries supplies for the boys - on days like this, plentiful supplies."

"Apples!" his wife exclaimed. "Robins like apples."

"Of course they do," Madam cried. "They come to the old orchards first. I knew that! Have we apples?"

Elizabeth shook her head. "Orange juice today," she said. "Apples are so very expensive in late winter."

"But I have some," Madam cried, and she started down the corridor toward the door, pulling on her mittens as she hurried along. She stopped in the porch, however, to adjust her hood, and I caught up with her.

"I'll go," I said. "There's no need for you to be out in the storm again."

"It's just across the street," she objected, "and you've already dug a path through the drift."

Before I could draw breath to argue further, she was gone. Behind her the door crashed back against the wall and banged several times. So much snow swirled into the vestibule before I could fight the door closed and follow, that I found it almost impossible to close the door at all.

"Madam," I shouted, but she paid no attention, and I ran after her.

The wind was worse, the snow heavier, and I had forgotten the shovel, but I took the short route - through the drift rather than around it by the path I had dug - and was in time to rescue Madam and a bemused young man from being blown away. They were clinging to each other and waltzing to the power of the wind. In two seconds they would have been down.

"Oh, Richard!" Madam cried with a joyous laugh. "What would I do without you. I ran right into this poor boy and nearly knocked him over."

That poor boy looked dizzy, the sour alcohol smell of him accounting for only part of his problem. I righted the pair of them, turned their backs to the worst of the wind so they could catch their breath, and Madam beamed at me and at her victim.

"I think you were right, Richard," she said. "You had better come with me... You," she said to the young man, "what is your name?"

He blinked. "What? Oh. Uh-h, Marvin."

"You had better go into the church, Marvin," she said. "You will be warm in there, and the vicar's wife has orange juice. I'll bring something to eat, and we'll make tea."

Marvin looked up at the church as if he wasn't sure it was there, but Madam gave him a little shove.

"Go on," she said. "Richard and I will be right back."

Marvin looked at me.

"Better do as she says," I told him. "I always find that works best."

He nodded and staggered up the path, that was rapidly filling in. Madam and I ran across the road and arrived buffeted and breathless.

"You *are* a godsend, Richard," she gasped, as we burst into the lobby. "Wait here. I'll be right back."

"You're sure," I argued. "Just a couple of apples now, and right back."

"Of course," she said, as if surprised I could question her intentions. "Of course. The rector will be wanting to start the service. It's Easter."

"An Easter I am not likely to forget," I muttered as the elevator doors closed. I was remembering the decorous Easter celebrations at home - one year just like another - with everyone dressed in their best and the church full of spring light and chocolate eggs for the children.

"Robins!" I muttered, and sprawled in a chair to wait. It was already twenty minutes past the hour when the service was scheduled to begin, and a good percentage of the congregation - a quarter if you counted the children, who would normally be in Sunday School; half if you didn't - was off hunting apples! I left Marvin out of the calculation entirely, never expecting to see him again, and I forgot about him altogether when the elevator doors opened and Madam appeared with a large picnic hamper on her arm.

"Good Lord!" I cried. "What now? I thought you were going to bring a couple of apples in your pocket."

"Oh, don't worry, dear," she said. "This is for the birds!"

"All of it!?"

"What? Oh, no! For the birds to live in!"

"But... they're in Gerda's box!"

"Ah," she said, tapping her temple, "but I am long-headed. Come along. You'll see."

I followed her out into the snow again and picked up another shovel at the door; but to my surprise Marvin greeted us at the church gate wearing a big grin and waving a shovel in the air.

"Come on," he called as we sailed across the street and almost missed the gate, my calculation of speed and distance off by a foot or so, no doubt affected by the wind resistance of the basket.

"Come on!" he shouted. "I've cleared the path, but it won't last long."

Chapter Seven:

Again there was sweeping down and chatter as we cleaned ourselves off, and more chatter as Gerda and Madam, with the help of the boys, arranged the two active birds in the picnic hamper and shut them in with some slices of apple and a handful of cracked corn. The rector and I supervised proceedings. He was already in surplice and stole, prepared for the service.

"If we're all ready," he said, "we can begin." And we trooped into the sanctuary, leaving the two living birds in their covered basket in the vestry. The dead one remained in the box on the radiator. Gerda covered him with a silk scarf and gave him a sad little pat.

Something had been niggling at the back of my mind all along - something fundamental to Easter - but I had been too busy to recognize what it was till I followed Madam and Gerda into a front pew and knew it: flowers. Easter lilies on the altar. The smell of them brought back Easters on the prairie in the little United Church we attended there. We always had lilies - lilies and the boy Jesus in the window.

When I was very small, I thought the boy Jesus was a girl because of his long curls and white dress trimmed with gold. He held a lily in his hand, as well, which, it seemed to me, was not a "boy" thing to do. I was sure Pete Yakovitch would never have anything to do with lilies. But, I recalled suddenly out of those long-gone years as I went into the church on that stormy Easter Sunday by the sea... but birds flew around the boy Jesus's head, and one had just landed on his shoulder. That, the boy Richard thought, was a "boy" thing, and one Sunday - it may have been an Easter - I tried in imagination to devise methods of enticing our birds to come and land on *my* shoulders. I thought perhaps they might like peanut butter if I spread some on my sweater. Actually that plan might well have worked had not my mother interrupted my preparations - the only time I tried to test my hypothesis - and, as we used to say, "had a fit."

As I followed Madam and Gerda into a pew and turned to face the altar, I could see that prairie window more clearly than I could see the one in front of my eyes. I suppose the memory showed in my face, for Gerda looked up at me almost as if she understood.

From Gerda I glanced along the pew and encountered the rector's two young sons sitting with their mother. And I remembered exactly what it was like to kick your feet in boredom because you could see nothing but the back of the necks of the people in front and understand maybe one word in ten. I almost felt my mother's restraining hand upon my knee.

I might have been back on the prairie but that Marvin had been left hesitating in the entrance. I motioned him to come in as if I had belonged to that congregation for years, and to my surprise, he did.

"Haven't been in church since my mom died seven years ago," he whispered as he settled down beside me.

"I know how you feel," I replied, "but it all comes back."

"Yeah," he agreed, and reached for a book from the rack ahead of us. Obviously he knew more about what to do than I did. In fact, it took both Marvin and Gerda to keep me abreast of events as we went along.

The organist, of course, was missing; and when the time came for the first hymn, the situation became acute. Even the rector was a little concerned. But he was a man of decision. "We'll just have to do our best," he announced. "On any other Sunday I might be tempted to suggest we simply read the hymns, but this is Easter. Madam, perhaps if you were to lead..."

We all sang. We sang with Madam, every one of us: "Both young men, and maidens; old men, and children." Even I, as much as I could.

The King of Love my Shepherd is
Whose goodness faileth never...

My mother used to sing that hymn. Often. Working in the garden. Preparing meals. Turning out the light and going downstairs when she had put me to bed. Even once, I remembered, when we were shovelling a path from our door to the street.

I saw myself again, following my mother, working with my small shovel. The drift that the wind blew back at us caught me full on the face. I worked with my eyes and nose screwed up against those frozen showers and found them almost more than I could bear.

I nothing lack for I am His
And He is mine for-e-e-ver.

"Only, God," the boy Richard whispered, "I would like to be bigger. Not much. Just enough so the wind would hit me on my snowsuit, not on my face."

Maybe that was why I never grew as tall as they said my father had been!

The middle-aged Richard smiled and sang; stayed more or less with Madam - till she came to the "streams of living water..."

Somewhere beyond the horizon the Red River was flooding. Slowly, inexorably finding new levels. Around our town, water was spreading onto the fields, filling every brook, every lake and slough and pond. The barbed wire fence between my mother's vegetable garden and the pasture beyond was partly inundated.

I think I was ten. I stood in my bedroom window and watched. Flood came like a rising tide, the old people said, and I wanted to see a rising tide. What I saw was a film of clear, clean water crawling toward my house. It was as I had imagined it, eerie and terrifying. For several nights I had hardly dared sleep, fearing that the water would come and get us in the night.

I felt I had to stay on guard. My mother and I might drown.

From my room that day I wandered downstairs and stood in the kitchen window for a time. Then, on impulse, I pulled on my rubber boots, my cap and jacket, and went out. I knew I probably shouldn't do it, and I hesitated a moment on the back porch. But it was necessary to learn about rising tides. I went down the steps and cautiously into the garden.

The loose dry ground where the vegetables grew had turned to mud; almost, in places, to liquid. I advanced slowly but without stopping - scientifically, like the flood. I tried to think like the flood. But halfway down, just where the cucumbers always grew in a cold frame, one foot sank deep. Mud oozed over the top of my boot and down inside. I was caught. I couldn't pull the boot out again. Only my foot; the boot and sock stayed.

Heart thumping, I glanced toward the water and saw it coming, coming with bubbles in it, like water running very hard into a glass - not bubbling like a pot when it boils, simply coming, with bubbles in it.

I stood a moment not sure what I should do, but what choice had I? As fast as I could, I limped home with one bare foot.

The ground was cold but yielding and full of pebbles that hurt with every step I took. That surprised me. Not the cold. I had already felt the cold through my boots and heavy socks; not that, but the coarseness of the soil. When it grew vegetables, it always felt soft and springy.

I expected the rough side of my mother's tongue to add to my troubles. Rubber boots and wool socks cost money. Besides, I had heard at school that there wasn't another pair of rubber boots to be had for love or money. Not in any store in town. I was sure my mother's tongue would be very rough indeed, but she didn't say a word. Not a word. She just pulled on her own boots that, for the past few days, had stood on a thick pad of newspapers by the cellar door, and went out.

Through the window I watched her walk slowly, carefully down the garden, stoop and pull my boot and mud-sodden sock out of the hole by the cucumber box, knock the worst of the mud off, and come back.

Even then, when she was in the house again, she didn't

say a word. She just looked at me with a worried expression and set my muddy boot and sock on another thick pad of papers near the central hot-air vent in the front hall.

"I won't go down there again, Momma," I said. "It scared me."

Then she smiled and I knew I was forgiven. If I hadn't been ten years old and almost a man, I would have run to her and flung my arms around her neck.

Later, with the mud cleaned even from between my toes and from under my toenails, and with warm socks and slippers on, I went back to the kitchen window and watched the rising tide. Nothing much had changed, but because I wanted a flood such as Noah would gasp at, I thought that one rickety post holding the barbed wire seemed a little deeper in the water than before.

But I was ten; not a baby of eight or nine, and the mechanics of the problem struck me.

"Why doesn't it go the other way, Momma?" I asked.

"It..?"

"The water. Why does it come up here?"

I found the course of the water impossible to fathom. Didn't one always go "down" to the United States from "up here" in Canada?

"Yes," my mother agreed, "but North Dakota is ever so slightly higher than Manitoba, Richard, and water runs downhill. It runs down out of the States to Hudson Bay."

"Well, I wish it would hurry up and get here," I sighed.

"You may have your wish soon," my mother replied. "It's beginning to seep into the basement. If it rises much higher than my ankles down there, we'll have to leave."

I hadn't considered that possibility. "Where will we go?" I cried.

"I thought we'd take the train to visit your Aunt Bessie in Ontario for a few days."

My eyes flew wide at that. I had never been on the train. I had seen trains, of course; nobody I ever heard of in those days lived far from the Canadian Pacific tracks. Rumbling, clanking CP engines crossed and recrossed the prairies, and the strings of cars they pulled were familiar, I thought, to the whole world. A trip on the train? Almost too good to be true.

I began to plan in my head what I had better take with me. But the water drained away. By the next morning the crest had passed, they said. Gone down to Hudson Bay, a place so far from Winnipeg it might as well have been on another planet. And Momma and I weren't going on the train after all...

This time, when I remembered where I was in present reality, Madam and the others had reached the "verdant pastures."

The pastures always came back after floods. In "bad" years the plowed fields didn't dry out in time for planting and hard times followed... Those were the years when the freshet came down out of North Dakota before the ice had melted in the northern "links of the long red chain," and that meant trouble. I saw that happen once and I felt the grip of fear. Water. Rising with nowhere to go. Slowly, ponderously finding outlets. Spreading over the land. That sight brings the plainsman a helplessness that is hard to bear.

The water drained away, of course. In time. Water always drains away. Rivers always run to the sea. Brooks and streams run to rivers. Water on the fields and in the spreading lakes runs to the brooks and streams - or evaporates in the summer sun. "His goodness faileth never..." Like the poor, I thought, the sea is ever with us to take the overflow - to be the one factor the old people left out of the equation, for it has seemed constant for so long.

As I wiped the corners of my eyes, I remembered a day in Winnipeg when the spillways filled quickly and we didn't know if they would prove adequate. I saw it all even as I sang with Madam that Easter Sunday morning in La Tour. And I saw, as well, as if superimposed on the flat Red River country, the beautiful river valley that led into the rolling hills behind my city-by-adoption. When the freshet came down this spring...

After the flood, the grass.

> And so through all the length of days
> His goodness faileth never...

Perhaps the wisdom to be watchful was part of that goodness?

Tears filmed my eyes. The altar wavered in my sight. The

colours of the window ran together. And a blur crossed the space between the congregation and the lilies.

I had reached for my handkerchief again, to rid myself of visual illusions, when I heard a gasp beside me and a small hand grasped my arm.

"Look!" Gerda whispered. "Oh, look!"

Another singer balanced on the rim of the communion cup. He looked out to the back of the church. He inflated his lungs till his scruffy red breast grew smooth and bright. And he filled the church with spring and new beginnings.

Our hymn ended on a note of jubilation.

The rector fell to his knees.

And Gerda, holding some slices of apple taken from her pocket, sidled out of the pew and approached the altar.

The bird hopped down from the cup to the table, cocked one eye, and accepted her presence with dignity and a flick of his tail. She stood still and smiled at him. Then, after a few moments, she placed the pieces of apple on the altar cloth and, returning, squeezed by me again to resume her place.

The rector, still on his knees, followed her every move as if mesmerized. But at length, perhaps because of her matter-of-factness and beaming face, he rose. He took off his glasses and wiped his eyes. He examined his lenses and polished them on his surplice. Having done that, he climbed into the pulpit - and did it all over again.

At last he held up a sheaf of papers and looked at each of us in turn. "Dear friends," he said, "here are my notes for the sermon I prepared for today. I worked hard on my sermon. It was a good sermon."

He folded the papers together lengthwise and dropped them on the floor.

"Instead," he said, "let me read to you from the Gospel according to St. Luke, Chapter 8, beginning at Verse 41:

> And, behold, there came a man named Jairus, and he was a ruler of the synagogue; and he fell down at Jesus' feet, and besought him that he would come into his house:
> For he had one only daughter, about twelve years of age, and she lay a dying...

> (But)... While he yet spake, there cometh one from the ruler of the synagogue's house, saying to him, Thy daughter is dead; trouble not the Master.
> But when Jesus heard it, he answered him saying, fear not: believe only, and she shall be made whole...
> And all wept, and bewailed her: but he said, Weep not; she is not dead, but sleepeth.
> And they laughed him to scorn, knowing that she was dead.
> And he put them all out, and took her by the hand, and called, saying, Maid, arise.
> And her spirit came again, and she arose straightway: and he commanded to give her meat...

"They gave her meat," the rector whispered. "They gave her meat. Slices of apple, perhaps?"

And he blessed us and let us go.

Gerda immediately and calmly walked back to the altar where the robin was still enjoying his breakfast. She watched him a moment, and he appeared to be watching her. Then, as if with his agreement, she scooped him up and carried him to the basket in the vestry to join his fellows.

Chapter Eight:

At my place in the pew, in disbelief as Gerda picked up the robin and carried him away... with Marvin in the aisle, at the end of the pew, waiting for Madam... passing down the aisle as the wind rattled the windows, and the roof pulled and creaked... as the two little boys, in shrill whispers, argued and appealed to their mother... I began to wonder, to wrestle with a problem I thought I ought to solve, with a question I should answer, at least to my own satisfaction. For the sake of the work that lay before me, for the efficacy of that work, I saw that I ought to know - if not finally, at least provisionally - whether the human mind had a limitless capacity for awe and possibility - or none at all.

The rector clearly believed in miracles; clearly believed that we well might have experienced a resurrection miracle of our own. His eyes shone with wonder. But when he raised them above our heads, he was not looking to heaven but to the roof of his church.

His sons, little more than infants, already argued whether the bird had been dead and come alive again or "must of been alive all the time."

Madam followed me out of the pew, her beautiful gray

eyes full of hope and clarity of mind, but she took my arm and murmured, “Richard, it’s lunchtime. I thought it best that we all eat here in the church before the Reegers started home. Now I’m not sure they’ll be able to start home at all - just listen to that wind! If it’s still snowing...”

“Perhaps we should go across now,” I suggested.

“I’ve thought of that,” she agreed, “but I asked Jenny to pack a picnic and bring it here. And on the whole... Well, till we know... You see, I’ve already explained my plan to Mrs. Reeger. Perhaps if Marvin would go with us...”

She smiled at both of us - Marvin and me - and for that smile Marvin would have walked to the ends of the earth for her. I knew that - from my own experience. But I put my foot down on one point. “Marvin and I will go,” I said. “You stay here.”

When we returned with Jenny and the food, I was already sorry I hadn’t put my foot down harder and insisted on going immediately to the NEPP building and staying there. The wind was worse - much worse - and the snow showed no signs of letting up.

While Jenny set out the lunch party in the vestry, I toured the building with the rector and Mr. MacKenzie. They discussed the age of certain parts of the structure, the likely direction a serious attack by the storm would follow, whether some areas would be better able to survive than others... I followed along but said nothing; the church was under stress, inside and out; they didn’t need me to tell them that.

“This is the church under siege with a vengeance,” Reeger said.

But we arrived back in the vestry drawn by the fragrance of baked ham, salmon mayonnaise, hot oyster tarts; above all, by freshly baked bread; and the storm was far away and unimportant.

Gerda and Marvin had moved some of the lilies into the vestry so that we wouldn’t forget, in spite of all, that this was Easter Sunday; and the boys, I’m told, ever since Reeger pronounced the benediction, had been dividing their time between peeking at the robins and sampling any food that became available.

I ate well, drank quantities of strong tea, talked to everyone, and endeared myself to Gerda by telling her about a pair of robins that built a nest outside my bedroom window when I was her age.

But the rector was worried by the weather. "Have you ever known such a storm!" he kept repeating.

"Really, Beth," he said, after one of his many forays to the door to stick his nose out and find that conditions were worse than ever. "Really, dear, I don't think we should stay much longer."

"Oh, you mustn't try to go home in this!" Madam exclaimed at that point. "We can put you up.

"Richard, I'm sure, between us..."

"I can do better than that," I replied. "The VIP suites on the ninth floor are empty this week-end. Nobody comes visiting over Easter. You can have one of those."

"Wonderful!" Madam exclaimed, and clapped her hands in that way she had. "Then we won't have to break up the family, and you can all come to my place for supper. Perhaps Richard will even introduce the boys to Perry."

"Who's that?" the little one wanted to know, and the children listened to Jenny's stories about Pericles Rex of Regina while the rest of us ate cake and strawberries and cream.

But the rector's mind was on his church. I doubt he knew he was eating the finest of Jenny's own baking and strawberries grown in Florida on our own local stock and flown "home" to be in time for resurrection.

"I've never heard the like of it!" he kept repeating.
Between the first and second cups of tea, "Listen," he cried. "That must be the roof creaking. And do you hear the windows rattling in their frames? There's even a hollow resonance from the pipes of the organ."

And after a sip of the second cup, "I have never seen the like of this! Have you, verger? You've been here a long time."

"All my life," Mr. MacKenzie told us. "Man and boy."

"And have you ever seen such a storm?"

"Not since the Groundhog Day Gale," the verger agreed. "And that's better than thirty years. We were building the new City Hall that winter, and the windows started popping out of the upper floors. Couldn't do a thing about it."

"My mom almost got hit by a sheet of plywood flying

through the air off that building," Marvin put in. "She said she never seen nothing like it."

"They closed the bridges and people couldn't get home to the west side," Mr. MacKenzie recalled... "And a ship blew right up against the causeway. Or was that some other storm?"

"My mom said all the power poles uptown snapped right off. That's why we've got everything underground now," Marvin explained, barely able to wait for his turn to speak. "But I don't know. This is pretty bad. We might lose our power this time."

"Will we, Grandpa?" Gerda whispered.

"I hope not, honey," the verger replied. "But if we do, we'll manage. You and me always manage, don't we, sweetheart?"

Gerda smiled.

"Perhaps, Madam..," Jenny murmured, "Perhaps we should go now, do you think, before the power goes out in our building and we have to walk up? It's a long way."

"That would indeed be a long climb," the rector agreed. "Do you think, Dr. Waterman..?"

"I think we should go as soon as we're ready," I said. "But, no. We have put in a couple of generators for emergencies. If the city supply is cut off, they're programmed to take over automatically."

"Well, of course!" the rector cried - with some relief, I thought. "You're in the power business, aren't you! I should have remembered that!"

I felt sure he was thinking about all the stairs and one small boy who would never finish the climb on his own.

The wind was stronger. I remember thinking that the isobars must be very close together. In fact, I had no idea. None of us had, at the time.

We arranged the transfer of the boys and their mother, and Madam and Jenny, across the street. The rector would carry the smaller of his sons; I would look after the other. Elizabeth, the rector's wife, would cross between us. Marvin would come behind us with Madam and Jenny. If anyone experienced trouble - that is, as everyone knew, if anyone could not stand against the storm - he or she should hold onto one or two of us and huddle low to the ground until rescue could be brought to bear.

Gerda and the verger would remain in the church till the

children and the women were safe indoors; then the men would come back and see them home.

It was a good plan. The only thing wrong with it was that it didn't work. The rector had no sooner stumbled through the doorway with his son in his arms than the boy began to cry. "I can't breathe, Daddy," he whimpered. "I can't breathe."

Hearing his little brother in distress, the older boy turned to his mother, white-faced and frightened. "Mommy," he said, "will we be able to breathe?"

"Change of plan," I shouted. "Mr. Reeger, come back."

The rector was only too glad to come back.

"This is what we used to do when I was a little boy on the prairies," I told the children as I knelt at their level and showed them, using myself as a model, how my mother used to muffle me up on bad winter mornings with a scarf wrapped around my head, cap and all, so close that only my eyes showed.

"You probably won't like this," I said to the little fellow... "By the way, what is your name?"

"Harry," he said.

"Oh, that's a good name," I told him. "What's your brother's name?"

"Bobby."

I winked at Bobby, who smiled back at me.

While I talked I was wrapping Harry in a second wool scarf, Ukrainian fashion - at least this was how Pete Yakovitch's grandfather used to do it, and what my mother called Ukrainian fashion. Never came loose.

"You may not like this, Harry," I went on, non-stop. "The scarf gets wet when you breathe through it. Then it feels nasty. But don't take it off... Did you know your breath was wet?"

"No."

"Well, there you are," I said. "You learn something new every day."

By this time Harry was muffled to the eyes, up and down, but his eyes were smiling.

"Now," I said. "One of the ladies. Madam?"

"Perhaps Harry would like to have his mother," she said.

I turned to the child. "Well, Harry," I said, "it's up to you. Mamma? Madam? Or Jenny?"

"Mamma," he shouted through the layers of scarf over

his mouth, and his eyes crinkled so that we knew he was not afraid any longer.

"All right, Mrs. Reeger," I said. "Hang onto me as tight as you can. Off you go, rector. Mar..."

"No!" Harry shouted. "Mommy needs a scarf too."

"Very good, Harry," the rector agreed. "So she does. A scarf for Elizabeth, someone?"

"You tie her up, Richard," Harry ordered.

I did so - Ukrainian fashion.

"All ready?"

The rector nodded and left carrying Harry.

"You next, Marvin," I said.

Then I turned to the others. "We'll come back as soon as we can," I promised. "Don't anyone try to follow us."

I knew they wouldn't. Standing in the porch with the door open was enough to frighten every one of us, and I knew I could trust Madam to see that my orders were obeyed.

I helped the verger wrestle the door closed, and we left the shelter of the porch.

Out there the wind hit us like a solid wall. For a moment Mrs. Reeger hesitated, even with a scarf covering her face, but Harry was watching her over his father's shoulder and she took a deep breath.

"Keep your head down," I shouted.

She nodded.

"Marvin?"

"Okay."

The path was drifted in again, but the new snow was still fairly loose and we won through, single file of necessity, holding to each other as tightly as we could.

At the church gate we huddled for a moment. Close together. Like cattle on the plains. Head down. Back to the wind. And close together. You learn something new every day.

"We'll go across now," I shouted, when I judged we would have to move or risk losing our nerve. "Mrs. Reeger, stay in the middle. Keep low and keep moving."

As fast as the storm allowed, we ran for safety. The drift in front of our building was deeper but, so close to our goal, in seconds we had kicked aside enough to allow us to squeeze through.

Harry's eyes were shining brighter than ever. The moment his mother freed him from his scarf, he started in chattering at the top of his voice. "I nearly got blown away, Mommy," he shouted. "Daddy nearly got knocked down by the wind. He nearly dropped me, didn't you, Daddy! Can I go again?"

Mrs. Reeger laughed. "Not on your life!" she chuckled. "You and I are not going out in that again. Not today, my lad!"

"But Daddy's going," he insisted.

"Daddy is going to help bring Bobby and the others," she said. "You and I will wait right here."

The lone security officer on duty that Easter Sunday galloped toward us - from her post at the monitors at the back of the building, I supposed.

"Wait, sir," she shouted. "I'll come with you, sir. Wait just a minute till I get my coat and boots."

I looked at her eager face, but I shook my head. "How much do you weigh?" I asked.

"Hundred and twenty? Twenty-five with my gear on?"

I smiled.

"All right," she agreed, reluctantly. "But I'm a good shoveller."

"Then let Mrs. Reeger and Harry into the reception office so they can watch us through the window," I said. "Then you can go out and clear the door. That would be a big help."

We left in good humour, but the return to the church was even harder. The storm was worsening. Worsening by the moment. And no doubt we were already tiring. My thigh muscles burned and my breath came in gasps.

We kept our feet - just - but we were blown off course and missed the church gate by a good ten metres. Fortunately we fetched up against an iron railing around the churchyard and could fight our way back, hand over hand, along the fence.

When we stopped for breath at the gate, I glimpsed Harry in the window opposite, jumping up and down and waving. He was barely discernible through the snow.

His father saw him too and waved back. "They'll remember this," he shouted to me, and his eyes laughed.

But we had taken twelve and a half minutes, door to door. Twelve and a half minutes to cross a narrow street and a few feet of churchyard. And we arrived exhausted.

Madam heard us in the porch and came running. “We’ve made tea,” she cried, “and the verger has found sugar. You must come and drink some before you start out again.

“Richard, your scarf has slipped and your face is covered with ice. Oh, you poor dear! Jenny...”

“That’s because none of you knows Ukrainian fashion,” I said, and laughed.

“Then I’ll learn before you go out again,” she declared.

Jenny had already seen the need and come running with an assortment of tea towels. Madam seized one and began to apply it to my face.

“Only red,” she said, after the first swipe. “No whitening. But Richard, you really must be more careful. A man from the prairies ought to know better.”

“And does,” I said quietly, and took the towel from her to finish the job myself. “It’s bad out there. Far worse now than it was. You’re going to have to go out in it yourself. Wait till you’re safe home again and then scold me.”

“As bad as that,” she murmured. “I was afraid so. Can we go at all?”

“Oh, yes,” I said, “but we can’t waste time.”

“Then come and drink your tea. Jenny and I will dress.”

* * *

There was a moment just after we entered the path through the drift in front of the church door when I wondered if we could make it. The onslaught of the wind was terrible. A gust came that stopped us where we stood. We could barely hold position by clinging to each other and bending low. For a moment we hung in the balance. Then suddenly the gust passed and left us in an unexpected lull, an area of low pressure that took our breath and left us braced against a wall of air that had gone down. Madam tumbled into the snow, and the rector stumbled with Bobby in his arms.

We were close to disaster, but a rush of adrenalin - possibly of the hot, sweet tea we had drunk - pushed us on. Marvin lunged for the rector and saved him from falling, but I noticed signs of strain in Reeger’s eyes, and Marvin doubled up for a moment as if in pain.

Jenny and I retrieved Madam from the snowbank and we struck out again.

The passage of the street and into safety was almost easy after that. My guard had the door cleared and open for us, and Mrs. Reeger and Harry were there to cheer us on. But it was clear that the rector was in considerable pain.

"What is it, Al?" Mrs. Reeger demanded, when she had seen to unwrapping Bobby, and the boys were comparing notes at speed - the story of our adventures was already being exaggerated out of all recognition.

"What is it?" Mrs. Reeger repeated. "I can tell there's a problem."

"It's nothing," the rector protested. "I'll be perfectly all right in a moment."

"Don't be heroic, rector," Madam ordered. "It's plain from your face that you're not all right. What have you done?"

"I believe I wrenched my back when we were caught in that sudden lull," he admitted. "Stupid thing to do. Perhaps if anyone has an aspirin tablet."

"Into bed with a heating pad," Madam ordered. "And no arguing.

"Richard, if you can supply a bed, Jenny can supply the heating pad."

She turned to Jenny. "You know what to do, dear," she murmured. "We'll leave Mr. Reeger to you."

I turned to the security officer. "Put Mr. Reeger in the west suite on the ninth floor, Anna," I said. "From there he'll be able to watch his church. Turn up the heat and show Jenny where everything is."

"And you must go out again, Richard," Madam said to me, speaking softly. "What do you think?"

"I think Mrs. Reeger and the children should go with you to your apartment and be diverted till this is all over," I replied, equally softly. "Marvin and I will rescue the MacKenzies."

"You should bring them here," she said.

"But I think Gerda is going to want to go home and take the robins with her."

"I'm afraid so," Madam agreed.

"Anyway," I said cheerfully, in a voice that could be heard by the whole company, "Marvin and I will soon have everyone stowed away. Come on, Marvin, let's go. St. Bernard to the rescue."

Marvin grinned, but I thought I detected a slight hitch to his gait as we crossed the foyer and fought our way out into the storm. So I had been right. He had hurt himself when he grabbed the rector. His knee, probably.

Chapter Nine:

We waited in the vestibule for a lull between gusts; then we ran as hard as we could and burst into the church ahead of another gust, like a couple of dry leaves lost and out of season. The wind had veered slightly, perhaps, though it was hard to tell. Up there at the top of the town, with streets and alleys running in all directions and the park in the middle, the wind seemed to come from every quarter at once.

While the verger made a last check of his church - he was worried about some of the old window casings - Gerda approached me. "We have a backyard," she confided, "and an apple tree. It still has apples on it... some."

"It will be a week or two," I said, "before this snow has melted..."

"They could live in our sunporch. It would be safe. It's upstairs. And it's at the back. I would feed them. We have good apples, I mean ones we bought at the Market, not the ones on the tree. Grandpa would let me, I think..."

"You could come to my building," I suggested. "It might be better. We have lots of room."

"Would there be a place for the robins to stay?" she asked.

"Well," I had to admit, "not really."

"Then I think we had better go home," she decided.

I wasn't surprised. I just wondered if we could make it. Gerda was small but too big to be carried, and her grandfather,

I judged, must be close to eighty and appeared rather frail.

I hesitated, wondering whether or not I should insist and what I could possibly do with the robins, but Marvin was standing beside me.

"I go that way too," he muttered. "We'll do fine. You run for it, Doc. We'll see you across the street."

That sounded like a good plan, but the storm was worse than ever, and it was evident, almost as soon as the verger had secured the church door, that it would take all of us to see Gerda and her basket of survivors safely home.

"Our house is just over there," she shouted into the wind, pointing in the direction of the street of wooden houses across from our parking lot. "We live almost next to the Green Dragon. It's not far."

It was not far. On any other day, Gerda could have skipped home in a couple of minutes. On that Easter Sunday, she clung to my hand and we ran - we had no other choice - ahead of the storm, down the street, heading for the corner where we would have to make a left turn and battle our way past the dragon, with the wind in our faces.

Sometimes both of Gerda's feet flew off the ground together and her weight pulled at my arm and shoulder. I learned to bring both arms to the rescue. That way she was more secure, but we danced in circles till I felt giddy.

At last we fell and the wind blew us along the street, twisting and turning us like empty plastic bags. I kept hold of Gerda by bringing my free hand around to grasp her wrist. Still, once or twice I thought I had lost her.

In the end we blew into a place between drifts where we were out of the wind and came to a stop.

Gerda laughed merrily. "You look funny, Mr. Waterman," she cried. "If you had more legs, you would look like a beetle on its back!"

"Well, you look like... You look like a Barbie doll. Your cheeks are so red they look painted on."

She looked pleased and rubbed at her cheeks with the backs of her mittens, but I helped her to pull her scarf over her face again. My scarf was gone.

I sat up and reconnoitred, and saw that we had already made the left turn I had dreaded. We were in the last of a series of troughs that ran mostly crosswise down Gerda's street. And we were very near the door of a rooming house on the corner.

Marvin and the verger, with the basket of birds held tightly between them, had set out behind Gerda and me. Cautiously we both raised our heads just high enough to look for them over the drifts, and saw them coming very fast. My heart stood still, but they were better balanced for size, and with the basket gripped firmly between them, they waltzed rather than ran and did not fall.

At the corner of the street a gust caught them, and the basket came close to sailing out of their hands. I saw the horror in Gerda's face when she thought the birds might be harmed, but I put my arm around her and hugged hard, and we watched - we could do nothing else - till the waltz out there in the street ended in our sanctuary.

Gerda's grandfather flew into the snow, and she slithered as fast as she could to his side. But he appeared to be unharmed and came up snow-covered but laughing.

Marvin had the basket. He had saved the birds, but whatever he had done to his knee had been compounded, and he shouted with pain as he and the basket came to rest beside me in the trough.

"Is it broken?" I shouted against his howls of agony, and against an agitated cheeping coming from the basket.

"I don't know," he gasped.

He moved his leg, and his face went white. "I'm sorry, Doc," he said. "I don't think I can go any farther. If you can crawl over to the door there, you'll be able to get some of the guys who live in the house..."

As he spoke, the door opened and two men appeared.

"Give us a hand, Gary," Marvin called to one of them, and they both ran out of the house, just as they were, and half-carried Marvin inside.

"The rest of you okay?" they shouted through the open door.

"We'll be fine," I shouted back and prepared to move on with the birds.

"We'll watch out for you till you're safe home," Marvin called to me. "Cross the parking lot and we'll be able to see you right to your back door. If you get in trouble, some of the guys will come."

I waved and bent my head to the wind, following Gerda and her grandfather, who were doubled over, too, but hand in hand were making progress - slow progress, but progress all the same - through the maze of drifts in the street toward their own front door.

In the cramped vestibule of their house, Gerda turned her big blue eyes to her grandfather. "Please may I keep them?" she whispered.

He nodded and unlocked the door to the stairwell up to their flat.

Her eyes, full of light, flew to mine.

"Please, Mr. Waterman?"

I released the basket into her care and turned away. Suddenly this child, the day, the storm, Rob's death so far from home... My mind was exalted and at the same time very, very sad, and I found the experience frightening. At Nepp we had been warned of days like this, days when, without warning, we would see life in different colours, different dimensions. Preparation for such occurrences was part of the training we had undergone, and it had prepared me well for Christmas Eve in Denver, waiting for a flight to bring me home. Nothing had prepared me for this.

"You'll come in and rest, Dr. Waterman," the grandfather said.

"No," I muttered. "No, I think I must go on while I can."

The old man nodded, expressionless, and opened the door to the stairwell, but Gerda looked at me, eyes bright, head on one side, not unlike her precious robins.

"Thank you, Mr. Waterman," she said. "The robins thank you too. When the storm is over, will you come and visit us?"

"I'll look forward to it," I said, and went out once more into the wind and snow.

* * *

To cross the street. To cross the parking lot. To open the back door. On any other day...

My scarf was gone and I began to see everything in a strong blue light. For a few minutes I rested in one of the troughs and risked taking off my mittens to warm my face with my bare hands.

When I felt driven to protect my hands again, I stood up to struggle on. But the wind was worse. A gust threw me a dozen feet off course into another trough.

I stopped for breath and tried again. This time I knew better than to stand. I crawled, flat on my stomach, like Gerda's beetle. I literally swam my way across the street and into the parking lot.

Several cars were in the lot, only mounds of snow now but big enough to provide the shelter I needed to make steady progress, if slow, toward my goal. I went bent double, no longer having to swim, but knowing I was not out of danger. The blue colour persisted; my chest was in distress - the air was too cold; and the stinging in my face had stopped. In the shelter of the last car in the row I once again risked my hands to save my face.

The treatment worked. Returning circulation to the tip of my nose and over my eyebrows brought the pain of thawing flesh. But I had to save my hands.

I was in grave danger.

Nonsense! I was almost home!

Pete Yakovitch stood before me.

"Come on, Dickie baby," he sneered. "Mamma's boy! Can't take a little cold wind, eh? You'll never grow up to be a man!"

"Damn you, Pete Yakovitch!" I yelled into the storm. "I'll show you!"

I pulled on my mittens to set out renewed, but the worst was yet to come. In the passage between the parking lot and the back courtyard of our building, the wind had free range. I could almost see it moving. The onslaught would be terrible.

Behind that last car I stood up and stretched, taking the cramp out of stressed muscles, waiting for a lull.

The lull came.

I ran.

But the next gust roared down too soon. It lifted me clear of the ground and slammed me down on bare pavement well on the way to the street in front of the church, to start all over again.

"Told you so!"

"No! Damn you, Pete Yakovitch! A man has his intelligence!"

A large dumpster stood close to the building. I grabbed one of its grapple handles, and the wind swung me behind it into deep snow piled high against the wall.

I couldn't breathe. Air swirled in there. I was in a pocket of low pressure fighting for life.

For some minutes I struggled to supply oxygen to my body and to control its reactions. Immediate needs first.

But those needs satisfied, I realized that the dumpster was not in its usual place. It had moved. Worse, it was still moving. It was turning - slowly turning - and grinding toward me. I had to get out of there or be crushed.

I hesitated. Which way?

But a rumbling began inside the dumpster. The lid was lifting.

Lifting.

Banging shut.

Lifting.

Banging.

"Clear out!" I yelled at myself.

"Which way?" I yelled back.

"Go!"

I fled along the wall toward the street, taking advantage of what shelter there was ahead of the dumpster.

The lid clanged up and down, up and down.

I scrabbled away.

The dumpster wrenched free of the wall. It was broadside to the wind now.

It ground toward me on bare pavement.

The lid clanged.

I went for the corner of the building.

"Wait!" my mind yelled. "Think!"

It could be death to rush out into that street, away from the protection of the wall.

I slowed myself against the bricks. I dragged every surface I could manage against that resistance. I spared nothing but the bare skin of my face.

The dumpster came on slowly, jerking forward as the gusts struck.

The lid clanged once, twice.

I yelled.

The lid screamed.

I held my breath.

The lid screamed again.

I glanced back.

The dumpster was balanced on one edge, going over, the contents spilling out.

I turned the corner plastered against the wall, my clothes gripping the bricks, ripping, abraded by the roughness.

The lid screamed one last time as the wind snapped its hinges.

I clung to the corner of the building.

The lid plunged after me.

It struck the corner of the building above my head, and a shower of broken bricks and dust fell around me.

I hung on, choking and gasping.

The lid sailed across the road.

With a shriek it bounced off the iron fence around the churchyard.

It rose into the air and cut through the second storey corner of a shop next to the church.

It plunged on past a convenience store on the corner, and smashed through the windows of a florist's shop across the way. I watched in disbelief as it came to rest in the midst of what had been a fine display of Easter lilies and hydrangea. I did not really comprehend what I was seeing.

The dumpster itself slid past me across the sidewalk, where it stopped, shuddering.

Again I heard the yelling in my head. "Go!"

I ran. Bent low against the slipstream of air in the street, I headed for the side door of our building, the same door we had been using during the morning.

A gust blew me back. I survived by catching hold of a window ledge and hanging there for my life.

In the brief lull that followed, I reached safety.

At the last moment I glanced back. The dumpster was moving again, on the incline toward the rooming house where Marvin lived, but with luck it would stay in the street and miss the building.

Chapter Ten:

Anna, the security officer, accompanied by the whole complement except the rector and Jenny, forced open the door against the weight of snow and wind, and hauled me in. Everyone talked at once. Everyone but me. I was busy breathing.

Anna prepared to secure the door but I stopped her.

"Don't lock the outside doors, Anna," I managed to gasp. "Inside doors, please. But leave all the vestibules unlocked. It's unlikely there's a living thing out there, but if there is, I want sanctuary available."

"The main doors, sir; the park entrance, will blow open, sir," she warned.

"Let them," I said. "If they're broken, I'll replace them out of my own pocket if need be."

"Yes, sir," she said. "And I'll keep watch."

I found the strength to walk to the parking lot door and go out into the courtyard, where one could stand against the wind, and wave till I saw acknowledgement from Gerda and her grandfather, and from Marvin and his friends in their various windows.

After that... Well, my authority seemed to end there. I was taken home and freed of my ruined outer clothing.

"Mommy!" Harry shouted. "Look at Richard's coat. I can put my head right through it!" And he did, right through the front of what had been the very best in Arctic-wear jackets.

"Wow!" Bobby yelled. "Can I, too?"

"No!" Harry fought back. "You can have his snow pants."

Bobby snatched my outer trousers as I pulled them off, and began to poke his hands through tears where reinforced knees used to be, and then to climb into the pants and prance around with his feet through the knees and the rest of the legs trailing behind him.

Their mother tried to object, but I objected to that. I remembered what their father had said: "They'll remember this!" Let them have all the good memories we could manage.

"Wow! Look, Mommy! We're Richard," Bobby shouted, and they both began to swim around on my new parquet. So they had seen me swim my way home across the snowdrifts. Good. They would remember!

"But you might scratch Dr. Waterman's beautiful floor," their mother cried.

"It's too new anyway," I muttered. "It needs a few marks here and there for me to remember things by."

I slumped back in my chair and Madam brought me a mug of Jenny's famous mushroom soup with a generous shot of single malt mixed in at the last minute. She said nothing, but her eyes questioned me.

"A narrow escape, but no permanent damage," I muttered, and she smiled.

At that moment a ripping, tearing noise drew a gasp from Mrs. Reeger, and even stopped the shrill play of the children. I was forgotten as the whole room, it seemed, flowed to the windows. A large portion of the church roof had blown off.

The kids raced back for me. "Richard," they shouted. "Come quick. The church is blowing away."

Each of them seized one of my hands and pulled, and I staggered to the window in time to see the steeple twist, rise into the air, then slowly sink from sight. A six-foot gilded fish that had been atop the spire hung, free-swimming, for a few seconds, then gracefully, almost as if purposefully, plunged headfirst toward the church. It was found a few days later resting unharmed on the altar.

Elizabeth Reeger turned a shocked, white face to the rest of us. "I must go to Al," she cried. "He'll want to get up and see what can be done, and he mustn't. Come Bobby, Harry..."

"Leave them here," I said. "I'll look after them."

"But you've been through enough yourself!" she cried. "And Madam has..."

"We'll manage," I said. "We'll have a great time. I'm too tired to say no, and Madam never says no till it's absolutely necessary."

I turned my head and grinned at Madam.

"Of course," she promised.

The boys looked at their mother with a question in their eyes. Then they consulted, eye to eye, with me, with Madam, and with each other.

"Bye-bye, Mommy," they said in unison.

We pushed chairs to the window where we could watch the disintegration of the church. Bits of metal sheathing ripped off the roof from time to time, but the old stone walls stood. Not very exciting.

I returned to my usual place and drank my soup. And then we all had our fill of Jenny's delicious chocolate chip cookies, as many as we liked, probably about six each. After that, milk and a pot of tea.

Drawn by the opening of the fridge door, I suppose, Perry appeared.

The boys stood back in awe. They recognized quality when it walked among us, and, of course, they had been well indoctrinated by Jenny.

Pericles Rex accepted a small drink of milk, even allowed himself to be watched while he lapped it out of his dish, and to be touched when he had finished. But no blandishment could keep him with us. He disappeared again.

"Cats don't like wind," I explained.

"Where is he hiding?"

"I don't know. He has his places."

We all sprawled a moment, me in my chair, Madam in her favourite corner of the couch. The kids perched on the edge of the couch between us, all filled up with cookies and excitement - quiet, but not for long.

"Can we look at your house?" Bobby asked.

"Sure."

"We never touch anything that doesn't belong to us," Harry promised.

"Okay," I agreed.

"I think you can take their word for that," Madam said, as they ran into the kitchen, "and I will run across the hall and see how dinner is coming along. Jenny had plans for an Easter feast, and now... with having to nurse the rector..."

"We'll be fine," I said with a flap of one exhausted hand.

She only raised an eyebrow at me and went out.

I found the strength to raise my stockinged feet to the table top, and to lay my head against the back of my chair.

The boys rummaged around in the kitchen. They already knew where the cookies were, and what was in the fridge, but I heard cupboard doors opening and gently closing. Apparently opening cupboard doors didn't constitute touching.

When they found the place where the groceries were stored, they spent a few minutes "reading" the labels on the cans and bottles. I dropped off, only to be instantly awakened by another shriek of anguish from the church and two sets of small feet rushing toward the window. But it was "just another piece of the roof," so they walked around my living room, examining everything, and finished by examining me from the other side of the table.

I struggled to wake up.

Harry stood simply looking. Bobby, however, hugged himself, and with his arms entwined, slowly turned to examine the end of the couch next to my chair. "Who sits there?" he asked. "*That's* your chair."

I agreed. "This one, where I'm sitting," I said. "This is my chair."

"Who sits there?" and he unwound himself and pointed to the unmistakable marks Rob had left in the couch.

"Nobody now," I said. "He went away. That was Dr. Robert's place."

I was in for grilling then!

"Where did he go?"

"He went to Honduras."

"Why?"

"Because he liked Honduras."

"Is it nice?"

"Yes. I think so."

"Where is Honduras?"

"Oh, a long way from here."

"Which way?"

"That way," indicating the direction of salt water.

"Did he go in a boat?"

"Yes, he did - at least some of the way."

"Why didn't he go in his car?"

"Because the road is pretty bad when you get near to Honduras," I said, "and he was taking too much stuff with him anyway."

"What stuff?"

"Medicine and things. He was a doctor."

"Oh."

"Are there kids in Honduras? Like us?"

"Yes. That's why Dr. Robert went there - partly. He wanted to look after them."

"Was he a missionary?"

"No. Just an ordinary doctor."

"Why didn't he take the couch?"

"He left that for me."

"Oh."

"Could we go to Honduras?"

"Yes. You could. But it's a long way."

"Could we be back for supper?"

"No. Much too far."

"Oh."

"What do people do in Honduras?"

I was running out of steam, and the idea of a nice nap under a waving palm... on a beach of golden sand... by a rich deep sea... was inviting me to sleep.

"Oh," I said, "I think they go swimming. Then they play on the beach. And after that they take a siesta in a comfortable little *cabaña* till dinnertime."

"What's a siesta?"

I heard Harry ask that, but I was too far into mine to reply.

"I guess it's a nap," Bobby decided. "Let's explore the rest of Richard's house."

Falling asleep, warm and full of cookies, felt wonderful. I

slid down in my chair and let my mind slide down into rest and replenishment. One... Two... Three, maybe.., before I heard a shout from my bathroom and the boys were back, standing one on either side of my chair, slapping my hands to wake me up, and jumping up and down to relieve their excitement.

"We found Honduras," Bobby shouted the moment I opened my eyes. "We're Honduras people. Can we go swimming?"

"Swimming?"

"In your swimming pool," they both shouted at once.

I frowned, trying to figure out what they were talking about.

"You know," Harry insisted.

"In your bathroom," Bobby explained. "In your swimming pool in your bathroom."

Oh. Of course. My swimming pool. The hot tub Rob had had installed for Sarah Jane. I never used the thing, and, of course, I had never thought of it as a swimming pool. But if one were four or five - or both...

"Please, Richard," Harry begged. "We want to be Honduras boys."

"Hondur -an. Honduran boys," I instructed them.

"Oh. Can we?"

I struggled out of my chair and followed the Honduran boys to my bathroom.

"There isn't any water in it," Harry said, looking up at me with perfect confidence.

"Oh," I said, and turned on the cascade tap, which fascinated them.

They began to peel off, and I had never seen kids with so many clothes on. They must have been half dead with the heat. Sweaters, shirts, and undershirts; pants, longjohns; oversocks and undersocks... They must have been feeling like Hondurans all along. At last they were down to little white underpants.

"We didn't bring our bathing suits," Bobby said. "We'll just have to swim in our underwear. How do we get in?"

"Oh. Of course. I'll have to lift you."

"Oh, boy! It's warm! Is the water in Honduras warm?"

"Oh, yes. Honduras is a warm place."

"Oh."

"I like Honduras."

"Yes, it's a nice place."

They might have been a couple of tadpoles but for their chattering all the time.

I made a cushion of a bathtowel and sat on the toilet cover. The room contained a comfortable chair but I didn't dare sit in it - I would have fallen asleep, and the Honduran boys might have drowned. As it was, my head dropped onto my chest more than once.

Eventually, in spite of the warm water, the Hondurans began to shiver, and I lifted them out of my swimming pool and wrapped them in towels. They squeezed out their underpants into the sink and we put them in the dryer to dry.

The dryer made a soporific hum in the background, and I could barely navigate from room to room.

"Now what do Hondurans do?" Harry wanted to know.

"Richard said they play on the beach now," Bobby remembered.

"But..." I was inspired. "But," I said, "they always have dry underwear to put on. In our situation I guess they would go directly to siesta."

"Oh."

"Okay," Bobby said. "Where's our cabin?"

"*Cabaña*."

"Oh."

"It's... Well, we'll have to make one."

"Where?"

"How?"

The need for a few minutes sleep drove me on. "We'll make one out of the table," I said. "Come with me to the closet and we'll find some pillows and blankets."

"Okay."

We spread a folded blanket for each of them on the Persian rug under the table. They crawled into the *cabaña* and prepared their nests like a couple of puppies circling a hole in a garden. Then I passed each of them a pillow.

They curled up.

They giggled.

They crawled out.

"What do we cover up with?" they enquired.

I provided blankets for covering up with.

They went into their *cabaña* and tried out these arrangements.

They came out again. "We can't keep our towels on," they said.

I got them into their longjohns and undershirts.

They disappeared into the *cabaña* again.

I settled down in my chair.

"Richard," I heard. "We need a door."

"A door?"

"Yes. Our *cabaña* has no sides."

We found more blankets and spread a couple over the table to make walls and a doorway.

They giggled, very pleased.

But just when I thought they would crawl in again, I heard, "Where's your *cabaña*, Richard?"

They made one for me on the couch. I stretched out at their direction and they made sure everything was *cabaña*-shape for me.

"Now shut your eyes," they said.

I was only too happy to shut my eyes.

They watched me for a moment, then shushing each other noisily, they tip-toed to the door of their *cabaña* and crawled in. I heard wriggling and giggling and sorting out under the table, then silence.

Silence!

The last thing I remember was a feeling of surprise, then of gratitude...

A full hour later, greatly refreshed, I woke to find two small Hondurans in long underwear standing side by side and looking at me with misty eyes.

"We want to see our mother," Bobby said.

* * *

In spite of what was going on in the world, dinner at Madam's table was a delight, as I knew it would be. With the drapes across the windows, shutting out the storm, we forgot for a time the stresses of the day and the coming stresses of tomorrow. Even the rector, although far from comfortable, was well enough to join us for an excellent meal and, for short periods, to forget to mourn the state of his church.

"Richard, I'm going to put you in my usual place," Madam told me quietly. "You've had your turn with the children. They can sit one on either side between me and their parents."

"If they can sit at all," I replied with a chuckle. "I haven't seen much evidence."

But I was surprised, and pleased, too, to sit at the head of Madam's table and carve the baked ham and spiced chicken, and to supervise the service of the fine white wine she had provided.

Much later, when we had come to the lemon meringue tarts that Madam held to be traditional for Easter.., and Harry had asked what was "trajnal," did it mean very good..? And they both had said, Yes, please, they would like another too... At about that point, Mrs. Reeger turned to me.

"I want to thank you, Dr. Waterman," she said, "for looking after my children this afternoon."

"I thoroughly enjoyed it," I told her truthfully, "though you may have noticed some changes in the returned articles. I apologize for that."

"Changes?"

"You gave me Bobby and Harry," I explained. "They returned to you Roberto and Enrico from Honduras."

She smiled at them fondly; they were busy telling their father - not for the first time, I'm sure - that Ricardo had a *cabaña* and a pink swimming pool in his house.

Their mother turned back to me. "You are very kind," she murmured.

"Not at all."

I had a feeling this young woman was not your typical rector's wife, if there is such a person. And I was not surprised when she turned the full gaze of fine dark eyes on my face and said quietly, "I wonder if you are kind enough to answer a serious question."

"If I can," I hedged.

"Oh, I'm sure you can," she went on. "It's about this problem of climate change. I wish to know exactly what is going on."

"I wish I could be sure," I replied, "but I don't think anyone can be. I've read that the models show a wide variety of possibilities."

"But you do think it's happening."

"We have certainly had bad storms the last few years," I muttered. "But perhaps they may not... I know very little about it, really."

Her face told me she didn't believe me.

"But you do think that we are beginning to see it happen," she insisted, and looked me straight in the eyes. "Otherwise Lepreau would not be a possible threat and the government would not consider spending so much money to shut it down completely and decontaminate the site."

Another intelligent woman, I thought. Much more acute than her husband. I would have to watch my step.

"Lepreau is getting past its usefulness," I said. "It may need to be shut down before it starts to cost the tax-payers more than it will ever be worth again. It was good technology in its day, but we have moved on."

Her eyes never left my face. She didn't believe a word I said.

When I had stopped speaking, she turned away. "I don't think it's the technology, Dr. Waterman," she said. "It's the site. The plant is too close to the water and too close to a fault line that runs down the bay. Is it true that the weight of water as the sea rises could destabilize the sea bed?"

"I really don't know," I said.

Then, when she turned troubled eyes to mine again, "Nobody knows," I added softly, for her ears alone.

I was sure she understood me. I had spoken with authority: "Nobody knows." I who had been trained to prevaricate. I who could turn on a plausible lie almost at will and enjoy the game of wits. I spoke the truth to this young woman I had known for an hour or two. And she understood.

"Have you children, Dr. Waterman?" she asked.

"No."

"Ah. If you had, I would not need to explain to you," she said. "Since you have not..."

"I envy you your children," I heard myself tell her.

"I worry about them," she murmured. "About their future."

"They may be more resilient than you know," I said. "*They* call me Richard."

"Oh, dear!" she said, and giggled. "They're little monkeys."

Eventually the boys began to flag and to cling to their mother - but thanks to our long siesta, not till about nine o'clock. At that time, darkness having long since shrouded the wreckage around us, the rector was persuaded to go back to bed with a hot pad for his pulled muscles - much to Elizabeth's relief, I thought; she must have been dead on her feet.

Madam and I herded them all, still chattering, to the elevator and waved them down to the ninth floor.

Quiet.

At last.

We couldn't even hear the storm very much, there in the centre of the building.

Madam turned to me. "What a day, Richard!" she exclaimed. "What a wonderful, stupendous Easter Day to remember! But not a sensation more! One more experience today and I'd..."

She stopped mid-sentence because I, without conscious volition, had drawn her close and kissed her.

For a moment neither of us reacted. Then Madam drew back and looked at me a moment with those wonderful eyes of hers.

"That's done it, dear," she said. "Every circuit in my brain is running blue fire. Can you smell the burned out wiring?"

I kept one arm around her and walked her to her door, where I repeated the experiment with even better results. But that was a moment when it was absolutely necessary - and wise - that Madam should say no.

I retired to my own room. I expected to face an irate conscience. I didn't. I went to bed and slept.

Chapter Eleven:

Three weeks - or thereabouts - later, a brief respite from melting snow and mounting problems brought me to the side door of our building on a morning of heavy rain. Water pounded the metal roof of the portico.

I was waiting for Al Reeger to let me into the church to see the damage done by the storm, and the measures taken to secure the building while repairs were made. As I waited, hoping that the rain would let up before I had to leave the porch, Marvin came up the street, his walking cast protected by a system of plastic grocery bags. He hobbled into my sanctuary, hunched against the rain.

From inside the building Madam appeared, smiling, dressed in silver gray except for a pink umbrella half open in her hands.

"Good-morning," she cried. "Isn't this wonderful!"

"As always, Madam," I said, "you are a ray of sunshine."

"Sunshine!" she exclaimed. "With all this beautiful silvery rain in the air?"

Marvin grinned ear to ear, as he always did when Madam was around.

"Al Reeger called," I told them both. "A few visitors are

to be allowed into the church for a tour of inspection. Want to come?"

"Sure," Marvin agreed. "I heard about that. Thought I'd come along - if I can get around in there with this cast on."

Madam looked disappointed. "I'm off to a luncheon at Ravenswood House," she said. "And I have a fitting first. There won't be time. You must tell me all about it later. Be sure to remember everything."

"Of course. Ravenswood House," I said. "The dress-maker..."

"Designer," Madam corrected.

"...designer in the next street down."

"I'll go through the churchyard," she said.

Al Reeger drove up at that point, and I accepted a crossing of the street under Madam's pink umbrella, just about big enough to get us both soaked. Marvin stumped along behind.

"When is Frank going to go away?" Madam asked as we ducked across arm in arm.

I chuckled. "I thought you and Frank were getting along like a house afire," I said, and glanced at her. I expected to see laughter in her eyes - and I did.

"Frank is all very well," she said, "but I never see *you*, and we have a great deal to work through. Do you realize, Richard, that we have never yet said a word about Robert's passing? You haven't had a minute."

"I don't think he would want us to mourn for him," I said. "Of course you knew him much better than I did, but..."

"No, he wouldn't," she agreed, "but we need closure, as they say nowadays. I suppose I feel a need to say good-bye. I'm not sure what, but something must be done."

Arrived on the other side of the street, Marvin sought refuge in the church porch, but Madam and I stopped, in spite of the pouring rain and in spite of Al Reeger's hails and the greetings of members of the vestry, insurance agents, some of Marvin's pals - who lounged out of doorways along the street, and several others, all strangers to me. They began to emerge from buildings and from parked cars up and down the street, hats pulled down, collars turned up against the rain.

Madam and I made a bright oasis under the pink umbrella, discussing a memorial service for Robert. I argued for a ser-

with a Catholic priest.

"Yes, I know," Madam agreed. "But I can't seem to make up my mind about it. How would one proceed? He wasn't a religious man."

"Frank is leaving on Friday," I said, to answer her earlier question and to change the subject. "Lift off at four."

"Then I claim an hour or two of your time on Friday evening," she cried.

"You shall have it all," I promised. "From six on you shall have my undivided attention. How about dinner somewhere?"

"Lovely," she murmured, and squeezed my arm... "Oh, here's Mr.MacKenzie. How are you, Mr. MacKenzie?"

"Better, better," the verger declared.

"I hope you're dressed warmly."

"Oh, yes," he chuckled. "Wool next the skin, Madam. Don't worry. Don't worry."

Madam laughed merrily and left us with a wave. I watched the pink umbrella. It alone remained visible as she hurried away into the silver rain. The light seemed to go with her.

When she was gone from sight, I turned to Mr. MacKenzie and found him still looking after her too, and smiling to himself. For some reason his smile made me feel better, but I was careful not to let myself know why I felt better - and myself, frankly, wasn't asking.

Mr. MacKenzie and I splashed through puddles and streams, and entered the church together. Everything was changed. The light was different; translucent plastic sheets that covered the ruined part of the roof took away the shadowy reverence. The colours were different; some of the stained glass was gone from the windows. The entrance at the back had shattered, probably when the steeple fell, and the whole of the far end was boarded up and dark. The building was cold, damp. And water was seeping in at some of the temporary seams, and running down the walls from cracks that hadn't been identified before this day of heavy rain.

Mr. MacKenzie turned sad eyes to me. "I was baptized in this church," he said. "Seventy-nine years ago in August. Man and boy. Boy and infant, you might say. And now... I don't believe I'll stay. Damp in here. Not good for old bones."

"Will you join us for lunch?" I suggested. "Al Reeger and some of the others are coming across..."

"Thank you, no," he said. "No. Not today. You'll understand."

"Of course," I said. "I'll come with you."

I did understand. I felt bad about the church too. I had no claim on that church. That church had no claim on me - no claim, but that it had become a pivotal locus in my life.

We left together and hesitated a moment in the porch before facing the rain, much as we had hesitated on Easter Sunday in the wind and snow. My mood was gloomy. But Mr. MacKenzie brightened as he took a deep breath and raised his umbrella.

"The birds are sitting on eggs," he said with a wide smile. "Gerda can hardly wait. She's up at the crack of dawn every morning to check on them. And she wakes them up again last thing at night, shining her flashlight on them, before she'll go to bed and settle down."

"She has promised to ring me the moment they hatch," I told him. I was sure he already knew.

I walked across with him, under his umbrella. He was still smiling. And he left me with a jaunty step, in spite of the church, the rain, and arthritis in his knees.

I watched him down the street and still felt sad. I, who had no special reason to feel gloomy, except that heavy rain was beating a tattoo above my head, I stood another moment on the doorstep and felt sad. I could have told myself where and when the light refused to shine, but at that time I was not looking into the future farther than a few minutes every now and then; I had too much on my plate. From that moment, though, I began to look forward a little more, first to Friday evening, and then to the hatching of the robins; and life took on a rosier tone.

* * *

Heavy rain fell again on Friday, heavier as the day progressed, and Madam and I chose to eat at the little restaurant in the corner of our building and to spend the evening at home. The sky was very dark for the time of year and we were happy to sit sipping a good white wine in a corner of the cafe, letting the past three or four weeks burn away in the flame of a candle and the fragrance of roasting lamb and herbs that drifted from the kitchen. We had given our order for a share of the lamb and had the evening before us.

"This feels right, Madam," I sighed, as I stretched my legs under the table and reached for my wine glass. "I feel as though I've been walking in a storm ever since..."

"I was terrified that day," Madam murmured.

I studied her face, surprised. "You didn't show it," I said.

"You didn't see it," she replied, and slowly turned her wine glass in the candlelight.

"When you were in the storm, alone," she said, "and I couldn't see you anymore, that's when I was terrified. For you. And for myself. I was terrified of losing you."

Her face was full of the memory, and I reached for her hand.

She smiled, and I was beginning to lose myself in her approval and to feel very good about it, when, without warning, a gooey voice oozed around my head from a point just behind my left ear, "Dr. Waterman. Madam Justassen. Do you come here often?"

Madam slowly withdrew her hand and looked up. "Good-evening, Shelley," she said with a smile I hoped was forced. It didn't look forced, but she had spent most of her life on the stage and I hoped - perhaps rationalized - that it was forced.

I collected my legs, that had been so comfortably stretched out under the table, and stood up.

"So nice to see you both," Shelley gushed in her sticky voice, that she accompanied with a supply of syrupy smiles. "I'm here with Dr. Farrinburg and Edna. They're just hanging up their coats. Oh, here they are. Edna, do you think..? Perhaps we could ask the waiters to put two tables together."

My one outstanding talent came into play automatically. "We dropped in only for a drink and to watch the rain in the square for a few minutes," I said. "Perhaps you and the Farrinburgs would like to sit here. It's a quiet corner, very pleasant on a dark evening."

I reached into my pocket for a bill, which I dropped on the table. And Madam gathered up the sweater she had hung over the back of her chair and picked up her bag. Almost in the same movement she extended her free hand to Edna, then to the professor. Her ease in the situation concentrated all attention on her, and gave me the chance to slip a bigger bill to the waiter and mutter, "Upstairs. My place. 10 West."

He nodded and bowed us out.

We said good-night and walked through the restaurant with straight faces. We crossed the foyer soberly, as if someone might have been watching - there were always the monitors. But once the elevator doors closed...

"That was a wonderful performance, Madam," I hooted. "If you didn't want to sing anymore, why didn't you take up straight acting?"

"Me!" she cried. "You missed your calling altogether."

Perry came to the door to meet us, but Perry doesn't understand hilarity and soon stalked off looking dignified and disapproving, which made us laugh all the more. I was very happy.

My apartment struck me as another secluded corner, bigger than the one we had left downstairs but similar in "feel." I had no candles, but the lights worked on a dimmer. I had no welcoming fragrance of rosemary and thyme, but we already had that in our clothes, and more would be right along. We had been enjoying some Brahms in the restaurant. No Brahms at my place, but my radio had come on with the lights, playing soft, slow, old dance tunes from even before our time.

Madam turned to me. Her face was still full of laughter, but I found an intimacy there, as well, that I wanted very much to see in her. I took a step toward her, and she reached out to me.

"I have been longing to dance on your new floor, Richard," she said. "You *can* dance, can't you." It wasn't a question.

She looked at me for a moment with speculation added to the fun and the softer undertones. "You must be a dancer, Richard," she murmured then. "I need you to want to dance with me."

I wanted to dance with her. For weeks I had wanted to dance with her. For weeks my new floor had been demanding that I dance with her. I felt it was a mistake. I knew it was a mistake. Well, perhaps not so much a mistake as a choice. A choice of paths. An irrevocable decision. A decision that would lead us...

I knew where it would lead us, and I had accepted as fact that I would go there long before the waiter arrived with the soup. His appearance startled me, in fact. I had forgotten all about him and our order for food. I jumped and froze.

But Madam laughed. "You *can* dance, Richard," she whispered. "I knew you could. It was important to me that you should... What soup did we order?"

Women! *I* was shaken to the core. But not Madam. She was soon in consultation with the waiter about table settings. Had he brought soup spoons? Rolls and butter? Would it be necessary to reheat the soup in my microwave?

We placed a small table in front of a window where we could sit and look out at the rain and the lights of the town, coming on early as the evening darkened. They ran like the rain down the hill to the water, where they spread out around the harbour and crossed on the bridges. The sodium arc lights on the long, soaring spans glowed red as they warmed.

While the waiter set fresh flowers on the table and arranged the places, I stood in the window thinking about stability - the human mind being what it is - and watching a flight from Montreal heading for the airport, port and starboard lamps flashing, cabin lights already extinguished. It was a flight that by then I knew well, and I felt for a moment almost as if I were one of the passengers, coming home.

I enjoyed those flights down east. Always someone one knew. Always someone others knew. Returning from business, from vacations. From visiting children and grandchildren. From a sitting of Parliament. Coming home.

I smiled at Madam. "I like this town," I said.

She nodded and took her place at the table. "I knew you would," she said, "as soon as you got over being afraid of the water. This is where you *are* now."

I wondered whether I had, in fact, recovered from that appalling introduction to the harbour, the bay, and the power of the sea. I thought it unlikely. I was a plainsman. There was no cure for that. I had no background of... water stability - there was that idea again.

We were quiet for a few minutes after the waiter had gone. Madam sat watching me. At first she didn't even look at her own soup. She simply sat, not moving, watching me as I began to consume my share of an excellent lobster bisque. After a while she looked down at her plate, took a spoonful, seemed to enjoy it... But then she set her spoon down again and continued looking at me.

"I thought the soup was very good," I said.

"It is," she agreed, "and hot enough to wait a moment."

I sat with my spoon ready to descend, waiting for her to join me, but she placed her elbows on the table, leaned her chin on the backs of her hands, looked me straight in the eyes, and said, "Are they going to fire you?"

My spoon remained suspended. "Fire me?" I echoed.

"That's right, fire you. Are they?"

"I don't believe so," I said. "In fact, I'm pretty sure not. Why do you ask?"

"I know there's a great deal you're not telling me, Richard," she said. "I'm not stupid. Actually I'm rather canny. And I've met a few of your colleagues in the last week or two: Frank. Jack Davidson. The Irish one - what's his name? Barry? That woman you don't like very much - Dame Nancy Sventhorpsen, isn't it? And I've heard you, and them, speak of others. They're all single, Richard. Every one of them. That seems strange to me. Does it not seem strange to you?"

We had had a spate of visitors after the Easter blizzard. The violence of the storm, the damage it had done to old and new buildings alike, the unusual time of year for such an event - well into spring - especially the ferocity of the wind brought the experts upon us in droves. The crowd from the other side of the Atlantic came to study the town that could survive the attack of a storm that recorded isobars so close together they half suspected technical error in the measurements. Those from the American side, I suspected, came to escape their various employments for a few days, and to see the show. Frank, I was sure, came to investigate Madam. Whatever their reasons they came, and I wasn't surprised by Madam's observation.

"There's Jon Carmody," I reminded her, though as a sort of last ditch stand.

"But he isn't really one of the NEPP people, is he," she said. "Frank treats him... differently. More at arm's length. With you he's easier, more brotherly. So I ask you again. Are they going to fire you?"

"Canny" was hardly the word for this woman. She had even picked out the fact that Frank was head of our enterprise - at least of the Canadian end of it - in spite of his insistence that he was only an old cop on an interesting beat.

"And if they did?" I hedged.

She merely waited, still leaning on her hands and watching me.

"No, mignonne," I said at last. "They're not going to fire me. I'm too good at the job. Besides, they know if they did I'd go right to work with Alexa Carmody and become another thorn in their flesh."

She laughed. "You could, you know," she said. "Robert left you this suite."

Now that came as a complete surprise.

"I'm executor of his will," she explained. "You'll be notified officially in a few days."

* * *

We had been invited to dinner - Frank, Madam, and myself - at Jon Carmody's home, where the guests were, besides ourselves, Rob and Lindsay Tate and Lady Maggie Murchison. I knew, of course, who Rob Tate was. Everybody knew about the La Tour Project, though nobody knew what it was. And I knew that Lexie Carmody was his right... hand, I was going to say, but right arm would have been closer. Lady Maggie, I had found out by discrete enquiries, was not only a close friend and frequent visitor of Mrs. Carmody's but President and CEO of the Murchison shipping interests in the UK - extremely wealthy interests invested heavily in the "Project."

I would be in high-powered company, and I suffered moments of doubtful anticipation, when I had flashbacks to the little town on the prairie where I grew up, where nobody was better known than Dr. Verachuk or richer than Henry Wong, who ran "The Wok" and, according to schoolyard legend, had five thousand dollars in the bank.

Having arrived at the door, however, I was relieved in my mind, as I was relieved of my coat, to hear Alexa say that now we were all here - the Tates, ourselves, and Lady Maggie. No other people. No Shelleys, thank God. Perhaps I would be able to hold up my end of the proceedings after all.

We spent an interesting evening, all playing our cards close to our chests, circling each other like dogs at a cat fight - except Madam, of course, who had no cards to play and held the party together. Interesting, too, because of an impression I formed that we all liked each other very well, enough to be friends, given the chance; that we would like to be open with each other. At times the stress of caution brought us to the point of silliness.

I enjoyed the evening very much, actually. So did Madam; there was no doubt of that. Hard to tell about Frank, though he played the game very well. I didn't know what he was thinking till we killed a bottle of whiskey in my flat after we came home.

We three arrived at the party to find the others already drinking single malt or China tea in a warm, comfortable study at the back of the house. A wood fire burned in an old-fashioned grate. A lot of dark leather-upholstered furniture gave itself up to the comfort of the guests, as it must have been doing for generations. A grand piano stood in one of two deep window embrasures. Books lined most of the walls. And between the windows a locked cabinet held a couple of fine old skeet guns and a beautiful .303 rifle in prime condition.

I gravitated toward the gun rack as soon as I had a chance, and Frank and Jon followed me.

"*You* shoot?" Jon asked Frank - it was obvious that *I* wanted nothing more than to get my hands on that rifle.

"No," Frank said. "Not for sport. I'm a cop... I haven't been above taking life for food in my time. But not now. No, Dick is the marksman. I've never met anyone as good with a rifle as he is."

By this time Lady Maggie had joined us. "Oh," she said to me, "I was hoping your salivating was for the skeet guns. Aren't they beauties?"

"He's shot skeet too," Frank said, "but it bores him. Too actuarial for an old accountant like him. He cut his baby teeth on a rifle stock back in Manitoba."

"Speak for yourself," I said. "I only shot rats in old man Yakovitch's barn. I've heard you used to bring down eagles."

"Tried to," Frank muttered, and shook his head. "Though

maybe I was trying not to, if the truth were to come out. I rarely hit them and always felt bad when I did."

"So you gave up shooting altogether?"

"Yes, but not for that reason."

His eyes sparkled, as they always did when he felt baited, and he gave Lady Maggie the full aboriginal profile nobody could miss, before he leaned toward her and said, "Unless I'm starving or in danger of my life, I can't hit the broad side of a barn. Not since I was fourteen and the old chief of my mother's clan caught me with fresh flight feathers in my hatband."

I suspected that he used the word "clan" for Lady Maggie's benefit - the Murchison connections were in Scotland. But she didn't rise. Instead, "Eagle feathers?" she howled.

"Yes."

"Then bravo for the old chief!" she exclaimed. "What did he do?"

"Cursed my gun for life."

She took him by the arm and led him to the fire, where she plied him with warmth and attention and probably found out a good deal, though not, I'm sure, what she was looking for - if she was looking for anything in particular.

I knew they were talking about me by the way they both kept looking in my direction, but I couldn't hear what Frank was saying. By that time Lexie was telling me what a deadeye Rob was and he kept chiming in with disclaimers, something about an old cougar and foal flesh.

Rob's eyes went distant for a moment, and Alexa turned to me and murmured, "He's back in the foothills of Alberta. You can understand how that is."

I nodded.

Frank started, then, telling Lady Maggie about the time we were out on Chesterfield Inlet with some Inuit friends and I had to shoot a polar bear. Before I could shut him up, everyone had heard "polar bear" and they were all listening wide-eyed to his account of the incident - a well embroidered account. I felt a familiar twinge of remorse. But it had been the bear or us.

"You shot a polar bear?" Madam whispered with her hand on my arm.

"To my eternal regret," I whispered back. "But it raised me to hunter status and a share of the choicest parts."

"You didn't eat it!"

"Great hunters eat their kill. It's a way of assuaging the departing spirit."

* * *

After the party I walked Madam home from the elevator - Frank had a key to my flat - and went in with her. That seemed to surprise her, but she let me hang her coat in the hall closet and then turned to me with interest but questions in her eyes.

"I know," I said. "I have a house guest who is no doubt already rummaging in my liquor cabinet looking for my best single malt. He'll be all right. I have some things to say to you first."

"Things that can't wait?"

"Yes, things I have to say now. Before... I'm afraid... Well, I'm afraid they may want to make some changes... unwelcome changes... in my life... which I don't think... I mean I hope... I don't want them to do."

"Come into the living room," she said.

"No," I objected. "I haven't time. That is..."

"Then you had better just tell me."

"I know," I muttered, and took hold of her arms. "And I wish... I mean this is not something... You see..."

"Dear Richard," she said - she was trying hard not to laugh at me. "At least come into the lounge. We don't have to do this on the doorstep like a couple of kids in grade school."

She took my hand and led me into her dark living room and to the window where we had met. Below us the town sparkled with light; above, the sky with stars; and the lighthouse on the island turned its green eye on us every ten seconds regularly.

"Madam," I began again. "I don't want to put this off any longer. I..."

She rested her hands on my shoulders. "How wonderful, Richard," she said, "to find the love of one's life when one is past anticipation."

"Yes," I said. "Will you marry me?"

She gasped and opened her mouth as if to speak again, but I said, "No. No, I don't want you to answer now. I just need to have asked the question."

"Richard, have you lost your mind!" she cried. "This whole evening has been full of innuendo and sentences left unfinished, but I thought you and I might have been spared."

"I know," I muttered.

"Kiss me, Richard?" she said.

I did so.

"Yes-s," she said. "I believe you do. Now you'd better go before Frank can't find the whiskey and comes looking for you."

"Yes," I agreed. But I didn't go. I didn't go till I had to force myself away when I was pretty sure neither of us wanted me to go.

Madam didn't come to the door with me. I left her in the window where I had first seen her...

* * *

"That business when we got home last Wednesday night," she said. "When you had to speak to me right then. That was because of Frank's authority, wasn't it."

"Yes," I admitted. "I wanted... I mean I didn't want..."

She looked at me soberly. "You wanted to tell me how you felt about me before Frank backed you into a corner and you had to admit it to him first."

"Yes, I..."

She smiled then and turned her attention to her soup as if nothing had happened.

I took a few moments to recover, to think of something to say, to try to explain to her. What I said was, "I love you."

"Yes," she said, "I thought that's what you meant. But I'm too old for you, Richard."

I found my tongue then! "No!" I said, decisively and with authority of my own. "No, mignonne. Don't deny me the love of *my* life because of six years, in whatever direction."

"Really, Richard?"

We were still sitting with fatuous grins on our faces, neither of us able to say a word, when the waiter came with roast lamb and new potatoes. Neither of us had finished the soup.

Chapter Twelve:

I woke early but in bright light, feeling happy. I had been dreaming.

I had been watching myself as I sat with my back against a lichen-covered inukshuk on a shore of shale slabs. There was something odd about that inukshuk. I felt it ought to have been clean.

The sea stretched before me. Deep. Transparent. Turquoise. And still. But the tide was coming in.

On the surface of the water and below, icebergs glinted with refracted light from a weak sun that rolled low in the east. Reds and purples flashed from the ice, but the dream world glowed green - the green of new-mown grass in springtime. I could smell the colour.

Above the water, among the bergs, coming closer and closer to the beach, ribbons of fog twisted, warm and harmless as the spirits of departed friends.

As soon as I woke I forgot most of the dream, all but that general impression and Frank's parting shot: "I didn't hire you for some woman to steal you out from under my nose... But I know how it is."

Frank was there in the dream. I didn't see him, but I knew

he was there. We were on the western shore of Hudson Bay, well north - still south of the Arctic Circle, but close.

"I know how it is." Frank had muttered those words after the dinner party, when my mind was already made up and I faced him with the problem.

"Do you want my job?" I asked him.

He scowled at me sideways, across that aristocratic nose.

I didn't flinch.

"This nose," he growled, and tapped the bridge. "This nose goes back fifty thousand years. Maybe fifty million. How the hell would I know."

I didn't say anything.

He tapped his nose again. "Long before there were Murchisons in Scotland. Or anybody at all in Scotland," he muttered. "Though I liked her well enough. Smart girl, her ladyship. Wouldn't mind seeing her again."

I tried to bring him back to my question. "I need an answer, Frank," I said. "Do you want my job?"

"What would I *do* with it?"

"Give it to somebody else."

"So you can marry Madam?"

"I'll marry her anyway, if she'll have me."

"I suppose you've asked her."

"Yes."

I braced myself for pungent remarks about fools, women, and the world going to hell and nothing to be done about it. Instead he leaned back in my chair, which he had appropriated for his visit, closed his eyes, and seemed to go to sleep.

We were sitting in dim light, the only illumination in the room the small spot over the painting of the grebes. I loosened my tie and gazed at the birds.

Maybe five minutes went by before Frank spoke. I had almost written him off for the night.

"That will all go, you know," he said.

"I know," I replied. "That picture haunts me. When I forget the fight we're in, it takes me back to the good times on the prairie when I was a kid... When I remember, my heart bleeds."

"Won't be long," he said. "The new figures show a strong rise in probability. We're up to seventy-nine percent on the fresh water-loss models."

"What on the salt?"

"Hard to tell. Still too many parameters. The level of the bay will almost certainly rise, but by how much isn't clear. Enough, though. I'll have to move..."

I waited for him to continue. He didn't. And he had drunk enough for me to hesitate to pursue the thought.

He was silent a few more minutes. Then he swallowed what was left in his glass and poured another shot.

"Suppose you want out of your contract," he growled then.

"No," I said.

"You could get on with the La Tour people tomorrow if you wanted to. And they'd pay you a helluva lot more than the government ever will."

"Yes," I said, "I know. But I don't want to. And I won't till you fire me."

He snorted. "For God's sake," he said, "you're the best man I've got. I don't want to fire you. But it won't be easy for you."

"No," I said. "I realize that. But Madam is reliable and discrete. I'm pretty sure... Maybe I'm not the best judge of that, but I think I can trust her with anything she may find out. I know I can trust her not to ask."

"A rare woman," he rumbled. "Too good for you."

"I know that."

He finished his drink and stood up, a little unsteadily, which he corrected by placing one hand on the back of my chair for a moment.

I stood too and faced him. "So I'm still working for NEPP," I said.

He gave me a disgusted snarl. "You're a fool," he growled. "But you won't be alone in that. I tell you because you're my friend. It was probably a mistake recruiting you in the first place. And I didn't hire you for some woman to steal you out from under my nose... But I know how it is."

He turned away at that and went to bed.

* * *

As the sun flashed in my eyes early that Saturday morning after the rain, the dream and the conversation with Frank flashed through my mind. I felt happy. I felt a mild surprise. I felt something different about my bed...

I turned my head. Madam was leaning on her elbows watching me wake.

"What are you going to call me now?" she said.

I laughed from sheer joy and reached for her - just as the phone shrilled in our ears.

I didn't know the voice. "Sorry to call you so early, sir," she apologized, "but they said to let you know. The ice is moving."

"Ice?"

"Yes, sir. In the river."

"Oh. Yes. What time is it?"

"Ten to six. Sorry to wake you, but they said..."

"That's all right. Where are you?"

"I'm on the copter pad at Macktaguac. But they're patrolling up-river, north of Woodstock. They think the ice will jam there. There's no copter here, but we could call one down."

"No," I said. "Don't take them away from the job. I'll drive up. Should be there in a couple of hours."

I hung up and turned to Madam. "The ice is coming down the river," I said. "Want to watch?"

The sparkle in her eyes gave me my answer.

* * *

Leaving town, Madam drove. I ate egg sandwiches and orange sections, and watched cormorants and gulls in the harbour.

The lower reaches of the river lay full to flood stage and bright blue under a cloudless sky. The tide had recently turned and was falling. That would mean pressure was coming off the stream. With my hands full of sticky breakfast, I calculated in my head the effect a tide falling through nine or ten meters would have on the ice as it came down. We were developing models for everything, but I knew we couldn't have accounted for every possible factor. At best we were guessing. At worst we would be taken completely by surprise. I hoped we weren't too far off. By the end of the day we should have some idea.

Madam left me alone to my breakfast and my figures.

She knew I was working. And I didn't come back to her, the car, and the road till we were nearing the dam at Macktaguac, and she spoke.

"We're almost there," she said then. "Where do you want to be dropped off?"

"I've made you drive the whole way," I exclaimed. "And you haven't had your breakfast."

"It's hardly breakfast time yet," she said. "Only a quarter to eight. And I've enjoyed the drive. It's a beautiful morning. I'm sorry you missed it."

"I'm glad you're here," I said. "I'll make it up to you."

"There's nothing to make up, Richard," she replied. "I'll eat while you do whatever you have to do. I'm only along for the ride, remember."

"No," I said. "I don't think you are. There's a reason... I think there's a reason."

She parked in the Power Commission's lot by the dam and I remembered again Frank's enigmatic remark, "I know how it is."

I felt I was just beginning to know "how it is." Then, for a moment, a blaze of enlightenment burned my brain and I forgot my models, my numbers, my reasons for being where I was, dressed as I was, employed as I was. I couldn't understand, but it struck me with force: I was going to keep my job. I was going to keep Madam. I was going to keep my home. Everything was changed and changing, but not so.

And the ice was running in the river.

As the excitement of the break-up coursed along my nerves, I pitied the hordes of human kind who live by rivers that never freeze, who never know the thrill of that moment in spring when somebody shouts, "She's moving! She's moving out!" and everyone rushes to watch.

Madam's eyebrows rose. My face must have told her my thoughts. She looked intrigued, puzzled; then her face cleared.

"I would hate to be the cause of your losing this job, Richard," she said. "You're having such a wonderful time."

"Yes," I said, as I began to open the door to meet two Commission employees who were running toward us.

"Yes?" she enquired.

The two who were coming - a copter pilot, I judged, and

probably the girl who had called me - stopped at a respectful distance, and I took another two seconds with Madam.

"Yes, I *am* having a wonderful time," I said. "And no, they are not going to fire me."

"You're sure."

"I'm certain. Frank doesn't have enough authority to fire me. This is my place. It would take more than Frank Quarters to get rid of me. More than the Industry Minister herself. More than the whole Government of Canada. This is my job. This is my life... And the ice is coming down."

I got out and closed the door, but I didn't walk away with the pilot and the despatcher; I walked around the car and opened the driver's door.

"Bring your breakfast and come into the hangar," I said. "You don't need to stay here."

"Perhaps..." she started to say.

"No, mignonne," I declared. "I'm not going to hide you away. We're in this life together."

* * *

The jam at Woodstock was spectacular. A wall of ice eight or ten meters high pushed down the main stream, moving glacially, feeding on the flow, thrusting up irregular blocks as big as small trucks, grinding their edges, folding them into itself and rolling over them.

Simultaneously the flow let go in the Meduxnekeag.

Out of the corner of my eye I caught a flapping of wings. And as my head jerked around in their direction, several large birds rose into the air and wheeled below us, hovering over a spot in the branch ice.

"Oh, oh!" our pilot muttered, and began a slow loop over a kilometre or two of the tributary. "That's a sure sign," he told us. "When she's about to move, the birds feel the vibration, or hear the cracking or something. It's nothing you or I would notice, but they know. If she settles down again, so will they. For sure there's something for them to eat down there. Don't ask me what, but..."

I trained my binoculars on the birds and counted a dozen or so crows and ravens, six herring gulls, and a bald eagle. They were hovering over a dark spot in creek ice. It looked to me as if they had found the remains of a calf or deer - probably a deer - partly in, partly clear of the ice. The meat would be well preserved, a good meal for large birds. They would be hungry this time of year - hungrier, perhaps, than usual.

"We can't go too close," the pilot said. "The noise might affect the break-up and make the situation worse. The Company would have my hide for that!"

I nodded. My attention was all on the birds. They were not settling, and I thought we must be far enough away that our rotors would not alarm them unduly.

As I watched the eagle drop toward the carcass only to flap away again, Madam leaned forward in her seat behind me, tapped my shoulder, and pointed down.

I swung my glasses around and watched a lead open up on one side of the stream, a dark, smooth, steadily widening crack in the dirty surface of the spring ice.

At that same moment the pilot shouted, "There she goes!"

I lowered my glasses and glanced at him. As I expected, his eyes were shining, his face split by a huge grin.

We all cheered.

And laughed.

And quietly Madam sang - as if to herself, as if she had forgotten we could hear her...

"For, lo, the winter is past
The rain is over and done
Flowers appear on the earth
The time of the singing of the birds is come.

The pilot turned and looked at her with respect. "That's nice," he said. "That's just how it is, eh?"

"That's just how it is!" she repeated.

"Is now," I thought. "And ever shall be? World without end? For how long?"

I turned right around so that I could look at Madam, and found the same sadness in her eyes that filled my heart. After a moment she placed her hand on my shoulder.

We were rushing downstream then, following the tributary ice as it broke and gathered speed and moved fast and free on one side of the stream bed. Below us the birds circled, still, apparently, keeping an eye on the carcass that was moving away. Now and then one of them settled, but only for a moment. Whatever they perceived going on down there was discouraging them from trying to continue their meal. Obviously the situation was unstable.

We looped away to gain altitude and turned our attention to the collision of the two streams that was coming fast.

I have tried since to think of a simile to describe what we saw that day, and what we heard, and felt through our bodies, even isolated as we were by the beat of the rotors. I have tried to think of something, but nothing comes to mind that satisfies.

Nothing I have ever seen... No, nothing in my direct experience...

We, here, east of the Rockies, see nature, like the mills of God, grind fine but exceeding slow. Hurricanes have blown themselves out before they reach us. Tornadoes are rare, and mostly small. Our landmass is pretty stable; we have no fear of earthquakes. Blizzards, of course. The odd ice storm. A flood now and then. But nothing we haven't learned to live with.

Hail, occasionally, on the wheat fields. Fire in the forests; there's that time in late spring and early summer when we have to be careful not to burn down our endless stands of trees. But once the leaves open out... No, nothing much happens here. A good place to live. Most of us, if asked, wouldn't be able to think of a thing extraordinary. And yet, every year, without fail, on countless rivers and streams, inestimable tons of ice move with the slow force of... What?

The best I can do for comparison, though it's weak, is the long trains of freight cars that used to pull out of Winnipeg when I was kid - heading east with grain for the lakehead, west with grain for the port of Vancouver.

For mass, for momentum, for power... As the railroads once were, river ice is, and always has been, this country. And like the trains... we just keep out of the way. That's how things are - or always have been.

As the three of us watched from the sky that clear April morning, tributary ice swept into the main river at the right moment, at the right angle, just as the slow-moving mass in the main stream stuck. The tributary ice piled up and over. It tumbled in front of the main flow. It spilled over the back. It broke the pattern. It started a flood that backed up the narrow valley of the Meduxnekeag, churning the flow rushing down; that spread into the low-lying areas of the town of Woodstock and onto farm land opposite, leaving huge blocks of ice stranded among the trees on the banks.

I will always remember that sight - the dirty white of the ice; the clear, bright blue of the sky; the sparkle of dark, open water; the black forms of the birds; and the cheering, pointing, dancing human watchers gathered at every vantage point - for lo, the winter had gone, the time of the singing of the birds had come.

We were still at our vantage point - or rather, we were back again after a meal in the town - when a provincial helicopter crew lowered explosives into three weak spots in the jam and the whole mass let go.

Chapter Thirteen:

After the break-up of the river ice, I expected summer. On the prairie we used to pass almost overnight from longjohns to bare legs and sandals. But here we were in May, and I saw no end to the protracted spring that had been going on since the middle of March. The unsettled weather: the fog, the wind, the rain, and a sense of clinging to the end of the universe, unsettled me.

On the day the robins hatched, fog filled the city again, and I felt claustrophobic and troubled. I had no reason to be troubled, that I could identify. In fact, my life was going particularly well at that time. I was secure in my job; and in spite of my employer's original stipulation, secure in my relationship with Madam - I felt sure we would marry before long. I had a good working relationship with my staff. I had many acquaintances in the town, and a few friends... I enjoyed respect and good humour wherever I went... I even had two engaging "grandsons," who called me Ricardo and spent every Sunday afternoon in my pink swimming pool - I had offered the Reverend Al the use of our theatre-lecture hall for his services while the church was under reconstruction.

But something was scratching at my mind. It seemed that

land's end was my doorstep; a blue-green mistiness hung over the city, and a raw wind blew along the streets. I wanted sun and the long road that leads to dust on the horizon.

Madam tried to distract me, and often succeeded. Moments with her could be like the shafts of sunlight on new grass that I sometimes glimpsed from my tenth floor windows; but still I felt alien, more alien than ever.

"When I was a small child visiting grandparents in this town," Madam said one afternoon, "we used to have a fog horn, a wonderful, deep bass fog horn."

She was standing in the parking lot when she said that, her arms raised as if in dedication, and she filled her lungs with air that felt to me like breathing cotton wool - cold cotton wool.

"You *like* this," I accused her.

"I *love* it," she confessed.

I could only shudder.

And so it was that, midway through the afternoon on the day the robins hatched, feeling restless, I left my desk and stood close to my office window, the one that overlooked the park. Fog clung to the pane. Fog filled the street. The old elms and the maples across the way were shrouded in it, close and thick; so close and thick that all the green had disappeared from their leaves and I could barely make out the shapes of their trunks in the mist.

As I stood with my hands in my pockets, scowling through the window, no doubt round shouldered and slumped, Madam sailed in, dressed for the street. Mischief danced in her eyes and brightened my spirits momentarily.

"We've been invited to a party," she whispered. "Lunch on Saturday. Aren't we going to St. Andrews on Saturday? I hope you're free; I have a reservation at the hotel for one o'clock."

I guessed the reason for the mischief and the whispers, and for the regret for the deception that I read in her voice. "Shelley?"

She nodded.

"You should give me an answer," I suggested. "Then we could announce our engagement. That ought to discourage Shelley, don't you think?"

"I doubt it," she said. "Then she'd bend every effort toward giving us prenuptial entertainments - to make sure of an invitation to the wedding."

"Let's elope," I said. "We'll go inland, away from this infernal fog."

She only laughed and waved at me on her way out.

My office door stood open and I watched her till she was gone. Then I returned to my gloomy study of the dull, damp afternoon.

Preoccupied with a limb of an elm that came and went in my sight - now there, now vanished - I only vaguely realized that the phone had rung in the outer office, till my secretary came and tapped on the frame of my door.

"There's a call for you, Dr. Waterman," she said. "A young lady. A *very* young lady, I think. She says her name is Gerda and that the eggs have hatched. I thought I'd come in and tell you instead of ringing through."

The sun came out in my heart and I dove for the phone.

"I saw them just a minute ago, Richard!" Gerda babbled. "As soon as I came home from school. Two babies. And the other shell is cracked. Grandpa says you can come over if you want to. Will you? I want you to."

She sounded as if she must be bouncing up and down as she talked.

"The robins have hatched!" I announced in a loud voice two seconds later as I passed like a strong wind through the office. I know I was smiling broadly.

"Not in your shirt sleeves, Dr. Waterman!" I heard from behind my back as I reached the corridor. "Not without your coat, sir. The fog is in again!"

It was only across the parking lot, and I was in a hurry. I opened my mouth to argue. But I checked my speed and accepted the jacket that came flying after me in my secretary's hands. She was a local girl, and I was learning that fog comes in cold.

That fact never ceased to surprise me: that fog would be cold. It looks so innocent. Even cuddly. But it's the visible breath of the north, and it can chill to the bone.

"Cold enough for you, Doc?" Marvin called out to me as I strode across the street toward the Green Dragon. He was sitting on the steps of the rooming house where he lived.

"Does summer ever come to this winter palace?" I shouted back.

"Oh, sure," he said, and there was amusement in his voice. "One of these days you'll wake up and find out the summer's been here all the time."

I waved and hurried on up the block. I didn't believe him. But the robins had hatched; that must mean something.

* * *

I liked Gerda's house. Each time I visited there, I liked it more. I felt at home in it. It was like no house I had ever experienced, but I liked it. From the narrow double doors that led into a narrow vestibule, to the stained glass skylight on the landing; from the cabbage roses on the front room walls and the uneven rolling floors, to the rickety sunporch on the back, I liked it. Perhaps I liked it because I liked the people who lived in it. Whatever the reason, the building pleased me and I never refused an invitation to come over.

Gerda was waiting on the stairs to the second floor flat where she lived with her grandfather.

"Come and see," she whispered. "They're the funniest little things. They have no feathers! Did you know they wouldn't have any feathers? I thought they would. I thought they'd look like the big birds, only little."

Up the stairs and through another narrow door off the landing, we tip-toed into the narrow sunporch that hung on the back of the house and looked down on a secluded backyard or garden. An old carriage shed extended back from the landing. And a high board fence shut out the neighbourhood on the other two sides, leaving an enclosure where coarse grass struggled to take over the ground. A few dandelions bloomed in clumps, doing pretty well in the leached soil. And in the corner under the porch, so close to the house that some of its branches touched the wall, a moss-grown apple tree sheltered. Its struggle to survive was evident and its ultimate failure obvious, but the palest of pink flowers had opened where life still clung to some of the branches; and in a rough little nest among the blossoms, just at the level of the porch windowledge, three tiny, featherless bodies waited in panic for the return of a parent with food. Wing stubs flailed.

Scrawny necks stretched. Yellow beaks opened wide.

"Oh, look!" Gerda whispered. "The other one is out. They're all there... They're Albert's babies, you know."

"You're sure?"

"Oh, yes. Albert. The one that came alive again," she said. "George lives in the maple tree over the fence. And I think Edward lives on a church windowsill in the next street. You can just see if you know where to look... Grandpa named them for King Edward the Eighth. He was a long time ago."

"Edward Albert Christian George Andrew Patrick David," I said.

She looked surprised, as if she hadn't realized I was *that* old.

"That's right," she said. "How did *you* know?"

I just tapped myself on the temple, and she smiled.

"We call the babies Andrew, Patrick, and David," she said. "But of course we don't know if they're boys or girls yet, so they may have to be Andrea, Patricia, and Davida."

She was perfectly serious, and I smiled - broader and broader with everything she said.

Mrs. Albert arrived home with a mouthful of earthworm which she rammed down one of the open throats. Hard to imagine that those scrawny little necks might ever produce the liquid notes of the rain warning, or be the first to announce the rising sun. I had to choke back some elusive emotion, but Gerda didn't notice - too busy watching the nestlings - and I was able to regain control before Mrs. Albert settled down on the nest and we couldn't see her family any longer.

Gerda looked around the porch then.

"This is how I come out to see them most of the time," she said, pointing to a window farther along the wall, where Grandpa MacKenzie was standing, waiting to speak to us.

"But today we'll use the door," she went on. "Grandpa says to come in now. It's time for tea. Will you stay, please? When you stay, Grandpa lets me drink tea. Mostly I have to drink milk instead, but I like tea. Please? Will you?"

She took my hand and looked up at me with the question in her eyes.

"Of course I'll stay," I said. "Thank you very much. I like tea too."

"I know," she said. "You drank four cups at Eastertime."

We went inside by the doors on the landing, not through the window, and I didn't object, though I would have liked to try the window.

I thought, as Gerda took my hand and led me to the kitchen table, that she and her grandfather had a wonderful life together. Probably it would have been better for her to live in a regular family with parents and siblings - I had no idea why she didn't - but only if she could be as free and happy there as she was with the old man.

I remembered my own childhood with only my mother - my father had died when I was three, a result of the war. I examined those years in my mind and found nothing to regret, though the memories brought with them another lick of the gloom I had been feeling. For a moment I was deeply depressed. But only for a moment - Grandpa MacKenzie's smile of welcome was too warm and his kitchen too full of the fragrance of fresh molasses cookies to support gloom.

We drank strong India tea, ate cookies straight from the oven, and talked of everything under the sun.

Where was Madam? Jenny said she was out when Gerda called to tell her the babies were here.

"Yes," I said, "but I don't know where she went. She'll be sorry she missed the celebration."

Was this a celebration? That was interesting... Were there pigeons on the prairies?

I guessed there were pigeons just about everywhere.

Yes. Probably there were. That was nice. Gerda liked pigeons... Had I been to the beach?

"No, I arrived on Boxing Day."

Oh! But I had a car.

Yes, would Gerda like to go to the beach when the weather was warmer?

Oh, yes! Would Madam come too? Was she my girlfriend?

Grandfather MacKenzie gasped a bit at that, but I replied with equanimity, Yes, Madam was my girlfriend. Did Gerda have a boyfriend?

"No!" with a snort of disgust. Gerda didn't like boys.

"Yet," Grandpa muttered, and smiled.

Did I have a mother?

No, my mother died. Her name was Elsie.

That was an old-fashioned name. None of the kids at school were called Elsie.

"There's Elsie Wayne, of course."

Gerda shrugged as if to say, Well, there you are! Anyone with hair as white as Mrs. Wayne's must be old as the hills!

"Mrs. Wayne is very important," she said. "She's the most important person in La Tour. She's our Member of Parliament, you know. And you can't be as important as Mrs. Wayne is till you're old and have white hair."

She looked at my hair and seemed satisfied. Gray, but not altogether. "Mrs. Wayne is more important than you are," she finished.

She even showed me her latest report card, and I was not surprised to see that she was a good student.

Now and then a stab of anxiety came back, but I ignored it, and Gerda almost immediately said something to make me smile.

"The fog is in again," she said after one such sally, sounding as if she were about as old as her grandfather and probably just as wise.

"Again!" I exclaimed. "Has it been out?"

"Yes!" she cried with a rippling laugh. "Didn't you see?"

"No."

She looked at me with solicitude. "I guess you don't like fog," she said. "I like it."

I shook my head and turned to her grandfather. "Madam has told me," I said, "that the way to tell a birth Maritimer from somebody transplanted here..."

He laughed. "We like fog," he said. "In moderation. A nice foggy day now and then is restful, cosy... stretching-out-for-a- nap kind of weather."

"I can't quite get it," I said. "You like fog."

"In moderation."

"In moderation," I agreed. "I suppose that's my problem. I haven't yet learned where exactly the line is - the line where moderation ends and too much begins. How does one recognize it?"

Grandpa MacKenzie took a sip or two of hot, strong Red Rose Tea while he pondered his answer.

"Well, Dick," he said at last, "that's hard to put a finger on... A fellah I used to work with at one time - the year we were putting up the new City Hall down there at the foot of King - Joe Nason, his name was - he was a terrible man to drink - but only in moderation, to hear him tell... To me, now, fog is in moderation if she lies out in the harbour most days, so you can see her out there, and you can feel the cold of the sea breeze that comes up from her late in the forenoon, but she mostly stays out and only comes in overnight, or now and then with the tide."

"Ah," I said, "then this year the fog is not in moderation."

"No, I'd say we're having a foggy spring," he agreed, "though not to a serious degree, you understand."

"And how will I recognize a serious degree?"

"Well, now, I suppose... when every second person you meet tells you we're having an awful foggy summer," he said. "That'll be a sign... When the children start being quarrelsome, and the mothers a little quick on the draw, that could be a sign... And if she goes into July and the strawberry farmers start prophesying about the crop rotting in the fields for want of the sun..."

He chuckled to himself. "I believe your strawberry grower is your indicator, Dick," he said. "For they're a nervous lot. For myself, I can't remember a year when the most of them weren't prophesying the end of life on earth as we know it."

I didn't enjoy his choice of metaphor, but... "A lot like the wheat farmers on the prairies," I suggested.

"I dare say," he agreed. "I dare say. For you see, neither wheat nor strawberries grow in this country by nature. You take blueberries now. If you was to try to stamp out blueberries, you'd need the entire population of this country working around the clock, and still they'd be back the following spring. For they belong here, do you see. They belong like the robins and the earth worms... And the fog... Let me fill your cup."

* * *

After tea and a final peek at the robins, Gerda invited me to come into the garden to feed the pigeons. Of course I said I would like that, and she instructed me to help Grandpa clear the table while she rummaged in a cupboard and came up with a basinful of cracked corn.

"In the summertime we go down," she explained, "but in the wintertime, if the snow is deep, sometimes I stand in the sunporch and feed them out the window... Would you like to see how I do it? First we have to go out the kitchen window."

Here was my chance.

"And now we have to stand in the sunporch - after we slide the window open, of course - and put the corn on the windowsill. It mostly falls into the snow and they can't find it if we throw it down from up here in the wintertime."

So after we had spread an experimental layer of kernels on the ledge and been rewarded by a flutter of wings and much satisfied cooing, Gerda firmly closed the window screen and announced, "We'll go down now."

"Yes, Ma'am," I said, and she laughed, but she led on anyway.

Grandpa was waiting on the landing, where green and golden light was pouring through the coloured-glass flowers of the skylight.

"The fog has lifted again," he remarked, and then, when I looked surprised - as if I hadn't noticed, which I hadn't - he nodded. "Clearing is always remarkable when you live on a fog-bound coast," he said.

How quickly I had forgotten. But I appreciated the brightness on the landing and then the scent of lilac that was heavy in the garden.

I looked around but could see no bushes. "Where is the lilac coming from?" I asked.

"Lots of places," Gerda told me. "They're just coming out."

"When the air is damp and heavy with fog," the grandfather explained, "the perfume lies close to the ground."

"So you can smell it better," Gerda explained.

We all stood still, breathing in the scent. I remembered lilac bushes that grew along the side of our house at home. My mother kept them low and uniform and never allowed them to bloom, which I could not understand; the thickets behind old man Yakovitch's barn grew almost as high as the hay-loading window in the loft and were full of flowers every spring. I remembered their scent, but the perfume here by the sea seemed heavier, sweeter. Perhaps the fog had something to do with it, as the grandfather said.

And perhaps because we all stood perfectly still, Albert began to sing on the fence at the back of the lot - or it may have been Edward, or George. I thought of cats, and another anxious icicle slashed my heart.

I was beginning to be concerned for my mental stability. The misty sunshine, the perfume of the lilacs, the robin-song, and certainly my special little friend were bringing me close to emotional crisis. I had to get away and reestablish control.

"I must go," I said, I hoped not abruptly. "Thank you both for this visit and the tea party."

"Will you come again?" Gerda asked.

"Indeed I will," I promised, "and I'll bring Madam. She'll want to see the babies while they're still brand new."

* * *

I moved swiftly, but not swiftly enough. I can still hear Albert singing me away. I can see Gerda as she was then, dancing beside me as far as the street. I can smell the lilac that filled the air as I stood on the sidewalk saying another good-bye while Marvin stumped up the street to cross the parking lot with me... I can feel Perry rubbing against my legs as he anticipated his dinner, which he accepted in his usual dignified way. Any of those memories - separately or in combination - can still bring tears to my eyes.

As if he knew I needed company, that evening when he had eaten, Perry came and jumped up on my lap. This attention was unprecedented. After his dinner he always curled up on the chair behind the kitchen table. That night he came to me.

As the fog rolled back over the town with the evening, I sat in my chair, stroking his fur, tears gathering behind my eyes and at the back of my throat, and I wept. For the first time in my adult life, I wept. I wept for the nestlings in the apple tree. I wept for the robin rain-song. I wept for the scent of lilac in the nostrils and the taste of fog on the tongue. For the rustle of aspen on the far wind. For the beach I had not yet seen and the sloughs I knew so well. For Gerda. For Pete Yakovitch. For Pete's grandfather. For Gerda's grandfather. For mine. For the bison, and the people, and the great rolling plains of grass. For the cowboys and the horses. For Wong's Wok and the freight trains, and the links of the long red chain...

And it was as if Rob settled into his corner of the couch again. I believed I saw the cushions move. And Perry left me and curled up there, and purred.

I leaned my head against the back of my chair. I closed my eyes. And I heard the "rain" of palm fronds and smelled blue seas and sun-warm islands. While sea fog off the North Atlantic chilled my windows and muffled the sounds of evening in the town, I wept. And in my darkening room my friend sat with me as I wept. For him. For Sarah Jane. For my mother, and old Doctor Verachuk, and the Persian rug.

"There was need," Rob said, after a time of silence.

I was suddenly furious. My head jerked upright on my shoulders, and I faced his corner of the couch, every muscle tensed. "What was that you said?" I roared.

"There was need," he repeated.

"And still is, for God's sake," I shouted. "The need goes on and on. Now that you're dead, it's worse than ever. You might have spared yourself the trouble."

"That need is met," he said.

"The need is never met," I argued. "You know it isn't. You knew that when you went. There are never enough doctors. There's never enough money, never enough..."

"There is enough," he murmured.

I was alone, sitting alone in a dark room, and I was furious with an old man who was dead.

"You will find there is enough, Dick," he said.

"Me!" I howled. "Leave me out of this!"

I was shouting at a memory.

I felt like an idiot.

I studied the cushions where he used to sit, studied them a long time. Then I sighed. "I can't *take* it from you, Rob," I said. "You're too late passing the torch. I'm not allowed heroics, self-sacrifice, self-immolation... insanity... Somebody has to keep both feet on the ground."

"But not you."

My living room became two dimensional. And still. No sound reached it from the street. No sound from the building.

Nothing moved.

I didn't want to believe it. Sound never ceases. Movement never ceases. But in that moment there was neither. I was alone. Only I. In peace. Out of space. Out of time. Alone. In peace.

At length a faint scent of lilac came to my heart, a faint cat's purr touched my mind; the taste of strong tea on my tongue eased my spirit. The grebes turned their heads on their long white necks and looked at me.

Perry stretched and let himself down from Rob's lap to the floor.

And Madam came home.

Chapter Fourteen:

June came, and toward the end of the month Madam and Gerda announced that no better day was likely to present itself for going to the beach. Gerda had been excused from school because "some of the kids had to write exams" but she didn't. The sun was shining. The tide would come in during the afternoon - a consideration they set great store by, that I failed at that time to appreciate. And Jenny had made strawberry tarts "with real berries."

"Much better than berries grown anywhere else," Madam explained.

"*Je t'assure*," Gerda declared.

We must go to the beach.

I looked out of my office window and discovered that summer had indeed been with us all along. Summer. So definite on the prairie; so tentative here. But the trees in the park were in full leaf; begonias filled the beds with red and yellow and white; and a couple of summer students were cutting the grass over there. How had I missed this transformation?

We must certainly go to the beach.

* * *

The day was warm.

As we left the city, warm air blew through the open windows of the car. I made an attempt to suggest that we might use the air conditioning, but I was voted down.

"No, no," they said. "Just wait till we reach the woods." And I confess that the air smelled very sweet among the trees, full of life and sap and flowers, and the damp pervasiveness of the sea. It was different from the smell of prairie, but very pleasant.

I slowed as we began to pass between stands of mixed forest: dark old-growth spruce unfolding fragrant light-filled tips; new- growth birch and poplar covered with young yellow-green leaves and hung with catkins; undergrowth rhododendron, leafless and brittle-looking brown stems raising flowers of the pink-but-not-quite-pink that I always saw in Madam's hair. And everywhere the smell of wild strawberries.

I don't suppose we were smelling strawberries in fact. No doubt the perfume was a compound of many fragrances from the complex of plants opening up to the sun. But we thought of it as strawberry and filled ourselves with it.

"My mother used to make strawberry jam," I said, remembering the taste of the first batch of the year. We could never wait for it to cool but must sample it straight from the stove. For a moment I thought I had burned my tongue again.

Madam closed her eyes as if remembering something like that too.

"Joanie Wallace's mother makes strawberry jam," Gerda said. "Only she makes them all pick the wild ones. Joanie hates it - picking, I mean, not the jam, which she assures me is very good, but the mosquitoes. Joanie says they like strawberries too, and if they think you're stealing their berries, they bite. One day she came to school with her fingers all covered with big red bumps that itched and itched."

"Oh, don't you remember!" Madam exclaimed. "Isn't this wonderful, Richard? We can talk all afternoon. Let's be quiet now and breathe in this wonderful smell, and remember."

"I thought we were going swimming this afternoon," I reminded her, after a few moments devoted to sniffing the air.

"And so we are," she said. "You'll see."

I supposed the delay in my seeing to have something to

do with the half-ton picnic hamper I had been required to carry down and stow in the trunk of my car. "After lunch," I suggested.

"You'll see," Madam repeated, with a knowing little smirk that she shared with Gerda, who was buckled up in the back seat.

"I see now," I muttered. "I'm along because you two only want someone to carry the baggage and drive the car."

"Oh, no," Gerda exclaimed. "You'll have to buy us ice cream cones before we swim, as well."

"What! After the lunch Jenny packed? We'll never eat again if we polish that off. It nearly broke my back."

"You'll see," they repeated, together.

Gerda giggled, and Madam turned as far as she could and held out her right hand, little finger crooked.

Gerda's little finger hooked into Madam's. "Bread and butter," she said, and giggled again.

"Make a wish," I advised.

"Naturally," they retorted, again together, and went off into gales of laughter and another round of "bread and butter."

"What did you wish for?" I asked. I didn't expect to be told. Telling, I believe, always cancels the wish. But I asked anyway.

"Oh, you can't tell or it won't come true!" Gerda declared, and settled down in the seat behind Madam to enjoy the drive.

I glanced at her, not for the first time trying to work out the hold she had on my heart. Gerda was a puzzle to me. I was drawn to her as to... I don't know what. Spring on the plains, perhaps. I felt about her as I think my mother felt about the first sign of crocuses poking through the snow in her garden. I thought I must have known her before, but try as I might I couldn't find anyone like her in my past. The problem baffled me.

That day her face shone. Her fair hair blew around her head. She was the picture of a supremely happy child. A dreamy, far-away smile glowed in her eyes. I shook my head and returned my mind to driving.

* * *

About half a mile of pale golden sand stretched between

the dunes and the water.

"Oh! It's a big beach!" I exclaimed.

"Yes, of course. Didn't you know?"

We three and a load of Madam's beach-visiting paraphernalia had emerged suddenly at the end of a boardwalk that led through sand dunes, and stood then with an expanse of shore and water before us - flat, unencumbered by trees, glittering.

I found it satisfying. My breathing slowed and deepened. "I like this place," I said. "I feel as though I could spread my elbows without knocking the two of you off the face of the earth."

They regarded me with interest.

"So speaketh a plainsman, Gerda," Madam explained.

Gerda nodded. "Someday I'm going to visit the prairies," she said.

"You won't like it," I told her, somewhat sadly. "Your kind never does."

"*I* will," she said.

"I'd like to think so," I agreed, "but I doubt it."

"Why? What's my kind?"

"The kind-that-lives-here kind," I told her. "Maritimers. You feel squashed by the prairies; like beetles trying to walk across a table cloth."

"We do?"

"Yes."

She studied me for a moment and I could tell that all the considerable intelligence she possessed was working on this problem.

"Well," she said at last, "beetles have six elbows."

Her reply pleased me strangely, but I dropped the subject and surveyed the expanse of sand. "*There's* a nice spot for our umbrella," I suggested instead.

"Where?"

Loaded down as I was with baskets, chairs, and all the rest of it, I could only nod to indicate the place I meant. "Out there," I said. "Where those people are walking. There's a mound. See where the sand is a little higher than it is in other places?"

Gerda giggled and glanced at Madam.

"Oh, *that* place," Madam said, and I saw that knowing smirk pass between them again. "Yes. There's probably a rock under that. We'll go and explore it presently, when we've set up our chairs and things... That looks like a nice spot just along under there. What do you think, Gerda?"

They had turned their backs on my choice out on the sand and were inspecting a small indentation in the dune that backed the beach. Grass and some pink and purple flowers grew on the bank. And a small tree, gnarled by the wind and a precarious position - a tree with thorns and small, dark leaves - overhung the place from part way up a low cliff of soft, reddish stone that began to rise out of the sand in that place. I thought we would be lucky if the tree didn't come down on our heads, but the ladies found no fault with the location.

Gerda cast an experienced nine-year-old eye over the place and pronounced it good.

"Yes," she said. "The tide is very high these days, but I think we'll be safe there. Last summer I lost my sneakers."

I was all at sea - not an unusual condition for me when Gerda was around. I concentrated on the picnic site.

"Are you sure about that place?" I asked. "It seems to be full of some sort of purple stuff all over the ground. There may be bugs."

"Bubbleweed," Madam announced. "It's dry."

"You'll see," Gerda said, and took hold of my arm to lead me to our place. "See, there's an old log there. You can sit on it if you want to."

I shrugged - or tried to shrug under my load - and allowed myself to be dragged along.

Once arrived, I dropped my lunch baskets, a green and blue umbrella, two orange chaise longues, and a lavender-coloured folding chair for Gerda. I dumped everything down on the bubbleweed, that crunched under my feet, and rubbed the circulation back into my arms before I began to set up camp.

"Did you bring your sweater, Gerda?" Madam asked.

Sweater!? My watch said ten past eleven. We were well past mid-morning and into the hottest part of what looked like being a hot day.

"Oh, yes," Gerda replied. "And my hat with the string under my chin. And my dry pants."

Pants? Surely...

Madam nodded approvingly. "Sunglasses? Sunscreen?"

"Yes."

"On they go then."

Gerda dropped a large backpack on the sand and brittle bubbleweed, and sent panic among the bugs I had predicted - a species of large, black beetle. But she ignored the beetles and almost disappeared from sight as she rummaged in the bag. Clothing and other articles began to fly out the top.

I looked at Madam. "Surely not a sweater," I objected.

"No-o," Gerda giggled, happening to have come up for air at that moment.

And Madam continued, "*Your* dark glasses, Richard?"

"Mine?"

"You brought them, of course."

"No, I..."

"I was afraid of that, so I brought a pair for you. You really must take care..."

"Thank you, mignonne" I said. I was grateful. I hadn't realized that the green and blue motif of the countryside would not continue onto the beach, and I was already feeling the glare.

"I know," Madam soothed, and patted my hand. "I know. You still have much to learn, Richard, but you're doing very well."

Gerda reappeared from her backpack. "It's starting already," she said, and laughed. "Your eyes are making tears in them, Richard."

"I brought a hat," I protested, in my own defence, as I adjusted the glasses over my ears.

"Good. Where is it?"

"Back in the car."

"I'll get it," Gerda offered, and giggled merrily.

"*You'll* get it?"

"I know how to open your car. All you do is push that little button on the remote."

I handed over my car keys and stretched out, as directed, on a chaise longue - what else can a man do. The glasses cut down the glare, and the orange straps of the chair - cotton, not plastic - gave comfortably under my weight. The place was peaceful, soporific...

Madam adjusted the umbrella for maximum shade and settled down beside me.

"This is very nice," I offered. "I suppose Gerda is safe?"

"She's safe," Madam replied. "When she returns we'll start lunch."

"Umm-m," I agreed, and closed my eyes...

The shouts of children came to me...

They came right into my ears, splitting my head into pieces.

My mouth opened...

I shouted too...

* * *

Our summer lake was cool under the sun, the water clear and bright. Loose sand shifted under my feet. I went down, eyes open. Every bottom grain shone from all sides in the filtered light. I sank toward it slowly, peacefully, holding in my mind only the interest of the occasion.

A shimmer passed over the sand and me: cumulus floating across the sky. The lake instantly cooled.

I touched down. The sand was rough against my skin.

"I'm swimming!" I thought. "I'm swimming!"

I wriggled like a tadpole. And I swam, straight for the surface, and burst through jubilant.

"I can swim!" I shouted. "Momma, I can swim!"

She didn't hear me.

"Momma!" I bellowed.

She looked up but didn't find me right away among the shrieking, splashing children.

"Elsie!" I thundered.

I would catch the rough of her tongue for that, but I must tell her.

"Elsie!"

She jumped to her feet.

"I can swim," I hollered. "Watch me, Momma. I can swim!"

* * *

"The water was two feet deep, I suppose," I muttered.

"Sound asleep," Madam murmured.

"Asleep?"

"I judged so."

"Dreaming?"

"Very likely."

I laughed. "I used to think, in those days," I said, "that our lake was as big as the ocean, probably as big as all the rest of Canada put together. And I had mastered it. I could swim."

"In two feet of water."

"I was less that three feet tall."

She smiled. "Hard on the knees, though," she said.

"I was five or six," I told her. "Younger than Gerda. Much. But that summer I swam all around the world. And then I swam up into the sky."

"How did you manage that?"

"By swimming down our river to the place where it met the sky, of course."

"Of course. Forgive me. I had forgotten your prairie milieux for the moment."

"Everyone knew that the clouds were filled with rain," I explained, "so naturally one could swim in them. And they were close together, so one could dive from one into the next. My only problem was how to keep my lunch from disintegrating in the water."

Madam seemed to like my story, but... "Here's your hat, Richard," Gerda called.

I dragged myself back to that warm day on a Bay of Fundy beach, and *two* little girls stood before me.

"This is Risa," Gerda said. "She's my friend. She's in my class in school. Her mother said she could come and play with me if Madam said so."

Madam, of course, said so, and we opened the lunch basket. Lobster rolls - lobster on fresh, white rolls with lettuce and mayo. Egg salad sandwiches on dark bread for Gerda - Jenny clung to the delusion that little girls didn't like lobster; my suspicion, soon confirmed, was that they liked it very well. Little girls, I find, can be as expensive as bigger ones.

There was potato salad with onion and a hint of mustard. A small roast chicken. Cold boiled frankfurters - Gerda liked them that way. A tossed salad.

There was food for a family of four for a week - or so I thought, still having much to learn about children. They had left only some of the green salad when they pronounced themselves ready for strawberry tarts, which they fell upon with unimpaired enthusiasm, and chocolate brownies.

No dessert survived, and a large thermos of tea was soon emptied. Gerda's eyes followed Madam's every move as she set out cups from the hamper, and shone with glee when she filled all the cups from the jug. Risa's eyes popped out onto her cheeks. "Tea? Real tea? Really?"

When we were all "stuffed to the gunwales" as Gerda put it, Madam sighed and looked out at the water. "The tide has turned," she said. "It's coming in, but we have lots of time for a nice rest... Risa, have you left your shoes on the beach?"

Risa glanced at her bare, brown toes and shook her head. "No, Madam," she said. "I left them with my mother."

"Good."

Madam stretched out on her chaise, and closed her eyes.

A few people strolled by, but they were well down the beach. A sparrow set up his sewing machine in the thorn tree. Gulls sailed overhead on updraughts from the hot sand. After awhile one of the gulls settled not far off and folded its wings.

Risa flopped down at my feet. "I wish *I* could fly," she said.

"I *can*," Gerda murmured.

I turned my head and found her sitting on the sand beside Madam, her eyes on the gulls that were still wheeling in the sky.

"Can you, dear?" Madam murmured, and reached out sleepily and stroked the child's wind-tossed hair.

Gerda turned and smiled at her. "Yes," she said. "If I shut my eyes and wish, I can. Yesterday I flew through our porch window and perched in the apple tree with Albert and the babies... They'll be able to fly one of these days."

Risa sighed.

"My grandfather says it's natural for people to fly," Gerda went on. "He lets me do it - as long as I don't really, of course... Can you fly, Madam?"

"Someday I am going to fly through the tail of a comet," Madam said.

My heart jumped. Was that what Madam thought? Many people did, still expecting Armageddon to be fire and brimstone, not dirty air and polluted water.

"What's *that*?" Risa was asking.

"What's a comet?"

"Yes."

"It's a... Well, it's a big snowball in space. Sometimes with rocks in the middle and snow on the outside."

Jason McCormack made a snowball last winter with a rock in the middle," Risa said.

"Yes, and he threw it at Peter Wilnex and broke his window," Gerda supplied.

"*His* window?"

"Yes, and Mr. Wilnex was mad and Jason had to pay, only he didn't, cause he hasn't any money - ever - so he had to shovel snow for Mr. Porterhouse every day all winter. Mr. Wilnex said so."

"Only some days there wasn't any snow."

"No, so Jason made us all stand in a circle at recess and pray, cause he'd be an old man before he finished if it didn't snow..."

"But we didn't. Pray, I mean. If we didn't want snow to come. Only we didn't tell Jason cause he would be mad."

Risa returned to the comets. "Snowballs don't have tails," she said.

"Comets do. They're going so fast they leave a trail of snow and ice pieces behind them," Madam explained.

"Wow!"

"I guess you have to hurry through them."

"Hurry?"

"Cause they wouldn't last long."

"They last for eons and eons."

"What are *they*?"

"Zillions and zillions of years."

"Really?"

Silence. And two rapt faces.

"Wow!" Risa said again.

"How big are they?" Gerda whispered.

"Pretty big."

"As big as my house?"

"Much bigger."

"As big as your house?"

"Bigger."

"As big as the world?"

"Bigger, some of them."

"Wow!"

I sat up and worked my shoulders loose of the near paralysis that had seized them. This discussion, though still wide of the mark, was coming too close for comfort. "Anybody for a swim?" I suggested.

"Richard," Gerda cried, "do you know about comets? They're big snowballs in the sky and they have tails and everything. And Madam is going to fly through one some day. Can we go too? Can we, Madam? Did you know, Richard?"

"Richard knows," Madam said quietly. "We'll let him come if he wants to."

"Will you?"

I made sure my voice was working. "If I can get away that day," I said, which may have been closer to the truth than anybody knew.

"What would happen to us?" Gerda wanted to know.

"Where?"

"In the tail of the comet."

"Nothing. We'd be in a space ship. They're tough."

"Tougher than the Titanic?"

"Oh, I hope so."

"I wouldn't want to hit an ice berg."

This *was* coming too close.

"How about a swim?" I bleated.

They stared at me as if I had materialized out of the tail of a comet with icicles hanging from my nose.

"It isn't time yet," Gerda said at last, patiently, as if I had the intelligence of one of the gulls she was watching.

"It must be an hour since we ate, isn't it?"

"Oh, I didn't mean that... Is there a tour, Madam?"

They chattered happily while I sat with one leg on either side of my chaise and studied the beach. I judged that half the sand that had been exposed on our arrival was now covered with water. I glanced at my watch. Two hours. And the tide had been still ebbing when we came. The water was coming in fast, I thought. But the beach was flat out there, only shelving steeply in the last third or so. The apparent rate would slow there, but I expected to find swimming water well in advance of full tide.

"How about we go and investigate?" I suggested.

"Not yet," Gerda said firmly. "Madam is telling us about comets. We never heard of comets before, did we, Risa."

"I'm going to walk down to the water," I said.

"All right."

I took off my shoes and socks, rolled up my pants, and sauntered onto the sand. It was hot, almost too hot for comfort, but I persevered and toughened up. The water was farther than I thought, too. Madam and the children under the green and blue striped umbrella looked very small when I turned at the water's edge and looked back at them.

I should not have turned back. A wave washed over my feet when I wasn't looking and I howled in agony.

A small boy playing with a toy boat looked at me and laughed. "You never been here before, Mister?" he asked.

"Never!" I said. "Is it always this cold?"

"Yes," he assured me. "Look out. There's a big one coming."

I was too slow. The wave hit me about knee height and exploded against screams of laughter.

I danced on the sand. "Do you mean to tell me people swim in this?" I demanded.

"Not yet," the child said with the same scornful patience I had suffered from my girls. "Later. You'll see."

I noticed that the child was careful to stay just ahead of the water. That seemed wise to me, and I patterned my movements on his. Even so, I leapt out of the way of the next wave with only a split second to spare.

As I returned to our picnic site over the blazing sand, my blue feet burning, I was glad to see Gerda and Risa running toward me with my sandals in their hands. They smiled kindly and watched me as I put them on.

"We'll come with you to the shop if you like," Gerda offered. "They have very good ice cream here."

"Already?"

"Yes. Madam said so."

But going for ice cream was not the simple process I imagined.

Madam was ready, waiting for us, and we strolled along the beach to a stairway up the cliff that backed thc place. That is, Madam and I strolled. The children ran ahead of us and were already deep in discussion of flavours, toppings, and combinations when we reached the canteen... I was consulted as to expense.

I gave carte blanche, which resulted in huge amounts of mixtures of bubble gum and Oreo cookie that I would have thought guaranteed to sink two small girls for a week, but they received the stuff with delight, and demolished with gusto what didn't drip onto their clothes.

I was concerned by the messes in progress, but Madam assured me that that was why we had the ice cream eating before the swimming. And Risa's parents, when we met them, didn't seem to notice anything amiss.

"I hear you're from Winnipeg," Risa's mother said, when I was introduced. "I'm from Brandon, myself. My husband is from New Brunswick, though - the northern part."

Seeing Risa's mother it was obvious to me that the child hadn't been named Risa for some ephemeral reason, but that the name was undoubtedly a common one in the maternal line. In the planes of her cheeks, broad rivers meandered under immense skies. Her smile came and went like the wind over long reaches of grasses. The stamp of horses rang in her voice, and in my plainsman's blood. And I felt that a man with twice the elbows of a beetle had not too much freedom, not too much space, not too much time...

I had always thought of myself as a Canadian of English stock brought up on the Great Plains of North America, which were my home. On my first day, though - Boxing Day with Madam - I had glimpsed a river I had never seen, which I supposed, because her words suggested it, was an English river. I had even tried to reconcile that fleeting vision with the Thames as I saw it on my visit to London during the winter. But that day on the beach I wondered if possibly that river had been the Volga; maybe even the Yenesey, Ob or Lena, and I began to see that my plainsman's blood probably came from eons of time on the steppes of Asia and was simply reawakened by the Great Plains of America. It made sense. Anything that went that deep could not be the work of a generation or two.

But while my imagination expanded my experience and ripped open my mind, I licked my ice cream cone and sauntered back down the steps and along the sand with Madam and the girls. The tide climbed the beach. The sea breeze raised small surf. The small surf grew to bigger surf where the shore shelved more sharply. The water warmed over the hot sand under the hot sun.

And *then* we swam.

"Now!" Gerda cried, and kicked off her shoes, too close to the tide after all.

The water lapped around the picnic hamper. The bubbleweed carpet rose and fell. Gerda's shoes, my hat, Risa's T-shirt all had to be rescued. We splashed and shouted and swallowed salt water. But still not too much space. Not too much time. Not too much life.

Afterward we needed sweaters. And dry pants - those of us who had them. We put them on and went home.

Chapter Fifteen:

That day at the beach and the events that followed were weighing on my mind when I went north that summer. I hadn't been at all sure I would go to Hudson Bay that year, though I knew I should for the sake of the work I was doing. I wasn't sure till I heard from Frank that I was to join Jon Carmody in Ottawa for a few days in July, then fly to Churchill with him. We would go on to Chesterfield Inlet for some birding - whatever I liked - after that, but we were to present ourselves in Churchill on the stipulated day to inspect damage from a leak of Bunker C from a storage tank at the old port. A carrot and a stick obviously, but an excuse so transparent, it seemed to me, that I thought Frank must have been losing his grip. What did a Queen's Bench judge and an accountant know about organic effluent? Come on, Frank!

What was the real reason? There was another reason, I knew. Perhaps he wanted to wrench me out of my comfortable niche in the east. He had authority to do that if he chose. Perhaps he wanted to separate me from Madam and Gerda, but no power on earth was going to do that! No, Frank. Not that.

I sat one evening at home, in my favourite chair, with Perry on my lap, and asked myself those questions - and answered them. "Don't you approve of my family, Frank?" Of course he didn't. And I knew, if nobody else did, that Frank Quarters was a wily old fox who was never transparent and never did anything without a substantial reason.

"All right, I'll go with you," I said aloud - loud enough to disturb Perry.

"He has a reason, Perry," I said, and stroked the old fellow's fur by way of apology. "We may never know what that reason is," I said, "but he has one."

At that I moved the cat to the table and set out to rummage among my belongings for the things I would need up Hudson Bay.

Jon would be making his first trip into the north; I, my eighth. Eight summers in the Arctic. I could do without it. But I would miss it, too, if I didn't go. I sat on the edge of my bed with a pair of insulated socks in my hands and conjured up trumpeter swans and polar bears. A white sea. Ice blue ice. The odd translucence of the sky. Old acquaintances. And the fear that I felt in my stomach every moment I was there. I had grown up in Manitoba. I didn't need the Arctic, but I was drawn to it.

Jack Davidson joined us in Winnipeg. I didn't know he was coming till he hailed us in the airport there, looking like a tourist who had just spent his life's savings on things to hang from his belt and stuff in his pockets. He had a US Marine's backpack that would have held all my worldly goods. He had gear to cover his head, his face, his ears; to apply to his hands, his nose, his lips; to rub on, to swallow, to spray. And because he had come from the States on a commercial flight into Canada, against his shoulder he cradled a hunting rifle he had rented in Winnipeg, and on his hip an empty holster - they wouldn't let him cross the border with a handgun. He said that empty holster felt like an empty bed flapping against his leg. What did a man do without a sidearm in this Godforsaken country?

Jon laughed. He travelled, like myself, without weapons. And Frank, when he joined us, only patted the left breast of his bush jacket and grinned.

As Frank turned away, Jack scowled at me. "What's he packing in that pocket?" he muttered. "I like the fellow, but ah cain't understand him, not a-tall."

I raised an eyebrow.

"Okay," he said, and grinned. "I'll cut out the sagebrush

if you'll tell me what Frank meant by that pat on his jacket."

"His only defense against the north," I said. "The only one he needs."

I wasn't telling and Jon didn't know, but the mystery was not long with us. We, all three Canadians, reached into our pockets as the plane came in to land at Churchill.

"Fer Gawd's sake!" Jack snorted. "What's this?"

"Where's yours?" I replied.

"Mine?"

"Your bug dope."

"Insect repellant?"

"Insect repellant. Where is it?"

"In my pack. Didn't expect to need it right off the runway."

I laughed and passed him my favourite concoction. "Use it," I said. "They'll be here to meet us."

"Yeah? This is *cold* country... Isn't it?"

"Not cold enough."

"Mosquitoes?"

"Or blackflies."

"Them *little* buggers?"

"Them. And no-see-ums. Which breed will come out to meet us depends on how far the season has advanced."

If I didn't know better, I'd swear those bugs come up to meet in-coming flights like squadrons of escort fighters. Their appetite for blood makes them capable of any malevolence. It festers in their genes all winter while they wait as eggs at the bottom of frozen streams. That thirst for blood - especially mine - is all that keeps them going in the dark. Just their thirst for my blood, to survive another year, to continue their lousy species. The first one got me behind the right ear before we had loped across the tarmac and entered the terminal building. I didn't notice the bite as it happened, but something in me registered the wound; I put up my hand and it came away bloody. I had already begun my contribution to the survival of the north as I knew it.

After only a few hours in Churchill - time to look at the oil leak! - we flew on to Chesterfield Inlet. Somebody Frank had to meet there. Fine with me; I liked the Inlet. The judge and the general, of course, had no preferences; every place was new to them.

Frank's contact had come across from Igaluit. "Southern vacation," he said, and laughed; Igaluit is hardly farther north than Chesterfield, but being on Baffin Island, it seems more remote and romantic.

This northener's name was Andy - Andy Starkovitch - and he was already there to meet us, low keyed and good humoured. He came to our guest house every morning from the home of friends where he was staying, and Frank and he spent hours ensconced in armchairs with their feet on an empty Franklin-style stove, talking in low, solemn voices. I went out looking for trumpeters and ducks. The others hired a helicopter and flew all over the place. Getting a sense of the land, they said. I insisted they were only escaping the flies, and they didn't deny it. They came back in the evening - though "evening" is only a courtesy word at that latitude, nothing to do with the sun but everything to do with the habitual need for food at regular intervals.

We arrived on a Friday. For the most part the weather was fine and clear with just a little mist at night. Only the Wednesday came in cloudy, and by midday a fine drizzle, cold and soaking, kept me indoors catching up on sleep and keeping an eye on Frank and Andy while pretending to read a National Geographic article about Ellesmere. Ellesmere. It made me shudder. The high Arctic fascinates me and repels me at the same time. I had all I'll ever want of that country every winter at home, standing on my mother's back porch, smelling the north on the wind, feeling its pinch in my nose, its push against my chest.

While I read a little and dozed a lot, Frank and Andy continued their slow, low-voiced talk by the stove.

Andy was a squat, tough, sallow half-caste with a smile that said "Brother" and an eye that said "Bad joke, this universe."

Frank swore their meeting was wholly friendship for old-times sake, but I didn't believe it. No more for old times than my presence there - whatever that was for - or the night we all five sat in a cafe in the town eating fish fresh out of the Inlet and McCain's frozen French fries out of the fields of New Brunswick... There's a lot we'll never fathom.

Frank was introspective that evening, his eyes far off, the eagle profile prominent over a black turtle-necked pullover. He ate, but he said little.

His silence didn't worry me, but it was awkward for the others till the diplomat in Jon took over. Without seeming to probe, he questioned Andy about Nunavut till the place began to take shape before us and we could almost see the far reaches, where most of us had never been - God willing, would never be. Andy spoke softly, as men of distant and primal spaces do, as if unwilling to stir the spirit of some quiescent power. I was enthralled in spite of my aversion. Jack Davidson sat with his mouth open, literally.

Andy spoke as I suppose the meek of the earth speak, with acceptance but not with false humility. He was attached to the Nunavut Development Agency, his opinion worth as much as the opinions of any of his counterparts in Ottawa, London, Washington, resting, as it did, on logic, experience, and truth - truth as, and in so far as, any of us understood it. He spoke slowly. He considered what he said. He made no wild claims or demands. He spoke well.

"Where the hell is this Nun's Foot?" Jack hissed in my ear when Jon gave him a chance - or perhaps lost him - by gently digging into Andy's store of knowledge about winds, ice conditions, and currents in the Davis Strait.

"Never heard of the place," Jack muttered. "What is it, Nun's Foot? What kind of a name is that?"

"NOO-nuh-voot," Frank whispered, as if he had heard - probably he had. "Noo - nuh - voot."

"Another name for his tongue to caress," I thought.

"The Arctic," he murmured. "Air the deaf can hear, whether it roars for the kill or croons like a nursing mother. Nunavut. Diamond on the finger of a pregnant bride when spring comes, and the birth of countless offspring in the night sky. Infinite meeting place of men and spirits. Wind shaking a hundred fists at the stars. Permafrost and ice, groaning. Bare crags, like whales breaching from a smoking sea. And a carpet of flowers when the sun returns."

As he spoke the room fell silent. Andy's eyes looked into a different space - perhaps a different time - and took on the fanatical light in Frank's, that light I had learned to recognize as love. Jack's held tentative understanding. Jon, I think, was hearing the poetry. I was sad to the roots of my soul.

When the world came back into the room, Andy shook his head. "The ice is melting back," he said. "More every year. The balance has been upset. We don't know what to expect. They say in a few years ships will come through the Passage on regular schedules every summer. Tankers first. Then cruise ships. I don't know... Maybe you and I won't live to see it, but our grandchildren will. In Nunavut we have to be ready."

The waitress came to clear our table.

"Where *is* this place?" Jack whispered to me under cover of the clatter of dishes as she took away the fish-and-chips plates and brought us strawberry ice cream in styrofoam bowls.

"It's a new, autonomous district of what used to be known generally as this country's Northwest Territories," I said. "Protected status. No full participation in Ottawa - regardless of what anybody tells you."

"Why?"

"Why not full equal status?"

"Yeah."

"It has always been supposed that the people would not be ready for full participation in Parliament."

"Aren't they?"

"Of course they are. You've heard Andy. But you know how it is."

"Yeah," Jack muttered. "If you prick me, do I not bleed?"

"Exactly."

He shook his head.

"But *little* brother," I said. "Needs his hand held. Doesn't know the language well yet. Might cross the road and be run down."

"Yeah. Would he not bleed! But it sounds to me like these guys have got it made if they can hold on a few years. Better climate by then. More in touch with the rest of the world. Untold mineral resources in newly exposed rock."

"Yeah!" It was my turn.

"Okay," he argued. "Good-bye poetry, if that's what you want. Good-bye good old days. Is that it? What's good about them? How big is this Nunavoot?"

"Your jets could criss-cross it in a day," I said, "but you

would know you'd seen it. We crossed into Nunavut about half way between Churchill and here."

"You mean I've been in it all the time!" he exclaimed.

"Yes," I said. "It begins at Manitoba's northern boundary and goes on to the North Pole - covers thirty degrees of latitude. And east to west it's about equal in distance at the broadest point."

"I see. Texas," he murmured.

"Not unlike," I said, "but almost three times as big. It's about one fifth of the land mass of Canada, which is..."

"Yeah, I know that! About the same as the continental States."

"Right."

"Cities?"

"The town - capital - is Igaluit."

"Town."

I grinned. "Not city," I agreed.

"Like Chesterfield Inlet?"

"Sort of, I suppose. A little bigger. I've never seen it... Population, about twenty-seven or eight thousand."

"The town."

"The whole territory. Think about it."

"My God!" he whispered after a moment or two. "Think about it. Texas three times as big. Cold and dark instead of hot and dry. And only twenty seven thousand people."

He was quiet after that. Didn't say a word till we were leaving. Then he stood for a few minutes outside the restaurant. He was the last to say good-bye to Andy, who was going home after a few hours sleep.

Jon and I had already moved away, and Frank was speaking in some archaic tongue that Andy seemed to understand, when Jack strode up to them. He stood like a Texan in a western film, feet apart, hands loose at the gun belt, eyes narrowed. You could all but see the Stetson and the star-shaped badge on the shoulder. He towered over Andy as Texas towers over the other united states, but Andy's black eyes met the gray of Texas levelly. The two looked straight into each other.

Jack recovered first. He grasped Andy's hand in a tight grip. "Friend," he said, "Ah've been hearing about this Noo-nah-voot of yours from Dick, there, and it's breakin' my heart.

Ah'm from Texas."

Andy grinned. Crinkles fanned out from his eyes and his mouth, growing deeper and deeper as they met and spread across his face.

"Thank-you, General," he drawled. "I grew up on western movies. But I never in my life dreamt of hearing a real live lawman, standing before me looking me straight in the eye, and saying to my face, 'Ah'm from Texas.' You've made my day!"

"Ah'm afraid, Andy," Jack said, "that you-all have made more than my day. Ah think you've probably made the rest of my life. And it ain't pretty. You and Ah, Andy, have come to say good-bye."

Andy nodded and squeezed Jack's hand. "Texas of the north," he said. "I'll try to pass on your wisdom to my kids and grandchildren. We can hope they'll learn."

We walked away. Andy watched us go, not moving, nor showing any sign of meeting the next moment before it came, watching without judgment in his face or his stance as we became smaller in his eyes and he in ours. We waved before we crossed the street to our hostel. Andy was still standing there.

Jack looked hardest and longest. Then he waved once and followed the rest of us.

"There's just too goddamn many people in this world," he said. "They'll swallow Andy's village whole. And there's not a damned thing anybody can do about it."

"Maybe," I said.

"Not maybe," Frank muttered. "Not maybe."

I stopped in my tracks. I had heard pain like his in a human voice only once before, on the day that Grandpa MacKenzie died. I had heard anguish like that in the voice of a child. My child. I was glad we had only a few more days to stay. I needed to be with my family.

Chapter Sixteen:

That day in June, driving home from the beach, the children sat in the back and chattered. Madam smiled and withdrew into her thoughts. I felt sun-warmed, air-dried, healthy. I was happy.

I let my mind wander among the sensations of the day. I lived again the first shock of cold bay water. I tried to explore that insight I'd had into possible beginnings in the flat expanses beyond the Himalayas. I thought of comets, icebergs, the weight of the sea... But I found my focus narrowing. Enchanted days end, and the coach reverts to the pumpkin. Among the "strawberry" trees of the morning I began to discern effects of acid fog. A shredded tire, shed along the highway, brought recollection of an insulated glove I had glimpsed in dry bubbleweed under the stairs to the canteen. Beyond a doubt it had come on the tides from the south. Gloves like that would be common on the project that was running traffic under downtown Boston.

Most of the trash on our beaches, most of the acids in our air, most of the summer haze over our hills - most of the colour in the sunsets I watched from my windows - came from down that way: Boston, New York, Washington. I was well aware; none better. How long? How long could we sustain this..? The magic of the day ended in mental wrangling, the interminable wrangling I endured in Colorado, London, Ottawa... How long? Oh, Lord, how long!

It was almost time for me to go north again. My mind moved into the future, to the receding ice, the rising water, the delicate eco-systems under stress... And this year, to whatever it was Frank felt he had to move.

"Where does Risa live, Gerda?" Madam asked as we recrossed the Harbour Bridge. Her voice was rich and soft, and quieted my mind.

"Oh, just on King Street East," Risa replied for herself. "I can walk from Gerda's house. I know the way."

I wouldn't let her run off like that now. Now I would drive the maze of one-way streets uptown and wait to see Risa's mother come to the door before I would let the child out of my sight. Then... in that time before September, 2001 - there was such a time; I remember it - before the world changed forever... Nowadays I watch. I read the message in a mother's wave. I send the same message to her: err on the side of caution now, take no chances.

When we had reached the house where Gerda lived and had said good-bye to Risa, Madam spoke again. She spoke in that same quiet voice she had used before. "I'll go up with her," she said. "Come when you have parked the car."

I knew what she was thinking. Nor did that surprise me. I was growing used to Madam's - whatever it was... prescience? and taking it in stride. Even instances of wordless communication between us no longer astonished me. But I still needed confirmation. I was often slow to accept and to react. And that afternoon I had parked in my space in the lot and was setting empty baskets, sandy chairs, a slightly damp umbrella, Risa's soaked T-shirt - among other things - on the pavement, when an anguished cry and a loud squeal of brakes sent me breakneck to the street.

Gerda was running toward me blindly, calling my name, "Richard! Richard!"

She cast herself into my arms and held on tight.

I lifted her to my shoulder and stroked her hair. "What is it, sweetheart?" I murmured. "Tell me what's wrong."

I asked, but I knew. Grandpa MacKenzie was gone. There had been a bout with pneumonia and a heart incident after the blizzard. The doctors had been hopeful, but the old man was frail and lived only for Gerda. Now... I felt he must have known that Gerda had other, younger, more able guardians now; that he might rest.

My first coherent thought was gratitude that Madam had gone up with the child. My second, that I was not surprised that she had.

I carried my *little* love across the street. She was still, barely breathing. But she wriggled out of my arms in the vestibule, and walked up the stairs without hesitation, though holding tight to my hand.

We found Madam sitting in a straight-backed chair drawn up to the feet of the old man where he lay on the couch in the front room. His eyes were closed. He had died peacefully. There was no reason not to let Gerda see him.

For a moment, in the doorway of that room with the cabbage roses on the walls and the white lace curtains stirring at the windows in a breeze from the street, she drew back against my side. But only for a moment, as if to catch her breath. Then she walked up to the body in which that fine old man's spirit had made itself available to her for as long as she could remember, and looked at him where he slept. She patted his hand and kissed his cheek. And taking a crocheted afghan from the back of the couch, she spread it over his shoulders.

"Grandpa always said you should never go to sleep without something over you," she said.

I waited for what would come next. It was crucial to my future. And I was well pleased. Gerda looked at me with her aching heart in her eyes, but she turned to Madam, who held out one hand to her, one hand only, for her to take or not as she wished. Gerda hesitated; then she walked slowly toward Madam, paused another instant, and threw herself into Madam's arms, and wept.

It was well. I left them to mourn and called Al Reeger and the hospital to set in motion public recognition of an old man's passing.

* * *

I have said it before; I will say it again: I will never understand women. Is it conditioning - selection of the fittest through centuries of subservience? Is it a more basic mothering instinct? Is it simply survival?

When the paramedics came, Madam took Gerda into the child's own bedroom and helped her to pack a bag. When the body of the old man had been carried downstairs, they came out of the bedroom and followed, to stand on the sidewalk and watch till the ambulance was out of sight. After that, Gerda locked the door and they walked hand in hand across the street and across the parking lot, leaving Gerda's bag for me to carry - along with the picnic hamper, the sunshade, the wet clothes... Fortunately a small crowd had gathered, in solemn conclave as they say, which included Marvin and some of the boys from the rooming house. They helped me to move back in.

Everyone had a good word to say for Grandpa MacKenzie, and a sympathetic word for "the poor little tyke."

"She hadn't anybody else, you know." This from an ample lady who appeared to live in the flat downstairs. "She was his *great*-granddaughter, actually. Her mother's dead and her father's no place - took off for Alberta before the poor little tyke was born. Broke her mother's heart. No, the old man was all alone, except for the little one. Brought her up from an infant. Good as any woman..."

"And all the work he done for that church!" somebody else put in. "Rain or shine. Night nor day."

"Yas, there'll be a welcome for him up there!"

And as all eyes turned piously to the bright blue sky, "But what's to become of poor little Gerda?"

* * *

"We're just waiting for you, Richard," Madam said. "Gerda has had a nice warm bath to wash off the salt, and we've shampooed her hair, and now we'll have a quiet supper together."

Which we did - a nice, quiet meal - but after several cups of tea Madam placed her elbows on the table in that way of hers. Business.

"Richard," she said, "Gerda and I have been thinking - about the future."

"Do I have a vote?"

"Of course."

They said this together and smiled at each other, little fingers crooked.

"But I think," I said, "that we are already two against one, so it won't matter what *I* think. What is your plan?"

"It's very simple," Madam said. "Gerda would like to stay with us forever."

"Good," I said. "The vote is unanimous."

"Then I will have parents like all the other kids," Gerda explained, as if she thought she still had to justify her position. "Only you and Madam don't live in the same house. Well, sort of. It's the same *house* really, but *not* the same. Like me and Grandpa live in the same house with Mrs. Gershwin, but not really. It's hard to explain, but I think you have to. Don't you?"

"We were thinking of doing that in any case," I said.

Gerda looked at Madam with a worried wrinkle between her eyes. "Do you think you will, Madam?" she asked.

"Oh, I think we will," Madam said, and reached out for my hand. "I think we have just been waiting for you to make things right."

"Did you know I was coming?"

"I thought it likely," Madam replied. She spoke slowly. "One day," she said, "when Grandpa MacKenzie was in the hospital and you were staying with me, I visited him. And your grandpa asked me if I would look after you if anything happened to him. So I said, 'Mr. MacKenzie, I've been wanting to talk to you about that.' And so we held hands for a minute and nothing else was said...

"Then, when I saw how fond you and Richard were of each other, I spoke to Jenny. Jenny has been with me for many years, you know, and I wanted to know what she would think."

Madam paused and Gerda watched her with big, half-frightened eyes. She was hardly breathing. "What... What did Jenny think?" she whispered at last.

Jenny appeared. She was, I believe, not very far away.

"Jenny," Madam said, "we need to know what you would think of having Gerda come to live with us forever."

Jenny looked at Gerda for several seconds. Her expression was impossible to read. She studied Gerda, but then she turned pointedly to me before she spoke. She turned to me, but she did not speak to me either. "What part is Dr. Waterman to play in this piece, Madam?" she demanded.

I replied. "General dogsbody," I said. "Name your terms."

"You ought to get married," she said. "Then you ought to adopt this child legally and make a proper home for all of us, including Perry."

"Done," I said.

Gerda clapped her hands. "Does that mean forever?" she squealed.

"Absolutely. Forever."

"I'll want a wedding," Madam warned.

"Naturally," Jenny said. "The social event of the season. Dr. Waterman won't like it, but it's the only way."

"I may not like it, but I'll go along with it," I conceded.

"Can I be a bridesmaid?" Gerda whispered, her eyes shining.

"Of course," Madam assured her. "We'll go to Joni Plenghorn for our dresses. She'll think of something beautiful. And Jenny too - dress, hat, shoes, everything - no housekeeping that day, Jenny; we'll leave everything to the caterers."

"We'll see about that," Jenny hedged, backing toward the kitchen door. She looked, I thought, a little shocked, a little shy, but vastly pleased.

"Do I get a say in *any* of this?" I asked.

"Of course, darling," Madam soothed with a laugh and a pat on my hand. "Anything you like - within reason."

"Just one thing, then," I said. "I won't be there if Jenny isn't one of the wedding party. Take it or leave it."

Jenny tried - and failed - to suppress a smile as she disappeared into the kitchen - but not far into the kitchen.

"Then that's settled," I said, and leaned over and kissed Madam.

Gerda clapped her hands. "When?" she cried.

"It will have to be a fall wedding," Madam said. "It's customary, you see, when someone near to one has died, to put off things like weddings till everyone is over being sad."

"I forgot to be sad already," Gerda whispered.

At that she left the table and walked to the window, where she stood for a few minutes looking out at the house across the street where she had lived all her life.

"I'm sorry, Grandpa," she said at last. "I'll miss you. I'll miss you every day. Only you always said, 'Life must go on.' And that's what I think you mean."

Then she turned and walked slowly back to the table. "Do you think Grandpa minds," she asked, "that I forgot just for a minute?"

"Never," Madam declared. "Grandpa never wanted anything but for you to be happy. We won't see him any more, but we'll never forget him, and we'll often speak of him. He'll like that."

"Will he have a funeral?"

"A small funeral next week," I told her. "And when the church is repaired, a grand memorial service. And in the fall, a wedding. He'd like that too."

"Do we have to wait for the wedding?"

"It will take awhile to prepare," Madam said, "and we'll have to see a lawyer about formal adoption papers and everything. And for a decent interval... Yes, it will be fall."

"But where will I stay till..?"

"Oh, but right here with us," Madam declared. "Tomorrow we'll bring all your things over and set you up in your own room."

Gerda gave her a big hug and a kiss. Then she did the same for me.

"It's been quite a day, Richard," she said, as she cuddled in my arm. "Quite a day. I'll always remember it. But now I need to go to sleep. Do you really want to marry Madam and have me for your little girl?"

"I do, Gerda," I told her.

"I love you too," she said.

Out of the corner of my eye I watched Jenny in the kitchen door watch Madam and Gerda walk hand in hand toward the guest room. "Poor little darlin'," she muttered. "But she'll be the makin' of this house."

* * *

That was the scene that ran through my mind as I watched Andy Starkovitch recede into the half light of that northern evening. It was time. I must go home.

But I still had not visited the place of my dream, that dream of being on the shore of Hudson Bay with Frank that came to me on a night of great joy and peace with Madam. I knew the place; it was near. I wanted to see it. And so on our last full day I approached it over a slight risc in the generally flat terrain, and paused at the top to study the slope of stone slabs that ran down to the sea.

Here and there a cupful of fresh water reflected the sky, or a clump of low plants sheltered behind a ledge out of the wind. Beyond, the bay lay bright under a clear sky. And dotted over the landscape between the water and me, the inukshuks. I thrilled to them.

Every time I visit inukshuks I feel the same thrill. We were here, they say; our past and our future came together on the shore of this unknown sea. We stand here through the years. We marvel. When the sun warms our faces, we wake; through the long nights, we dream in starlight. We are here.

The inukshuks, on that day, spoke to me almost audibly. I could almost hear them whisper, "Add Dick's name to ours. He is here. He understands." But Dick did not understand. Not yet. Dick shuddered, filled his lungs with Arctic air and started down the slope.

As I moved, one of my boots dislodged a small slab of stone, and as the sound disturbed the solitude, I thought I caught a glimpse of movement behind an inukshuk, as if...

A man rose from sitting position and showed himself, hands out at his sides in sign of peace. Frank.

"I knew you were coming," he said when I reached him. "I've been waiting for you."

"We could have walked out together," I said.

"I wanted time alone."

I sat down on the ground to rest, and reached into my pack for a canteen of water. "Drink?"

"Thanks," he said, and took a long pull at the bottle.

He squatted down beside me, and we sat for several minutes in silence, long enough for me to notice the bleached bones of a small bird nearby, and to begin to notice the insects that crawled or flew or burrowed around us.

Frank sat with his back against the inukshuk and closed his eyes. "Inscrutable" was the word that came to mind when I glanced at his face. Yet I understood the man a little; I sensed his heart; I had guessed at the strength of the emotions he carried.

He wanted time alone. So be it. But when I began to feel the hardness of the seat I had chosen and moved to try to find comfort in another position, he opened his eyes and studied me, long and hard.

After several minutes, he spoke. "This inukshuk is too close to the water," he said. "I need you to help me move it to higher ground."

I asked no questions, and I think I concealed my surprise. I merely examined the pieces of stone that would have to be carried up the slope, trying to judge their weight. Interesting that this was the inukshuk that had always bothered me when I thought of that dream. I recognized it now, and I solved the mystery. This was a new one; the others had been on this shore a long time, a very long time - long enough for lichen to colonize their surfaces. This was a new one.

"All right," I said at last. "Let's get to work."

It did occur to me that it would be a lot easier to move ourselves up the slope and make another inukshuk from pieces we would find there. But Frank would have thought of that. He knew what he was doing. There was meaning to this work that I didn't know.

Frank stood up first, and moved the head of his inukshuk from its place. It was heavy. We emptied out my backpack and used it as a sling between us.

That day we moved five large pieces of rock about five hundred meters up a slope that rose maybe six meters in that space. We carried them to the highest point of land for many miles around - five large pieces and I think about eight smaller ones. We carried the large ones in the sling between us; each of us singly could carry the smaller ones, but only one at a time. More than once during that day I complained to myself that Frank might have used fewer rocks to construct his damned inukshuk. I figured I could have made a passable attempt out of four or five. But what did I know?! He had his reasons.

We didn't talk. Grunted a lot, but didn't talk and didn't stop to rest or eat - even to drink from my water bottle - till the inukshuk stood safe and solid in its new place. Didn't even notice that the weather had begun to close in and that a few drops of cold rain were darkening the colours of the stones.

When the head piece was back in place, facing the bay and the flat horizon beyond the water, Frank stood for a moment looking around. His shoulders slumped. His eyes seemed weary and old. Then he laid a hand on my shoulder by way of thanks and trudged away.

I retrieved my belongings into my ruined backpack and followed, none the wiser. A couple of caribou - mother and calf by the look of them - stood out against the sky a mile or so away and watched us go. I thought of making a little inukshuk to myself and them, but I had done enough.

Chapter Seventeen:

I felt that I had done enough for all summer and deserved a real vacation, but work piled up and kept my nose to the grindstone. Much of the time I was away from home, inspecting outports I could expect to visit only in - I was going to say only in warm weather, but what I mean is only in non-winter. Either that or reporting my findings in Ottawa.

I was home in time for the Labour Day week-end, however, which, of course, was important, as school was about to begin again. Eight months since I had arrived in La Tour. Eight months and one day since I would have been too busy to shop for notebooks and pencils, too important to be needed home for such an occasion. I would have justified my absence by citing my level in the chain of command, my income tax return. I laughed at myself. The change in my life was going deep in me. A little girl, nine years old, needed me to help her shop for school supplies; I must therefore be home to help her shop.

In Ottawa I explained that I couldn't stay longer. I pleaded prior commitments, pressure of work, certain projects that were coming to a head, as, indeed, they were.

Frank saw through me, of course. "Madam having a dinner party?" he enquired.

"No," I replied, "Gerda is going back to school next week. Grade Four. Very important."

I expected snorts of disgust, but he surprised me. "Then make sure you're there," he growled, and walked away. "You don't know how lucky you are."

"I'll tell her you said hello," I called after him. "She thinks you're something special. Wow! Eagles. Ice bergs. Curses on your gun."

At that he turned back toward me, looking pleased. "I'll be down soon," he said. "Probably early October. Tell Madam to kill the fatted salmon - and get her to ask Maggie Murchison, if she's in town."

"Agreed," I said, and left to catch the last flight home.

* * *

Home. Home for Labour Day, the Labour Day of the year two thousand and one, which, that year I believe, fell on the first of the month. Of the month of September.

We were already past mid-morning in our time zone when I heard. Mid-morning on the eleventh. I went out into the park to absorb the news and to watch for Gerda coming home to lunch. Madam was nowhere to be found, and I didn't want Gerda to be left without at least one of us.

I sat in the sun on a park bench, looking down King Street hill toward the water. The morning was bright. The September sun gilded the red brick - some of it old brick and mellow - and the more recent concrete and marble around the square. The sky was intensely blue and cloudless. The harbour sparkled. Most of the trees were still green, and the grass was the grass of summer.

A street person sat down beside me for a moment. He needed a shave and a bath, but his good humour was unimpaired. "Trees don't seem to be turnin' as fast as they used ta," he observed. "Climate's changin'. No doubt about it... Couldn't spare a looney fer a cuppa coffee, could ya?"

I gave him five dollars. It seemed to be the day for it.

As I watched the old fellow... Probably he wasn't much older than I except in sad experience... As I watched him shuffle toward the nearest drink, a few yellow elm leaves floated around him. He looked as if he were kicking up gold coins as he went. Strange. I took off my glasses and inspected them for smudges, of which there were none. But when I looked again, the strangeness was still present and seemed to be a confusion of time as well as of space and colour.

I saw the trees, that in that place, at that moment, when my watch said eleven-thirty in the morning... I looked at my watch. Carefully I read the hour, the minute, the day, and the year. I even checked that the second hand was sweeping its perpetual treadmill path around the dial. But I heard - I would have sworn... I heard the clock in the Trinity Church tower strike the half hour, that clock that had been silent since the afternoon of Easter Sunday. I heard it loud and clear. I even smiled because I enjoyed the sound, though I knew I was hallucinating - in morning sunshine; in fresh, clean air; my body well rested, well exercised, well fed... I heard the clock.

Under the sound of the clock I heard the flight of many pigeons, and when I looked for the source of that sound they were passing over me, wave after wave of bright blue triangles of wings that, passing, left behind gold triangles of sunlight on green leaves.

I shook my head. I was a little frightened by what I was seeing - at least, frightened by my ability to see it. I would have preferred not to see it. I didn't know what it meant.

My eyes followed the trunk of an elm into its branches, where the first signs of colour change were appearing among the leaves. But I studied, instead, the wings of the Angel of Victory who stands high on the war memorial. She commands a view north and south along the streets and alleys at the top of the hill, and of the sharp incline west, down to the harbour and across to the hills beyond; her raised wings preclude her ever seeing east to the rising of the sun. I looked where she commanded. I saw the funeral pyres of another year igniting. We would, I supposed, eventually wonder at the glory as we did each autumn. Perhaps, though, we would not see the glory this year.

My mind cleared for a moment and I returned to the morning of September 11, 2001. This terrible act that had been done... It had brought our species to some threshold we had not foreseen, were not prepared for. In time we might be able to assess the totality of the event, but for now... now we were living in a moment of choice for the race, and I was chilled. I knew a little how we react to threat: how ready we are to deny, to blame, to strike out; how destructive we can be; how ready with our fists and unready to face facts. I had come away from representing NEPP at international meetings having heard little more than recriminations, denials of reasoned opinion, projections of blame; very little of constructive planning, though planning was our *raison d'etre*.

The angel gleamed in copper weathered to the green of the leaves around her. In her right hand she raised a cross high above her head. I shuddered and moved to another bench nearer the centre of the park, where the sun shone brighter, it seemed.

I sat facing a bed of marigolds and begonias. The colours leapt and flowed in the sunlight, and I was, at one and the same time, in the park looking at the carpet of flowers and in my flat watching Rob's Persian rug glow in ruby reds and pinks, yellows and blues, a deep purple, and a vibrant green. As well, at that same moment I was a small boy under Tom Verachuk's table, scraping away prairie dust from his carpet, astounded as the colours appeared and the dust rose into my nostrils - clean dust, healthful dust, the smell of home and childhood.

I rose from my park bench and walked toward the carpet of flowers in its bed. Beyond was another. And beyond that, more; more carpets of living colour, more beds of petunias, begonias, marigolds... As I walked, the sun rolled them out before my feet as if at that moment I had been a royal prince.

And then the children were coming. Their voices cut through the lunchtime sounds of the city like the piping of small birds. I had a fleeting vision of a flock of snow buntings I watched one bitter winter afternoon when I was home from school with chicken pox and stood disconsolate in my bedroom watching the birds and fogging the window with my breath, that instantly froze into snowflake patterns on the glass.

"Richard," I heard. "Richard!"

The snow buntings disappeared, but when Gerda rushed into my arms and clung to me, for a moment I couldn't understand why I was so much taller than she.

"Will they come here, Richard?" she gasped.

This little girl - my little girl... No little girl should be subjected to terror. I would see that this one was not terrorized, if it was the last thing I ever did.

"No, darling," I said. "They would have no reason to come here. We haven't anything big enough or important enough to make us worth their while. They want to make a *big* splash."

She looked relieved but still not quite convinced. "The telephone company has a big building," she said.

"But the buildings the terrorists attacked had over a hundred floors. How many has the telephone building?"

"I don't know," she said. "Maybe almost a hundred."

"Let's see if we can count them," I suggested.

We walked hand in hand to the edge of the park and sat on the same bench I had occupied earlier, but this time I didn't notice Victory on her plinth, having more immediate problems to solve.

Gerda began to count. One, two, three... five... ten...

We couldn't see the lower floors of the building because of the contour of the ground and because of the lesser buildings around it that obscured its lower portions from our view. But Gerda reached ten. Ten floors. Then she lost her place and had to begin again. One, two, three... five... seven...

"Oh, Richard!" she cried. "It's hard. It makes me dizzy and my neck hurts from bending backwards."

"Lean against my shoulder," I suggested. "Maybe that will help."

She cuddled against me and began the third time.

Eventually we compromised on an estimate. Allowing for hidden lower floors, for cricks in the neck, and for the really difficult task of counting rows of windows that are all exactly alike, we agreed on between fifteen and twenty.

"Good," Gerda said. "Cause I think I might fall flat on the sidewalk if I tried again. It makes my head spin."

"Well, then, rest a minute," I said, "and try to imagine five times as many of those windows, one on top of the other."

"Oh, I can't!" she protested. But it wasn't long till she was back at the puzzle. One, two, three...

Madam found us there. "What are you two doing?" she said, as she sat down beside us.

"Oh, Madam," Gerda cried, "we're seeing if we can imagine the telephone building five times higher in the sky. I have to put my head back as far as it will go and I come over all dizzy. Richard says the terrorists won't come here. Do you think they will?"

"No," Madam said. "I think there are many other places they would rather choose first... Have you had lunch yet?"

"No, we've been busy with important matters," I said. "Have you?"

She shook her head. "I thought we might drive to Gagetown for lunch and buy some apples," she said. "Jenny wants to make a supply of apple sauce and pies for the winter."

"That's a great idea," I agreed, and I thought Madam looked relieved. I took her hand and she gave me a grateful smile.

"Don't I have to go back to school?" Gerda asked.

We both looked at her, surprised. We had forgotten that school was in session.

"We're not very good parents, are we," Madam said. "You've hardly been in school a week and here we are forgetting. What would *you* like to do?"

Gerda thought a moment. Then she looked at each of us in turn and said, slowly, choosing her words carefully, "Mr. Murphy - that's our principal, you know - he said this was a black day for the world and things would never be the same again. He didn't know I was there. He was in the hall talking to Mrs. Colpitts - she's the Grade Three teacher in the room next door to ours - and I was coming back from the bathroom. Do you think he was right?"

"I'm afraid he may have been," I said.

"Do *you* think so too, Madam?" Gerda asked.

"It was a terrible thing to do," Madam said, "and I think it will never be forgotten, so in that way, yes, I think Mr. Murphy was right."

"Yes, but it isn't a *black* day," Gerda said, and opened her eyes wide. "Cause look at the sunshine. And everything is pretty. Is it black other places?"

"It is black in Lower Manhattan," I said. "Black with smoke and dust. And some of it will be here by suppertime."

"Really?"

"Yes. The wind is in the south today, and on days when the wind is in the south, morning pollution from New York comes in our direction and reaches us by the middle of the afternoon."

"It does!? I didn't know that!"

"No, well, we can't see it so we forget it's there," I explained. "But it's real enough. And today I think we'll see it because of all the smoke and dust it will contain."

Gerda thought another moment. "Then if it's all right with you," she said finally, "I think I'll skip school this afternoon. Can Risa come?"

* * *

Throughout the afternoon we managed to forget the troubles of the world for a few moments now and then. Fortified by a sandwich and a glass of milk each, Gerda and Risa enjoyed the drive that took us to an excellent cafe, where we all put away a delicious lunch of curried chicken sandwiches and blueberry pie - delicious, and copious enough for two small girls to declare themselves stuffed to the ears, after which they chased each other around Madam's favourite orchard and munched windfalls to keep topped up for the drive home.

Madam and I walked among the trees, sat on an old snake-rail fence in the sun, and gave ourselves up to the peace and beauty of the place. The corner we chose was quiet - till one had settled for a moment; then the sounds of insects grew in intensity till they were almost deafening.

"I love this time of year," Madam said. "My mother used to tell me the cicadas were practising summer songs so they wouldn't forget them while they slept in cosy nooks and crannies all through the winter. I think it was the cicadas that taught me to become a singer.

"Is that what we've been doing, Richard? Singing summer songs against the winter that was coming?"

I didn't know how to answer her. I think I stammered something about fables, and grasshoppers and crickets - and things.

She took my hand and held it.

"I know *you* haven't been singing summer songs, Richard," she said. "*You* have seen the winter coming."

"But not *this* winter, mignonne," I said. "Not this one. The winter I have been expecting has been eclipsed. Spectacularly. It will still come... But..."

"Funding will be cut," she said.

"Very likely."

"That will be bad?"

"Yes, but not as bad as the isolation. I mean the mental isolation. Our work will be sidelined. I will have to watch..."

She didn't ask me to continue, but she didn't move; she sat holding my hand and watching the expressions I knew were following each other across my face.

"Last night when you were at the church," she said at last, "through the evening - I was alone after Gerda went to bed - I experienced a very strange... feeling, I suppose.

"I know I'm inclined to be psychic, Richard. But this was different. Something new to me. Very intense. A difference in scale, I think.

"I sensed a terrible evil in the world, a depth of hatred enveloping the planet that I had never felt before. A general hatred. Not Arab for Jew or Jew for Nazi. Not Protestant for Catholic or Christian for Muslim. Not black for white or white for brown. A general hatred, a blanket of hate that almost suffocated me.

"Do you think it's possible, Richard, that I felt *this* evil as it drew near? You're not a fanciful person - not very! Do you think it's possible that I felt... *this*?"

I took a moment to answer her while she waited, still without moving, watching me. Consciously I was trying to find words to touch her heart and mind that would not altogether betray Frank's trust in me. I never found them.

"Mignonne," I heard myself say, "often, in meetings, when the delegates are at each other's throats, each trying to save the world on another's back, I sense something of this."

And I told her Jack Davidson's words to Andy Starkovitch: "You and Ah, Andy, have come to say good-bye."

"I think so too," she said... "Will NEPP continue?"

"Women!" I exploded. "I will *never* understand you."

Madam laughed. "Of course not, darling," she said. "We have two functioning halves to our brains. You men have only one."

"Maybe that's why the world is in such a mess," I said. "For too long we one-sided men had everything our own way. Think you girls can set things right?"

She answered seriously. “I don’t know,” she said. “We may have let things go too far this time.”

* * *

Back home with a bushel of old-fashioned Wolf Rivers that are, so I’m told, “great cookers,” the weight of the morning’s shock seemed to be lifting a little.

I had carried up the basket and deposited it in the kitchen; Madam and Jenny were examining the fruit and pronouncing 2001 a very good year... But then we heard, “Richard! Richard, come quick. Madam. Jenny. Quickly.”

Gerda was in the living room in front of the window that looked out over the bay. “Look!” she shouted, when we appeared. “Come look! It’s all funny!”

Even the light inside the room was strange.

The sun was going down, its rays shining obliquely across the town - a golden time of day as a rule, that I never tired of watching. But the gold of that day had reddened, as if by fire. The sky was the pink of brick dust. And across it, spreading from the south, dark streaks smudged the pink. Under that sky the harbour lay a red pool, dark as wine - the red of spilled blood.

None of us spoke. None of us had words for what we were experiencing. We stood in silence, close together, as the fire and the blood-red water worked into memory.

We stayed at the window till the sun had disappeared behind the hills and the pink had faded to gray. Then Jennie closed the drapes.

Later we listened to excerpts from President Bush’s words offered during the day. But for a few minutes only.

When I turned off the TV, Gerda sighed. Obviously she was thinking things over. I felt that she was not afraid, just looking ahead. After a minute she spoke.

“Do you think the president is right?” she asked.

“Right? In what way?”

“In the way that people should not let the terrorists win by being afraid of them?”

“Oh, yes indeed,” I said. “You can’t allow bullies to win.”

“That’s what I think too,” she said. “Last winter Zackie

Barrowmore used to throw snowballs at me. They hurt and made me cry, and I told Grandpa."

She remained quiet for a moment, seemingly remembering Grandpa and that life with him that must have been like something out of a story to her already. After awhile she smiled.

"Grandpa said that was because Zackie liked me and wanted me to notice him," she said. "But I didn't like Zackie and I didn't want to notice him.

"One day he chased me home and hit me all over with snowballs, and I cried, and he broke Mrs. Gershwin's window - downstairs, you know.

"And then Mrs. Gershwin came up to our house. And when she saw I was crying and all covered with snow from the snowballs in my hair and down my boots and everything, she went downstairs and brought up a great big chocolate cake she just made. And Grandpa made tea, and me and Grandpa and Mrs. Gershwin had a party and talked things over. And Grandpa said it was only cause Zackie liked me. But Mrs. Gershwin said love pats could be pretty hard sometimes and there was no excuse for bullying and maybe we should call the police. But Grandpa said no, not yet anyway, we'd try to take care of it ourselves first. And then he said you had to stand up to bullies. And I said, 'You mean I should snowball him back?' But he said no, cause that would be coming down to his level and we could do better than that. And Mrs. Gershwin said I should just put my nose in the air and walk right home, like Zackie and the snowballs didn't exist, and could I do that?"

There was another long break in the story. "And could you?" Madam asked, when the silence was stretched pretty thin.

Gerda looked at her.

"Could you walk right on by with your nose in the air?"

"At first I couldn't," Gerda said, "and I ran as fast as I could, but still sometimes a snowball hit me and hurt and I cried. And one day Mrs. Gershwin was waiting and she came out and yelled at Zackie, and he ran away to the corner and then he yelled back."

She took another deep breath. "So one night when I was saying my prayers," she said, "I asked God if He thought it would be a good idea if I walked right past Zackie with my nose in the air, and He didn't say no, so I did."

Madam and I waited. Were we not to hear the outcome of this story? But in a moment Gerda looked around with a bright smile that lit up her eyes. "And it worked!" she cried.

"But..." I started.

"But what happened?" Madam howled. "We must hear all about it."

"Oh, I just put on my coat after school and got all ready," Gerda said. "I pulled my hat down hard over my ears and put my hood up. And I zipped up to my neck. And I put my back-pack on by both straps. And I put on my mittens. And I tucked my pants in my boots and made my boots tight. And went home!"

"And Zackie didn't throw snowballs at you?"

"Oh, yes! He did! Only I was ready and they didn't hurt - not so much. And I pretended I didn't notice. And he only did that once."

"And that was the end of it."

"Well, almost. Cause one day Zackie passed me a note in school. It said, 'Did you tell Mrs. Gershwin I broke her win-dow?' Only Mrs. Colpitts - she was our teacher then - she saw the note, and Zackie had to go to the principal and then he had to pay Mrs. Gershwin for the window."

"But he didn't blame that on you!?"

"Of course not. It wasn't my fault!" she exclaimed. "And on Valentine's Day, at recess, Zackie said, 'Hey, Gerda, do you want one of my cookies? My mom made them."

"And you replied?"

"I said, 'Okay, and then you can have one of mine. I made mine myself!"

I exploded with laughter. Madam tried hard not to laugh but didn't succeed. "Poor Zackie," she gurgled.

"Oh, Zackie's all right," Gerda said. "He's going to grow up and be a bus driver. So as we were saying... Are we still going to get married?"

Madam looked at me, her eyes dancing. "Oh, yes," she said. "That is, if Richard thinks he can face the strain of living in a house with three female brains."

"Can you, Richard?"

* * *

We had quite an hilarious evening after that. But in the night - my bedside clock said a little past two in the morning - I woke and sat up in bed. Madam was standing beside me, in a pale gown that shimmered in the light of the city that was the only illumination.

"I'm lonely, Richard," she said. "Can you smell the stench? My room is full of it."

My room, too, reeked of wet ash, of active volcano. Rock, burning. The guts of the world metamorphosing by fire. The smell of a stricken city, a burnt out hut, a dead campfire. The work of men's hands, rubble.

"Thank God for you, Richard," Madam whispered with her head on my pillow.

Chapter Eighteen:

Madam and I married early in November, in the church across the road, on a clear day with no wind and not a cloud in the sky. When we walked across, the sun shone and hardly a breath of air stirred, as though Nature were trying to apologize for her tantrum at Easter. The day was the kind of wedding day we had hoped for.

But throngs lined the way, waving and smiling. As the wedding party stood for a moment under the portico over the side door, I felt almost that I should be wearing gold lace and carrying a dress sword. My mouth dried without warning, and my eyes blurred. Stage fright! I had not prepared myself for this! For an instant I forgot what I was doing there, till Gerda's hand slipped into mine and I glanced down and saw her eyes, blurred too with tears of unexpected fright. I squeezed her hand and winked. We were fine after that.

Madam, of course, rose to the occasion like Venus from the waters. A gasp broke from the crowd when they saw her, smiling, looking out at them with thanks and an invitation in her eyes for them to approve her marriage. Their gasp gave place to a buzz of conversation, then to a murmur of delight and gratification which soon became a cheer. I suspect, sometimes, that

Madam considers her wedding day her greatest triumph.

I identified some in the crowd. Everyone from NEPP was there, and many from the city and provincial power companies. All the staff from the restaurant. All the boys from the rooming house. Mrs. Gershwin. Amos and his increasing tribe. Most of the city's cops, on or off duty that day, grinning ear to ear and providing crowd control and security - a sign of the new times; we had met the police after the storm, when we opened our doors to neighbours who had no power and no heat in their flats and houses.

The people in the street were the overflow crowd, those who had not been able to obtain seats in the church. The church itself was full. Aside from close friends, admittance was supposed to be by special ticket only, tickets having been drawn by lucky winners: so many for the kids at school, so many for NEPP, so many for Trinity members... But a few who didn't have tickets slipped in anyway. The initial shock of the press of people as we tried to enter the church was almost overwhelming.

But in that moment when the wedding party stood under the west portico preparing for the walk across, I became aware, in a fleeting way, of developments in my life that I had not so far properly evaluated and would have to think through in the days ahead. I saw that, when the time came for me to reveal NEPP's core mission to the people of this town, they would be solidly behind me. I knew it, and a weight lifted from my mind. I couldn't have had a better wedding present than that.

Madam turned to me and smiled. "You have arrived, Richard," she whispered.

She was psychic? I wondered if she were not telepathic. And I wondered, as well, if she knew I was thinking that I owed my "arrival" to her and our marriage, that this wedding day was symbolic of my place in my world and in the universe.

My stage fright vanished. "Ladies," I murmured, "shall we go to church?"

Madam took my arm. Gerda held to my other hand, and so we led the way. Gerda was the only bridesmaid. Frank would stand up with me. And after much persuasion, Jenny had agreed to sit in the place generally kept for the mother of the bride. She followed with Frank, and the party was complete.

Jenny had appeared in a dark blue - but shimmery - dress

and small hat, that gave her style and dignity, and that, I thought - the shimmer, that is, and the flowers she carried, which I think were white gardenias but I couldn't swear to that - softened her usual... severity, I suppose; reserve, maybe. I had never seen Jenny look so well, or so happy.

Madam wore her favourite pink. Gerda's dress was cream-coloured. Beyond that I cannot describe what they wore. I can only record the impressions they made on me when I met them in Madam's apartment. They were beautiful. I felt them as superior beings who couldn't possibly want to spend the rest of their lives with me.

At the same time, on a practical plane, I realized that this Joni Plenghorn I had been hearing about, she who had made their dresses, was far from being "the little dressmaker in the next street" I had thought her, but must indeed be the world-class designer everyone proclaimed her to be. Madam's dress made her look taller and slimmer than I had ever seen her. And the colour... Well, her skin glowed, even in the pale light of a November afternoon. She wore a hat, too, but it was a small affair, nothing that would make difficulties when the time came for me to kiss the bride. I was grateful for that.

I felt humble before my ladies and couldn't find a word to say, but they laughed, pleased by their effect on me. Gerda made me bend down for a kiss, and Madam said, "Thank you, Richard. I couldn't ask for a more eloquent compliment." After that *I* kissed *her*.

I remember that Gerda and I stood with fatuous smiles on our faces when Madam came from her room with Jenny behind her. Jenny was glowing with pride. I suspect that she considers Madam's wedding day *her* greatest triumph as well.

Gerda was an angel in her cream outfit, with her strawberry-blonde hair under a crown of flowers, and her blue eyes sparkling. Even the freckles that peppered her nose in the summertime, but were fading as winter approached, had been coaxed back for the occasion by the creamy colour of her dress.

They were dazzling, all three of them, but when Frank appeared from my apartment where he was staying... I was going to say, that moment capped the day, but I would not be accurate, for there were many caps to our wedding day; Frank's appearance was only one of them. He looked handsome in a dark, well tailored suit, such as I wore myself, and he had on a silver tie, as I had. But around his brow... a beaded band... and in the band...

"Eagle feathers!" Gerda cried. "Richard, aren't they beautiful? Madam asked him to wear them cause me and Lady Maggie wanted him to."

Her eyes, I thought, were a little apprehensive. Was I going to disapprove? Should I have been let in on the secret?

"Am I allowed to hug my girls?" I asked. I said it, though I think my voice shook. "Because if I am," I said, "come here. I think you're wonderful, both of you. Too good for me! What other bride and bridesmaid would share the limelight with 'an old cop on an interesting beat' like him! I'm afraid he's about to steal the show."

Gerda turned from me and studied Frank and Madam. "No, I don't think so," she said. "He looks..."

"Very distinguished," he supplied.

"Does that mean..? Wow! Yes, I think so," she said. "But not as much as Madam. I've never seen anything as bee-ooo-tee-ful as Madam. Have you, Richard?"

"Never," I agreed. "Never once in my life."

Madam knew what I meant.

"And Madam and I won't let Uncle Frank steal the show from you, Richard," Gerda went on. "Cause we both love you."

A man should always have a nine-year-old daughter to go with him to his wedding.

* * *

The church was at its best, restored almost to its former presence. Some could remember it over many years, and missed a crack in their favourite pew, a familiar creak in the floor, the special red glow of a small patch in a side window, the smell of the old hymnals and prayer books... Others, however, Al Reeger included, thought - at least privately - that in many ways the building was now better than it was before the storm, that the storm had possibly been a blessing in disguise. The heating system, they said, had been long overdue for renewal; before long, too, something would have had to be done about the roof; and the organ had been needing a good overhaul for the past several years.

They were divided in their attitudes, but not in their belief that they were somehow obligated to me. They seemed to think that I had arranged everything single-handedly: storms on demand, or wish lists expertly handled up to and including restoration of the clock tower. Whether they looked back with regret, or forward with satisfaction to the new roof that would not leak and the new furnace that would keep them warm on dark and dreary mornings, they agreed that they owed their blessings to me.

Al had kept me apprised. On the day a vestry meeting learned that an anonymous donor had offered to rebuild the tower and restore the clock to a state as much like the original as was technically possible, he galloped across the road and burst into my office, eyes shining, arms and legs flying, to tell me all about it. I should have been there, he hooted. He had never heard such rejoicing in the vestry. He'd never seen the like of it! He had led them all in a prayer of thanksgiving and a motion to have the work finished in time for Dick's wedding.

That was the first time I was aware that Dick was having a "wedding." Until then I had supposed that Madam and I, with Gerda and Jenny and a few close friends, would stroll over to the church one day and legalize our arrangements. Until that day I had thought so. But no, no. Trinity's deliverance they attributed to me, and I must be suitably rewarded.

Al had always been inordinately grateful to me for NEPP's offer of a place to meet during the reconstruction period, and never missed an opportunity to thank me. In private he often burst out with, "We never could have accomplished so much so soon without you, Dick!" In public, he simply changed "Dick" to "Dr. Waterman" and went right on. He was convinced that it was my courage and generosity that had inspired so many donors to come forward - from all over the country. And as for the clock tower! He would never know how to thank me for that.

He allowed me the Sunday visits of his sons. That was enough for me, and so I told him. He didn't listen.

I - and Madam too, of course - had done so much for Trinity, both on the day of the disaster and ever since; in truth, we had done nothing. Think of the lives I had saved on Easter Sunday! I had been lucky to save my own! And living and working just across the street? It was as if we had been sent! Our tremendous influence for good, for success in the church's return to life - even though neither of us was a member of the congregation... The truth was that exaggerated stories of our Easter escapade had already entered local mythology and there was no escape. Short of running for our lives, we were going to be married by bishop and clergy, the bishop in full regalia and as many of the local clergy as could be sandwiched into the building.

It was the clock tower that pushed Madam and me into legend. We might have been the anonymous donors ourselves. Some townsfolk suggested that we might be. But whether we were or not, no matter who the donor was, his or her generous gift drove all hands deeper into pockets and gave new impetus to the reconstruction. I was surprised to learn how many people uptown missed the chiming of the hours, especially on summer nights when bedroom windows were open. Insomnia didn't seem so distressing, they said, when one could look forward to Trinity clock striking the hours, the halves, and the quarters. And it was thanks to me. I murmured disclaimers and went on with my work.

I went on with my work. The contractors went on with theirs. And the town planned a wedding. The congregation at Trinity clubbed together and ordered an enormous cake that caused almost as much stir on the day as Madam made on first appearing ready for church.

Very generous of the church people to give us a cake, I thought, and put the gift to the back of my mind except when I met someone who needed to be thanked. Nothing to a cake after all; every wedding had one.

If I had thought about the other ingredients a wedding needs, I might have been better prepared for other exigencies as they arose. Unfortunately - or perhaps it was just as well - I supposed that since Madam, Al, and I were the only essential ingredients, I needn't concern myself with anything else. Oh, yes, a couple of rings and a present for Madam and the other members of the wedding party. Not to worry.

It was the music that caused me the most anticipatory anguish when I found out what "they" were doing. Madam must have the full choir, I was told. A singer of her stature and fame - perhaps I didn't know how great was her fame? No, a singer like Madam must not be allowed to be married without the best music that could be supplied. The string quartet, whose members also played in the symphony Madam worked so hard for, would play prelude to the ceremony, and the tympany and brass sections of the orchestra would enrich the organ, as it accompanied the massed choirs of several neighbourhood churches, augmented by several of the younger clergy and their wives, along with local soloists - and even some from away - who had been delighted to accept invitations to sing. The organ still wheezed a little, the restoration parts not yet having been installed, but the organist had mastered any storm-generated idiosyncrasies, and the music would soar and roll under the new roof. I would be impressed. Even with my well-known knowledge of modern music and my deep appreciation... Since it was Shelley who told me all this, I dismissed most of it. A mistake.

The musical machinations were supposed to be a surprise for both of us, but Shelley, having been in on one of the planning sessions, of course let the cat out of the bag. No matter how sticky her utterances might be, Shelley's thoughts always managed to escape into sound no matter how sincerely she had promised to keep them caged.

I met her in The Market one afternoon. So clever of Madam, she told me, to have chosen McWharton's "Wedding Song Suite" for the occasion, but, of course, one expected exquisite taste from her darling friend Charity, if she might be allowed to describe her so.

"Charity?" I wondered. "Who..? Oh, of course, Madam. That was her name. Charity."

I laughed at myself. Here was I, proclaimed saviour of Trinity Church, and I didn't recognize the name of the woman I was about to marry!

While I chuckled inwardly, I missed the rest of Shelley's words that gushed at me - which, at the least, saved me a few hours of painful anticipation.

I went home still chuckling and told Madam the story. She laughed too. "My darling friend Shelley," she said, "will describe me so, whether I allow her to or not."

"Is she to receive an invitation?" I asked.

"Oh, yes! I think we will end by inviting everyone in the city and county," Madam replied.

And we very nearly did. Well, when the quartet of strings, the drums, and the brass instruments are to be invited to a party, one must also ask the woodwinds and the rest of the orchestra, including the harp.

I forgot Shelley's disclosure till one day three or four weeks later when I said to Madam, "By the way, who is this McWharton person, composer of the wedding song thing? Friend of Virginia What's-her-name and Jeremy Squill, is he?"

"As a matter of fact, yes," Madam said. "*She* is. And it's the Wedding Song Suite - lasts a good fifteen minutes."

"No!" I howled. "They wouldn't put me through that! I thought a wedding was supposed to be a happy occasion. I thought we'd catch Edward, Albert, and George - if they hadn't gone south by then - and let them loose in the place with a few slices of apple and a handful of cracked corn. Keep it in the family... Let's elope."

"Would that we could," Madam said with a sigh. "But take heart, dear, Debbie McWharton is not as - to coin a phrase, not as bad as Virginia and Jeremy. Her Wedding Song is quite pleasant, really. And you will be busy and probably won't have to listen to much of it... Did you know we're having the bishop?"

"And massed clergy," I replied.

The phone rang right after that, and when Madam hung up from a lengthy conversation with someone called Ruth, she said to me, and she was serious about it, "Are you sure you want to be married, Richard? Because it sounds like we're going to be stapled together like..."

"I can see that," I said, with something of a groan. "Like Henry the Eighth and that first wife of his. What was her name? Ann? Catherine?"

"Catherine," Madam said. "Poor soul. I hope I don't face a fate like hers."

"Don't worry," I said. "I'll never play Henry. He would have enjoyed all the hullabaloo. All I want is to marry you."

I hoped for the best, but in the end our wedding was not too far short of the revels of royalty, at least of minor royalty, if not of Henry himself. And to tell the truth, I enjoyed all the hullabaloo. It was great fun, a bash to remember.

Along with bishop and clergy, symphony, choir, friends and relations, by the time the day came we had asked everyone we knew and, so as to avoid hurt feelings, everyone *they* knew. When we had a problem, Madam simply invited more guests.

When Frank came down from Ottawa, he had Andy Starkovitch with him - Andy just happening to be in Ottawa at the time with his wife, two grown daughters, and a son-in-law, who also came. Jack Davidson showed up with one daughter, a son-in-law, and two small grandchildren, a boy and a girl. My Honduran grandsons took to the two little Texans like long-lost brothers, and Jack found the four of them skinny dipping in my pink swimming pool one afternoon when they slipped their mooring lines for a few minutes and escaped the tired grand-dad who was supposed to be looking after them. Finding the pool unoccupied - though it was empty of water, by then Roberto and Enrico knew how to make things work - they were having the time of their lives.

Everyone was happy on the day. Our wedding was home-coming for the congregation, as well as the first celebration of holy matrimony in the repaired and rededicated building. The organ still wheezed a little, but, with the help of several trum-pets, as promised, the music soared and rolled under the new roof. I don't remember much else, though I am sure there was a great deal more.

Fortunately we had chosen to be married on a Thursday, when many we invited had to work. Otherwise the church, though much strengthened by the renovations, would probably have collapsed into irreparable rubble by force of numbers. Guests, with or without tickets, were as numerous as the leaves that had again fallen from the trees in the park.

Madam and I... But let me not forget Gerda... Gerda had claims all over town too. The church owed her grandfather for a lifetime of service. Therefore, she must be specially blessed by the bishop, and the children's choir should sing. Some confu-sion arose as to which children's choir was meant. The church naturally assumed that the church children would sing. Gerda's school, however, believed that their choir would be chosen. After all, had they not come first in their class in the Music Festival last spring? Besides, the school children had been told and would be terribly disappointed if... So had the church children, like-wise... Madam followed her simple plan: the church choir sang at the church, and the school choir at the reception.

The locus for the reception had to be changed several times from smaller to larger accommodations, till we hired the whole convention centre attached to the Hilton Hotel down at the foot of King, and hoped it would be big enough. We issued blanket invitations. All we asked in return was that people should RSVP, and hordes did, but we were still adding numbers when we reached the deadline a day or two before the wedding. Even so the hotel reported afterward that there must have been a few gate crashers, as they had run out of carefully counted champagne glasses and had to serve late comers in punch cups.

Madam and I might have been paying for our wedding for the rest of our lives - not that either of us would have begrudged a penny for it. But people wanted "to give us something," which we had asked them not to do, both of us already having more than everything we needed as we were. So they compromised by sending donations to the church restoration fund. This influx so greatly delighted the vestry members that they dug deep into their own pockets to provide flowers. Word got out, others wanted to help, and I have it on good authority that four large refrigerated trucks had to be hired to bring in all the blossoms for the day. Frank and Maggie Murchison gave the champagne, and Jon Carmody and his wife and Jack Davidson hired the services of T.T. Trevithian, a local photographer with a worldwide reputation. Madam and I had not planned to have portraits, but when everything was over we had some excellent stills and a video of the day, from the time just before we appeared at our door till we had driven away to a secret destination - that was also banked with flowers for our arrival! Copies of the video were made available for purchase, proceeds to the restoration fund - more rejoicing in the vestry! And more rejoicing in local service businesses, which hadn't had such a windfall since the Canada Games.

Joni Plenghorn, the designer, had so much business from the female population of the town that she had to bring in extra help from Montreal to have all the dresses finished on time, and she refused to take a penny for the wedding gown. Madam, of course, allowed her to use photos in promotion campaigns, and for a few months I appeared in glossy fashion magazines, though I suppose nobody gave me a glance at all. Joni shut up shop for the day and came to the wedding with husband, children, relatives, staff - with husbands, wives, children, and so on...

Everybody who wasn't there at the beginning came as soon as possible after work. At one point, I'm told, even the buses that pick up and discharge passengers around the square stopped running, not so much because the drivers wanted to be in on the party, though they did, but because the passengers weren't ready to leave till there was nothing more to see. Anyway, when we left the church, buses couldn't have forced their way through the press of people if they had wanted to.

Some of the passengers, I guess, never did climb back onto the buses. Somebody had to account for all those champagne glasses.

Chapter Nineteen:

Without my logs, and excepting the events recorded in this account, I remember my first year with NEPP as a collage of airports overlain with meetings, meetings overlain with airports; everything angular, everything out of sequence. Only three other days stand out, the three days I spent on Sable Island.

"Oh, Richard, you are so lucky," Madam sighed, when I told her I was going there. "So few people ever see Sable Island... Be sure to take your dark glasses. It's only a sandbar, you know."

She wanted very much to come with me. She and Gerda would have loved it. To me, Sable Island was mental and physical torment. Had it not been for the birds and a couple of young Newfoundlanders, I might have curled up in fetal position and stayed that way till somebody manhandled me back onto the plane to go home.

I flew out with the two Newfies - ecologists from a university on the mainland - and a load of boxes, bales, canisters, and cartons of beer, Coke, and drinking water. I sat up front with the pilot; I would gladly have sat back with the groceries instead. It was noisy, rough, and terrifying. I had never been so... head on, perhaps... to the ocean. My experience of the Atlantic, to that point, had consisted mostly of night flights to Europe at thirty thousand feet, dinner and movies laid on.

The others, of course, didn't notice anything. One of them later told me a story about flying kites with his friends when he was a kid. Very nice. I flew kites on the prairies. He flew his from the deck of a fishing boat! I was horrified.

An hour or so into the flight, when I was becoming, perhaps, a little used to being out of sight of land in broad daylight, and so low to the water that I might have had to get out and swim before very long - or so it seemed - the pilot leaned toward me and shouted over the noise of the engines, "There she is!"

"Where?"

"Over to your right."

He pointed. "Over to your right. See that line of surf?"

My stomach sank on a bungee cord, and I heard Madam's voice, "...to the right of the island... a line of surf..."

"My God!" I thought. "Is he going to try to land on that! Am I going to have to spend three days on *that*? A man who grew up north of Winnipeg and has been accused of having six elbows?"

From that moment, my mind went blank till I was inside a metal shed and able to breathe again - except that I remember the very rational fear that I might pass out or throw up. Maybe both.

As I have already said, had it not been for the Newfoundlanders and the birds I think I might have lost my sanity on that handkerchief of sand, in the wind, with the constant rumble of surf on the beaches, and the suffocating sense of being lower than the sea and unable to breathe.

On the second afternoon I climbed into the dunes with Michael, a student from Carbonear. We had gone out to examine the flow of the sand. I wanted to form some idea, first hand, of how to set up models for measuring how various changes in climate and ocean currents might affect the island.

That part of the day's work didn't take long. As I braced myself against the wind and the shift of sand under my feet, I felt almost giddy, as if the island were dissolving away beneath me. As a statistician, I would never admit it, but I knew in my bones the answer to the question I had come to ask: Sable would not drown in rising water; it would be swept away.

I felt a deep sadness.

The wild ponies would have to be removed.

The birds and the seals would go, and come no more.

Nothing but memory would be left of the romance of the Graveyard of the Atlantic. A light-ship would mark the spot for a few years, to warn of the shoals that would lurk a little while beneath the sea - till that most desert of desert islands had sunk from sight; till a last refuge, if only in imagination, from an over-populated, polluted, and tired world had vanished forever.

As I stood there, lost in thought, observing how the dunes lay to the wind, and the drift from them where ground cover had been worn away; understanding them because I understood snow on the Great Plains; a hissing drew me back to present place and time. I looked up. Slightly above me, Michael was down on the sand and energetically demanding my attention.

"Come d'I, Dick," he hissed. "Come d'I."

The words meant nothing, but the gestures were clear. Keep low. Come up here.

I crawled up beside him and found, in a shallow scoop out of the white sand, lined with a few blades of stiff, dark marram grass, three late chicks, tiny little fellows, warmly dressed in sandy-coloured down. Least Sandpipers, I believe. Beautiful children of earth and sky and sea.

Michael and I lay motionless side by said, each smiling as if we had found a fortune in pirate's gold.

There would have been four eggs.

Chapter Twenty:

About a year into my tenure... It was St. Patrick's Day, I remember - we had broccoli soup and a green bean casserole for dinner.

I was happy then, but tired, troubled. More and more I was disagreeing with NEPP's governing directives as they came onto my desk in steady progression. More and more I disagreed, and I often thought these - I came to call them encyclicals - pointed at me. I may have been overly sensitive on that point, but still the encyclicals came, and still, I sensed, Frank often went to bat to keep me on his staff. I was going to have to make up my mind: to go or stay; to stand up in defiance or to cut and run. To be or not to be. That *was* the question.

At the end of St. Patrick's Day, I took the elevator upstairs feeling weary. But, as often happened, something was coming right along to lift the burden from my mind. Our front door had no more than clicked behind me than Gerda came bouncing from her room with Risa right behind her.

"Oh, Richard," she cried. "You're home at last! Risa and I need you in the worst way. We are working on our science project and we don't know how to start."

I laughed. A statement like that was guaranteed to cheer me up. "How can you be working on a project when you don't know how to start?" I demanded.

The bouncing stopped. Both of them stood rigid before

me, the question in their eyes, their mouths open but the flow of their words stopped.

"Hello, Risa," I said.

She grinned. "Hi, Dr. Richard," she said. "Can't you?"

At that all of us stood in the foyer looking stunned. Finally, "Can't I what?" I asked.

"Not you," Gerda scoffed. "*You*. You know."

"No, I'm afraid I don't."

"Of course you do," she cried, and began to laugh. "You do it all the time."

"What?"

"Start second."

"Impossible," I declared.

"But you do!" she insisted. "Last night you said so."

"Never!"

"Yes, you did! Madam said 'Richard, we must work on your trip to the north this summer.' And you said, 'Yes.' But that trip hasn't started yet!"

I evaded that hook. "I don't know if I'm going this year," I said. "Maybe I'll stay home with you girls and Madam. Or maybe I'll go somewhere else. That trip hasn't started yet."

"It must have," Gerda argued, with an eloquent shrug that engaged her whole body, especially her hands, "cause Madam is working on it. She told me."

"Is she? In what way can she possibly be doing that?"

"She has ordered a whole bunch of catalogues, cause you have to have new clothes, cause you wore out your old ones when you were out in the storm. Remember? And you didn't buy new ones last year. And your knees leaked. So Madam told me we must work on Richard's trip to the Arctic this year; we must send him off with a new suit; and then we girls will go somewhere and shop, how would we like that? Madam says it's like walking up to a brick wall and saying, 'Hello, there. Get out of my way, please.' And then you walk right through it. So we have to work on our science project, which we need you to help us with, and Risa is staying at our house tonight, so we walked up to the brick wall and said, "Hello, there..."

"Get out of our way, wall," Risa put in.

"Yes, so we said that, and then we stood there looking at the brick wall and I was saying to Risa, 'I don't think this wall is going to listen to us..."

"And I was saying to Gerda, 'This wall is pretty thick..."

"And then we started to laugh cause... Get it? Thick?"

"No," I said.

"Yes, you do!" Gerda declared. "Of course you do. Thick wall. Thick head! Get it now?"

"Oh! You mean..."

"Of course!" she cried. "The wall was thick."

"Thick in the head," Risa explained.

"Yes. So of course that didn't mean thick in... in..."

"...in the bricks!"

"Right. Cause thick in the head isn't *thick*! Right?"

"Right."

"So we looked at the wall again and it wasn't there any more..."

"Then how could you look at it?"

"We couldn't. We looked at where it was."

"Only it wasn't."

"And then the light went on over our heads and we said, 'Richard!' Right like that."

"At exactly the same time!" Risa declared, and beamed at me.

"So, of course, we waited for you!" Gerda finished. "And don't say we haven't been working on our project, cause we have. Cause we've been waiting for you."

"And you can't say we haven't started yet," Risa said with finality, "cause we have!"

"And all you have to do is walk up to the brick wall and it disappears? Is that right?" I probed.

"Right!" Risa exclaimed.

"I think he's got it, Risa," Gerda said. "So let's start now."

I led the way into the living room. "So what is the subject of your project?" I asked.

"Nunavut," Gerda said. "Cause that's where Andy Starkovitch lives, and we like him, and he's going to send us some pictures."

"Is he? Have you asked him?"

"Oh, yes. And he said he would. Cause he remembers us. And we got his e-mail address and sent him a letter."

"And we said," Risa told me carefully, "we said we were

working on a project and couldn't start it yet."

"That's *right*!" Gerda cried. "And he never said we couldn't, cause we were!"

I laughed then. "Got me," I conceded. "But you really have started, because you have been writing to Andy and finding out things."

"Oh, yes, I see *that*," Gerda agreed. "But... Is that part of it?"

"Of course it is," I said, "and I am very grateful to you for your insight. You have freed my mind for me. This is very interesting."

"That's because we're girls," Risa said.

I knew it. I would never understand them, but they were a source of delight with their incomprehensible female logic.

To establish a little control of the situation, I said, "So you are doing a project on Nunavut."

"Cause we know Andy and cause you have been to the North Pole."

"No, not that far north," I said.

"Yes, but almost," Gerda argued. "A lot farther than we have... Can we go someday?"

"Yes," I said. "You really must. You must see the north. But let's not wander from the subject. If you are doing a project on Nunavut, that's geography. Where does science come in?"

"Oh, that's easy," Risa said. "Cause you remember the day we went to the beach? Well, I didn't *go* with you; I went with my mom and dad. But I came home with you. And you bought us ice cream and talked to Mom about the west."

"I remember," I said.

"And Madam told us about comets and we said we'd all go fly through a comet's tail. So..!"

"Nunavut is not a comet's tail."

"No!" They laughed at me.

"Of course not," Gerda giggled. "But a comet fell on Nunavut once a million years ago, and..."

"On a place called Devon Island," Risa explained.

"And it left a great big hole in the ground. And now some guys think it's like Mars up there and so they're trying to find out what kind of suits they'll need and everything before they go to Mars. Which..."

"I wonder if they have Mars Bars," Risa mused.

"Had your supper yet?" I asked, but in a quiet voice, because I didn't want to utterly wreck the train of thought.

"No!" they both cried, suddenly back from Devon Island and ready to tear into whatever Jenny had for us to eat - even broccoli soup and green bean casserole.

Madam came home about then too, having been at one of her interminable meetings in support of the symphony, but she never even guessed that I had dragged myself up from my office. By that time I had rejuvenated, almost to a point to match the two little girls, and I was able to do my part to lift Madam out of her doldrums and get her smiling again. She only knew that I was a little abstracted during dinner.

"A penny for your thoughts, Richard," she suggested, when we were drinking coffee in the living room and the girls were sprawled on the floor scribbling industriously on papers held to clip boards, and appealing to us whenever questions came up among their flying thoughts.

"*My* thoughts, mignonne?" I asked. "Have I been woolgathering?"

"A little, " she said, "but you look as if rain had cleared off and left the sun shining from under a layer of cloud just as it was going down behind the hills. You know how everything shines in a special light at times like that."

"Yes, the wheat fields are bleached like straw, and the river is slate blue, and every bird stands out in the sky like... like..."

"Like me and Risa when we win first prize for our science project."

"Oh!" Madam exclaimed. "Is there a prize? Then maybe Richard and I should not be helping you."

"Oh, no," Risa said. "Everybody! I mean, I know at least a hundred kids whose moms and dads are helping them."

"A hundred?"

"Well, maybe thirty."

"How many in your class?'

"Thirty-two."

"I see," Madam said. "And what about the other two?"

"That's Mikey Greensward and Tommy McVane."

"Who helps them?"

"Nobody. They live on farms. They know already."

"When comets make holes in the ground, Madam," Gerda asked, "how do people know?"

Madam fielded questions about comets. And meteors. And meteorites. And what was the difference? And where? And when? And, Wow! Really? Did Sudbury really get hit by one? Well, no. Sudbury wasn't there then. And would La Tour be hit by one? And so on and so forth.

Madam didn't need my help. I stretched out in my favourite chair and worked out a plan for *my* science project.

Did I want to stay with NEPP?

Yes. I did.

Wouldn't I rather join the La Tour Project and make a lot of money?

No. I wouldn't.

...probably work shorter hours...

No.

...wouldn't have to be away from home so much...

I would like that, very much, but... No. Thanks.

Wouldn't I like to work with dynamic, creative, dedicated people; people I already knew and liked?

I already did. Some.

But Rob Tate? Alexa Carmody?

I shook my head.

In God's name, why? You're a fool, Dick!

Granted. I'm not going.

I chuckled. I had been arguing with a brick wall.

The arguing stopped. The wall faded away.

All right, then, I told myself. Either accede to all the encyclicals, keep a meek countenance and your tongue in your head; or stand up and be counted - whether the count ever reaches two or not.

That brick wall, too, was behind me. Had been for some time.

Then all I need, I thought, is a plan of action.

I began to invent models of behaviour and to follow them to their logical conclusions. No surprise that every one of them led through Frank to Dame Nancy - who was head of the whole North Atlantic Group then - to what I had wanted all along: the day I would rise to my feet and present the official Canadian point of view with a whole heart because it was also my personal point of view.

I "woke." My ladies - all three of them - were watching me.

"You're thinking something very funny, Richard," Gerda said.

Risa agreed. "I think so too," she said.

"And I will pay a *nickel* for your thoughts this time," Madam offered.

"Only a nickel for *my* thoughts?" I said. "Surely *my* thoughts are worth more than that."

"I have twelve cents," Gerda said. "I'll bid a dime."

"Do I hear fifteen cents?"

Risa shrugged. "Don't look at me," she said. "I'm broke."

"I *might* go as high as a quarter," Madam said, "if I were sure I'd understand what you were talking about when you told me."

"No guarantees," I said. "As is, only. Take them or leave them."

"Then I withdraw my bid," she said.

"Gerda?"

"Ten cents if I understand what you're talking about. Two cents if I don't," she hedged.

"Sold," I said, "to the strawberry blonde in the front row... My thoughts, my dear, were: 'Okay, Dame Nancy. Come d'I."

They looked at each other; shrugged; and with a sigh Gerda rose, went into her room, and returned with two cents, which she handed over without a word.

"Thank you," I said. "Now, who would like to go to the St. Patrick's Day party in the Atrium?"

"That's a wonderful idea," Madam exclaimed.

"Oh, good," Risa said. "They have green ice cream. Can we..?"

"If you agree to a dish and spoon," Madam decreed.

Later, while an Irish jig filled the Atrium and Irish noise and conviviality raised the clerestory windows, Madam took my arm and mouthed at me, "Come d'I?"

I winked at her, and brought mischief to her eyes and a slight flush to her cheek bones. "Don't *do* that," she whispered. "Not in a public place!"

Chapter Twenty-One:

Five years went by. Good years. Not easy, but good years. Sometimes when I looked from our tenth floor windows at the harbour and the bay, I thought that the currents of my life were as chaotic as the currents I observed in the water. Still, I felt I was held in no little respect for swimming against those currents, especially when NEPP's funds were cut year after year and our hands were tied with more and more red tape wound about us by special interests in Ottawa and around the world.

One never knows, till one tries to effect change in some procedure, how entrenched we all are in habit; what strength inheres in a hypothetical model that shows us what we want to see; how many men and women of mature years and superior intelligence will hold to the untenable, will support the insupportable, will defend the indefensible...

"It's like that story the priest used to tell us in school," Frank growled at me one day when I was allowing myself to boil over.

I kept right on ranting.

We had gone north again - Frank, ostensibly, to fish; I to study the birds, as usual. No-one went with us that year, and we spent most of our time apart. I was hoping for a little personal peace and quiet among the ponds, while the birds struggled to raise their chicks, and the rules of sun and planet conspired to allow them too short a time for the work. Frank spent his days on the water with old friends, who also worked to feed their families while the sun allowed open water and the planet gave a short respite from the grip of winter.

I tried not to think about the changes I saw taking place in the nesting grounds but to concentrate on finding advantages to the birds, if any. I found few - if any. Every possible advantage seemed threatened by a flock of probable disasters: warmer water, but more fog; a longer season, but stronger winds; possibly an increase in the number of nesting sites, but more than likely a few strong species to move in and take them over; more hatchlings in the nests, but more avian predators... The odds were against the little guys, the beautiful, shy, hard working little guys. And my hands were tied.

On our last day we sat... we had been sitting with our backs against Frank's inukshuk, the one we had moved five years before. Frank sat there still, but I was on my feet, pacing back and forth on my hobbyhorse.

"There is no need of all this secrecy, Frank," I argued. "I never thought there was - now less than ever. People have to know. They're not children. We haven't the right to protect them from something they will eventually have to face, each one individually.

"How do you think it makes me feel to watch my daughter becoming a young woman right under my nose, and not to be free to warn her of the greatest danger her generation has to face?"

"It's like that story..," Frank started - the second time.

I went right on.

"She's a bright girl, Frank. She's ready for high school. She should be choosing her future from all available data. But I can't tell her. I can only hope she won't waste her school years.

"She was with us, you know, on St. Lucia, when that rogue weather phenomenon rose up out of the sea and obliterated most of the island.

"I'll never forget her eyes. Full of interest, Frank. Not fear. Interest!

"While the rest of the world looked on in horror, and the

people in the hotel screamed and moaned in terror, Gerda wanted to know why.

"Why, Richard?' she said. And she trusted me to tell her. But I couldn't. I knew, but my tongue was shackled. All I could do was explain to her the event as it was happening.

"I knew. But I couldn't tell her why."

"Yes. I know..." Frank muttered.

"Nor could I tell her why half of Bangladesh drowned one terrible night."

"No."

"Or why the sun was darkened, even in La Tour, by dust from Turkmenistan."

"Or why we're always on the verge of war somewhere in the world," Frank sighed.

"She's growing up, Frank," I raved on. "I suppose one of these days she'll want to have children."

Frank shifted his weight on the shale slab where he was sitting against the inukshuk.

"It's like the fellow said..." he muttered.

This was the third time. I stopped pacing and glared at him. "Are you trying to tell me something?" I demanded.

"No, no," he said, and held up one hand as if to ward off my wrath. "No, no. Carry on if it's making you feel better. I just thought you might like to hear the story the priest used to tell us...."

"What story?!"

"The one about the farmer who went out with a bag of seeds to plant a garden."

"Yes?"

"You went to Sunday school. You know the one."

"Sunday school was full of seed stories," I barked. "Which one do you mean?"

"The one about the fellow who just went out and threw the seeds on the ground," he said. "And some of them fell on rocks and the crows ate them. And some of them fell in with the blueberries, and the berries wouldn't give them room on their ground..."

He stopped speaking for a moment then, and seemed to be thinking.

"Once I asked the priest what happened to *those*, seeds,"

he muttered then, "and the old bastard said they just stayed where they landed till they rotted in the rain.

"But I didn't believe that. He was an Irishman, that priest. Grew up on the old sod itself, so he said. What would he know? I figured maybe that would happen in Ireland, where everybody knows it rains all the time, but in Manitoba? Naw. The mice would have eaten them first."

My anger blew away.

"And some fell upon stony places," I quoted, "where they had not much earth: and forthwith they sprung up, because they had no deepness of earth:

And when the sun was up, they were scorched; and because they had no root, they withered away."

"That's it," Frank rumbled. "And the rest of the seeds fell on good garden plots."

"And brought forth fruit, some an hundredfold, some sixtyfold, some thirtyfold," I finished.

"That's right."

"And your meaning?"

"Oh, I wouldn't presume to know any meaning," he said. "Any more than our old Irishman did. He'd tell you the story, but if you asked him what the hell it meant, he'd say, 'He that has ears, darlin' boy. He that has ears."

"Let him hear. Yes. You're right."

"I don't know about that," he muttered. "My track record isn't good. You'll do better."

"*I'll* do better!" I laughed. "I'm likely to have a chance."

"That's up to you," he said. "But I think you'll pull it off."

I looked at him sharply.

He reached out a hand for me to help him to his feet. I had never known him do that before.

"Are you all right?" I asked.

"Of course. Yes... And no," he said.

I waited.

"Yes, Dick," he muttered at last. "I'm all right. I'm home. Home at last... And, no... No, I'm not. Not in the way they think in the south. But all the arrangements are made. You report to Ottawa at the end of August. Give you time to get Gerda into school for the first of the term."

He turned as if to walk away, back toward the town.

"And that's all?" I demanded.

"Do you want it spelled out for you?"

"Yes, I want it spelled out," I roared. "What the hell are you talking about?"

"All right, then," he said, and turned back toward me. "You never were much in touch with what's really going on, were you? But you'll be a better man for the job because of that."

I couldn't understand a thing the man said!

"Call on Lady Maggie," he told me. "She's been a great help to me - next to you. Smart girl, her ladyship. The two of you will do just fine... And don't worry about me. Madam will know when the time comes."

"Frank! What time? Come on. We've been friends for years. Don't talk to me in riddles."

At that, he placed one hand on my shoulder and one on the rock shoulder of his inukshuk.

"Dick," he said, "meet Brawna - I won't tell you her true name; that's for her to do.

"And this..." He laid his hand, quite tenderly, where the woman's hood would have been... "This is her child.

"I never knew whether we had a son or a daughter. Or what name she gave the little one.

"She was my wife. It was a bad winter. I was away on patrol. When I came back, the people were gone. I never found them...

"See to her inukshuk now and then, will you, Dick?"

"Frank..."

* * *

I couldn't move him. The next day I boarded the plane alone. He disappeared into his last winter in the north.

* * *

The official letter was waiting for me in Ottawa. The committee had accepted with deep regret the resignation from the directorship of the Ottawa bureau of NEPP, for health reasons... and following the advice of Mr. Quarters, and having consulted their own records, now offered the position...

I sat for a few moments at Frank's desk, now mine.

I thought first of him. I would not see him again, and my heart was heavy.

Next I thought of Madam and Gerda, and of the advantages to them of the new nest I had to offer them. My heart lifted.

Then I thought of Dame Nancy and the battle ahead.

A rush of joy pulsed through me. I picked up the phone and called Maggie Murchison. I didn't think we could win the war, but Oh! how I would enjoy the battle.

"Okay, Nance," I chuckled, as I waited for the call to go through. "Come d'I, old girl. Come d'I."

"Dick!" Maggie shouted when I reached her. "Where's Frank? Is this about the ice?"

"Ice? No. I'm just back from the bay. Haven't had a chance..."

"A Murchison ship in Davis Strait has reported strange activity in the Greenland icefields," she told me.

The world will end in joy, because it is a place of sorrow. When joy has come, the purpose of the world has gone. The world will end in peace, because it is a place of war. When peace has come, what is the purpose of the world? The world will end in laughter, because it is a place of tears. Where there is laughter, who can longer weep?

Manual for Teachers
A Course in Miracles

Yvonne Wilson is a writer, a book editor, and a teacher of the craft of fiction; a birder, a world traveller, and the very lucky mother of two fine daughters. She lives and works where she was born, in La Tour (Saint John, New Brunswick.)